A Mysterious History

Mysteries of Sparrow Island

A MYSTERIOUS HISTORY

Charlotte Carter

Guideposts Books
CARMEL, NEW YORK

www.guideposts.org
1-800-431-2344
Guideposts Books & Inspirational Media Division

Cover and interior design by Cindy LaBreacht
Cover art by Gail Guth
Map by Jim Haynes, represented by Creative Freelancers, Inc.
Typeset by Nancy Tardi
Printed in the United States of America

I'd like to extend my gratitude to Priscilla Drobes for reappearing in my life, and my appreciation to my fellow Sparrow Island authors Carolyn, Susan, Krysteen, Ellen and Lorena.

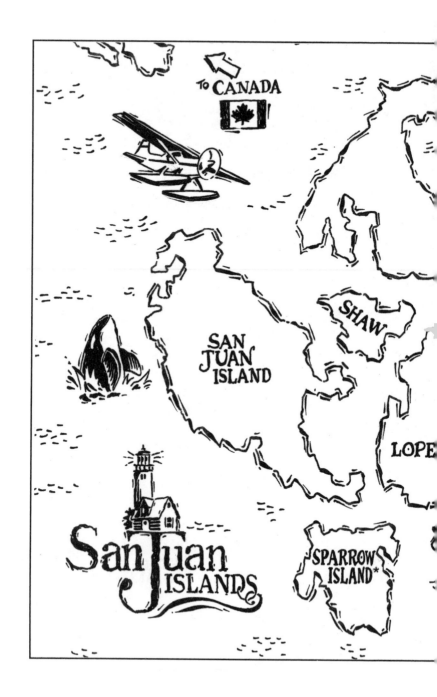

To U.S.A.

LUMMI

ORCAS

N
W E
S

CYPRESS

GUEMES

To ANACORTES

FIDALGO ISLAND

*SPARROW ISLAND IS FICTITIOUS

A Mysterious History

CHAPTER ❦ ONE

Amazing grace! How sweet the sound
That saved a wretch like me!
I once was lost, but now am found,
Was blind, but now I see.

JOHN NEWTON (1725–1807)

I'M TERRIFIED."

Abby Stanton almost laughed at her sister before she realized Mary was entirely serious.

Placing her morning cup of coffee on the kitchen table, Abby removed her glasses and wiped them with a cleaning tissue. "You'll do just fine. The church's Vacation Bible School for the children will be just like teaching Sunday school." She put her glasses back on, returning everything to focus.

"Which I haven't done since my own children were in elementary school. That's more than twenty-five years ago."

Despite Mary's bright pink sweater, which made a striking contrast to her silver hair and blue eyes, Abby could see how distressed her sister was. Normally Mary, who was age fifty-eight and three years older than Abby, was pretty laid back. But the accident last year that had landed her permanently in a wheelchair had changed many things, including Abby's life. She'd returned to her childhood home on Sparrow Island in the San Juan Islands in Washington State to care for Mary, but she had also found a new purpose as well.

"I don't think teaching children is something you forget how to do," Abby said, trying to bolster her sister's flagging spirits. From what Abby understood, the church camp had become a mid-June tradition, a treat for children after their regular school let out for the summer vacation.

"What I apparently 'forgot' when I agreed to teach for the program is that I can't walk." She rolled her chair back from the table where she and Abby had been eating an early breakfast together in the cheery kitchen. The action roused Finnegan, Mary's service dog, a handsome golden retriever-Labrador mix with amber eyes. Never far from his new mistress, he stood and stretched, eager to aid Mary in any way he could. Mary's son Zack had learned of Finnegan through a friend and had thought the dog would be a help to his mother. As it turned out the dog was a true godsend.

"For today's craft," Mary said, "I foolishly decided to have the children gather the little cones that have fallen from fir trees around the church as well as driftwood and other natural things to turn into dry arrangements that would help remind them of God's beauty here on earth."

"That sounds perfect to me. After all, you've spent most of your adult life running a florist shop. You make beautiful flower arrangements—"

"But what happens if a child goes running down the hillside by the church, falls and hurts herself." Anxiety sketched a frown on Mary's forehead, and she twisted her hands together. "How could I help an injured child or even get to her?"

Sympathizing with Mary's concern, Abby took her sister's hands in hers and gave them a squeeze. "You're borrowing trouble before it even happens. There will be other adults there, won't there?"

"Well, yes, of course. Rev. Hale will be there every day. And Janet Heinz is helping out. There's a new young man, a teenager, who's doing odd jobs around the church—Josh Nicholson. He's to come in about eleven to help Bea Ungar make the children their lunches and then do the clean up after class is over."

"They could all help an injured child, couldn't they?"

"I suppose. But I should be able to—"

"And Finnegan could go for help, if necessary."

The dog's ears perked up at the mention of his name.

"Yes, he could . . ." Mary conceded.

"Is it possible you're nervous about today because you'll be doing something you haven't done since the accident?" Abby suggested softly, the threat of her sister's tears tugging at her own heart. Between the two of them, Mary had always been the outgoing one, the sister who was ready for any social occasion, while Abby had grown up being shy and bookish. As a teenager, she'd also envied her older sibling, but maturity and Mary's dreadful accident had given them a chance to fully appreciate the love they shared.

Abby pursed her lips. "I'm so very sorry I can't come with you this morning. I had hoped to help out more—"

Mary waved off her apology. "You did plenty to help by recruiting volunteers for the Bible camp, like Ida Tolliver. She'll be wonderful as a snack lady."

"Still, I wish there were more I could do for you."

"I tossed and turned half the night, fretting about the

children and the day camp," Mary admitted. "I never should have let Rev. Hale talk me into this . . ."

Holding her sister's hands tightly, Abby said, "Why don't we say a prayer together? I'm sure God will help you get through today and take care of the children too."

Mary sighed and gave Abby a half smile. "You're right. As usual. I never used to be such a worrywart." Closing her eyes, she bowed her head. Finnegan seemed to understand the seriousness of the moment and rested his muzzle on her thigh.

"Dear Lord," Mary began, "help me, Thy servant, to have the strength and wisdom to keep the children at the day camp safe from harm. Lend me the knowledge and the words to help them see all the beauty of nature that You have blessed us with."

Abby added, "Please, Lord, help Mary to learn again the joy of sharing the gifts You have given her."

"Amen," they said in unison.

"Thank you," Mary said sincerely.

"You'll be fine." Releasing Mary's hands, Abby stood and carried their empty cereal bowls to the sink, which had been modified along with the counters to allow Mary access in her wheelchair. Past the window curtained with a vibrant Rhode Island Red print, the morning was already beginning to warm, and the sky was a cloudless blue. An early summer blessing.

Mary's pure white Persian cat, Blossom, responding to the activity in the kitchen, strolled in from the living room to see if anything new had been added to her dish. Disdainfully, she sniffed at the remnants of her breakfast, decided the dry cat food wasn't of any interest and minced over to the chair Abby had vacated. She jumped up, circled the chair cushion twice, then curled herself into a ball and settled down again. She gazed at Finnegan, almost as if she wanted to ask what his plans were for the day. Amazingly, the two animals had become fast friends since the dog's arrival in the household.

The wheelchair made a whooshing sound on the hardwood floor as Mary wheeled to the counter to dry the dishes as Abby washed them. "You know," Mary said, "you could save me a lot of worry if you'd agree to go in my place."

Abby laughed out loud. "I'd be happy to, except I don't have your artistic talent and would probably make a hash of the craft project. And I have a group of college students arriving on the early ferry this morning for a bird walk up Arrowhead Hill." A particularly interesting area on Sparrow Island with a variety of bird habitats, Arrowhead Hill was one of the many favorite places she had discovered growing up on the island.

"Part of a conservatory project?"

"Yes. We're working in conjunction with the University of Washington to offer course credit for students in wildlife biology and related fields. The students tour several of the San Juan Islands. This is the first year Sparrow Island is included. It's the kind of program I used to organize in New York."

"That must be exciting for you to replicate it here."

"It is." She glanced at her waterproof watch, one that she always wore on her birding expeditions—just in case. As an ornithologist and Associate Curator of the Sparrow Island Nature Conservatory, her typical work clothes included twill pants and hiking boots, suitable for walking through rough, brush-covered terrain. And she always wore her hair in a short, practical style for ease of care. Add to that her bifocals, and it was pretty obvious that she wouldn't make any best-dressed lists anytime soon, which was fine with her.

"I've got to go if I'm going to meet the ferry on time," she said. "Are you okay now?"

Mary idly petted Finnegan's head and scratched behind his ears. "I'll be fine. You have a good time with your birders and we'll share the day's news at dinner tonight."

Bending slightly, Abby gave her a quick hug, then went to find her high-powered binoculars, sunscreen, a sun hat and her birding vest where she carried, among other items, her compass, as well as her camera to photograph any birds she might spot.

Adjusting to Mary's new life in a wheelchair hadn't been easy for anyone, including their parents who lived on the east side of Sparrow Island. But the whole family supported Mary with their help and love. Each new activity provided another challenge for Mary. If she sometimes faltered, it was understandable. And it was admirable that she had learned to cope with her new circumstances as quickly as she had.

By the grace of God, Abby had been in a position to leave her job at Cornell University's Lab of Ornithology and return home to help out. Every day she realized again that she was in exactly the right place; this is where He wanted her to be.

Here on the island, she'd not only used her skills as an ornithologist, she'd been able to use her natural curiosity and deductive abilities to uncover the answers to some troubling mysteries. At odd moments, she was beginning to think her amateur sleuthing efforts were a part of God's larger plan for her.

Dear Lord, thank You for bringing me back to my family and to the embrace of their love. Help me to be worthy of You and let my work here on earth reflect the glory of Your name. Amen.

Abby had driven the conservatory's big, ten-passenger van home from work the prior evening. It was ten years old and had an assortment of dents and dings, but it was still serviceable and could carry a mob of birders or a load of cement bags and plywood for the conservatory.

Climbing in behind the steering wheel, she set off across the island to the ferry landing.

At this early hour only a few vehicles were on the streets of Green Harbor, the only town on Sparrow Island and home to many of the twenty-five hundred year-round residents. By afternoon, summer tourists would fill the sidewalks, stopping to shop at Bayside Souvenirs or to get a milk shake at the old-fashioned soda fountain in Willoughby Pharmacy.

Like most locals, Abby preferred spring and fall when the town wasn't overrun by tourists. Still, the businesspeople relied on visitors for their income, which meant the town council and county government had to balance both the quaint nature of the village with economic opportunities.

Abby cared about the businesspeople and knew many of them. One of the benefits of returning to Sparrow Island had been a chance to renew acquaintances with the townspeople, many of whom she'd known since childhood.

She pulled into the parking lot at the ferry terminal just as the ferry bumped against the dock and sounded its horn to announce its arrival.

As she hopped out of the van, she glanced at the sun, thinking that the island birds had been up since dawn. It would have been much better for bird-watching if the birders could begin their trek at six o'clock instead of later in the morning. But there were no accommodations on the island that could handle overnight groups of any size at a price students could afford.

Since the new arrangement with the university seemed to be working out so well, she'd have to give some thought to how she could accommodate students better. But not today. She had enough on her plate at the moment with conservatory projects, helping Mary and keeping a loving eye on her aging parents.

The pedestrians whose destination was Sparrow Island walked off the ferry first and then the vehicles exited. The ferry system was quite amazing, the workers sorting vehicles front and back on the two parking levels by their destinations, which allowed for efficient boarding and disembarking at the various islands or on the mainland.

Abby had no problem spotting the students as they came ashore. They all carried daypacks, had water bottles holstered at their waists and binoculars dangling around their necks. She counted an eager-looking crew of five women and three men.

"Over here!" Abby called to them, waving. "The Birder Express awaits."

Spotting her and the van with the conservatory logo on the side, they jogged in her direction. With a zing of nostalgia, Abby remembered how excited she'd been on her many forages into new birding territory. Sparrow Island had been her first, however, and her father had been the one who had most influenced her interest in nature. The hours she'd spent with him hiking through the woods were among her sweetest memories.

Abby welcomed the students to Sparrow Island and had the young people introduce themselves. The men were Adam, Oscar and Nigel; the women were Beth, Karen, Dottie, Tiffany and Valery. In an effort to remember their names, she tried to associate their appearance in some way with their names. Adam was the shortest boy, so he came first, and Nigel the tallest. Valery's face was heart-shaped like a Valentine, and Dottie had dozens of freckles dotting her nose and cheeks, complimenting her short, carroty-red hair. The name association was a technique one of her professors had taught her when she was a graduate lecturer at Cornell.

Sometimes it even worked, she thought with an inner smile.

"We're going to drive partway up the east side of the island," she told the students. "Then we'll park and hike up to Arrowhead Hill. We'll observe various habitats along the way."

"Can you find arrowheads on Arrowhead Hill?" Nigel asked.

"It's possible. Legend has it that a battle between two Indian tribes occurred there, which is why they named it Arrowhead Hill." Boys of all ages, she noted, appeared to be fascinated by weapons of every sort. College students were no exception. "We have a small display of bows and arrows in The Nature Museum. You might want to stop there on the way back."

Nigel seemed quite pleased with the prospect as did Oscar. The young women appeared uninterested.

The students climbed into the van while Abby settled herself behind the wheel again. She drove out of the parking lot, angling over to Primrose Lane. As she passed the Stanton Farm where she'd grown up, she glanced down the long drive that led to the house and barn. The back acreage was devoted to raising alfalfa as feed for her father's cows plus a small field of lavender he raised to be sold in Mary's flower shop. A stand of fir trees provided a backdrop for the buildings. Beyond the trees, a powder-blue sky stretched into the distance.

Spotting Samuel Arbogast, the farmhand who helped her father maintain the farm and care for the free-range chickens and milk cows he raised, she tooted her horn. Glancing up, he waved back.

Her parents had moved to the island in the 1950s, bought

the property and renovated the old farmhouse. The two-story, wood-and-shingle home was a landmark on this side of the island. Along the edge of the property, cheery white and yellow oxeye daisies lined the roadside, their heads bobbing as cars passed them by.

Just beyond the Stanton Farm, she passed the entrance to the Sparrow Island Nature Conservatory and The Nature Museum. The land encompassed an area of wooded terrain, which included towering cedars, bigleaf maples and madrone trees that bore colorful red berries in late summer.

"We'll stop back at the conservatory after we visit Arrowhead Hill," Abby told the students. "In case we don't spot all the birds we want to—which will probably be the case—there's a small static display of resident and migrating birds in The Nature Museum."

"What kind of birds are we likely to see today?" one of the girls asked.

Abby glanced into the rearview mirror and saw that it was Valery who had asked the question. "I think I can promise you a sighting of a house wren or two. As we move up Arrowhead Hill, there should be soaring birds that like to hunt in what was once farmland. Cooper's hawk. Red tail hawk."

"What about migrating birds?"

"June isn't very good for sighting migrating birds," Abby admitted. "Most of the ones that nest here have already fledged their young and moved north for the summer. If we're lucky we may see a purple martin. Or more likely, hear one. They're pretty shy."

"I've decided birds are a lot easier to identify when they're stuffed and have name tags around their necks," Nigel quipped. "Somebody would make megabucks if they could figure out how to catch them in the wild and stick name tags on them. Velcro would probably be the humane way to go."

The other students laughed at the image of birds flying along with the name of their species stuck to their breasts.

Karen said, "Why don't we let you out now so you can start working on that little project?"

Looking in the rearview mirror again, Abby saw the students smiling at the good-natured teasing. Apparently they had already coalesced into a bird-watching group.

Before Primrose Lane turned into a dirt road, she turned left onto Cross Island Road. From there she turned right onto Hickory Road, which ended a thousand feet or so before Arrowhead Hill. She pulled over to the side of the road to park.

"We'll walk from here," she announced as the students joined her in front of the van. It was amazingly quiet even though they were only a few miles from town. Spending time in the stillness of the woods with the sky above her and the birds trilling their songs always had a peaceful effect on Abby. It was as though she were closer to God when His wonders were all around her. Perhaps that was why one particular stanza from Psalms was a favorite of hers:

The heavens declare the glory of God; the skies proclaim the work of his hands. Day after day they pour forth speech; night after night they display knowledge. There is no speech or language where their voice is not heard. Their voice goes out into all the earth, their words to the ends of the world (Psalm 19:1–4).

She had an artist friend in New York who had shown her that forests and trees weren't simply green. Instead there were myriad variations on the color. Spruce trees were actually a blue-green and firs were streaked with purple shadows. Spring greens on the tips of spruce or pine trees could be dazzlingly bright. And through a mist, a forested mountainside appeared a milky gray-blue. And God had given human beings the eyes to see all those differences and appreciate them, if only they'd take the time to fully use their abilities.

"We'll be seeing three distinct habitats today," she told her students. "Who can describe this area?"

Karen spoke up. "It's a dry coniferous forest."

"And how do you know that?" Abby asked.

"Well, um, there are Douglas firs with lodgepole pines mixed in."

"Good. What else?"

"There's a red alder up the road," Oscar pointed out. "That's typical of a dry forest area."

"All right. Tell me what you hear."

Abby listened too. The soft buzz of insects sounded like a harmonica being played softly in the distance. The man-made roar of a motorboat revving up in nearby Paradise Cove interjected itself like a naughty child having a temper tantrum, and she tried to tune out the noise.

Then she heard what she'd been waiting for—the militant scolding of a wren. Lifting her binoculars, she scanned the trees until she spotted the neighborhood's angry resident perched on a broken branch of a fir tree. The aggressive house wren, common to the San Juans, didn't care much for visitors.

She pointed to the perch for the others. "See him? On the bare branch near the top of the tallest tree?" When she'd been a child growing up on the island, there had always been a wren perched in that tree. By now there must be generations of the wren family that had shown a preference for that particular spot, which meant Abby was confident when leading birders in the area that they'd receive the family's unfriendly greeting.

After all the students located the wren, Abby led them through the dry forest until the woodland became more open, hosting scattered oak trees, low shurbs and a ground cover of thigh-high grasses. She heard the high, unmusical trilling of a chipping sparrow coming from somewhere in the tall grass but couldn't convince the bird to reveal himself for the others to enjoy.

"We're very proud of our sparrows on the island but sometimes they're a bit shy of being seen," she apologized to the students, who laughed with her.

Two hours later when they reached the top of the summit, about 650 feet above sea level, the students had seen enough species of birds to make their trip worthwhile and were hot and tired. So was Abby. She sat on a partially shaded boulder and took a refreshing sip of water from her bottle.

The students found similar spots to rest. Adam sprawled out on the ground, tipped the bill of his baseball cap over his face to block the bright sun, tucking his hands behind his head.

Abby pointed to three red-tailed hawks soaring over the grassy hillside. "What are those?" she asked.

"Even I can spot a red-tailed hawk," Nigel said. "Those puppies are everywhere."

Karen smirked. "Better watch out. Those *puppies* have got sharp claws."

"Just like you?" he asked, giving her a wink, then leaned back on his elbows to watch the easy glide of the three birds of prey.

In areas that were formerly cultivated, field mustard provided a bright slash of yellow blooms. In the rockier areas, clumps of scotchbroom grew, their yellow flowers contrasting with the dark green stems. But for the most part, tall grass covered the ground under and around scattered oaks at this elevation. A little higher on the hillside, the landscape changed again to a mixture of spruce and fir trees.

"What's that big ol' house?" Valery of the heart-shaped face asked.

Abby followed the young woman's gaze across the open ground. The house, built of limestone blocks mined on a nearby island, boasted a tower room above the second story and a covered porch that spanned the width of the first floor. The black slate roof with a lightning rod at the peak was striking in contrast to the white-gray stone walls. The house was so much a part of island history, Abby rarely thought about it being here at all.

"It's called Winchell Manor," she explained. "As I recall the story, a man named Beauregard Winchell built it in the late 1860s. He lived there until around the turn of the century, when he died. It's been abandoned ever since."

"Why?" Valery asked. "It's got to have a terrific view. You can probably see the harbor from that upper window if the trees aren't in the way. I'd think a lot of people would be eager to buy it."

"The view might be great, but the house is said to be haunted." In certain light, the limestone exterior seemed to shimmer as though it were a living creature, which added to the manor's ghostly reputation. And when the wind was blowing just right, people reported hearing a woman sobbing. All of which made the place downright eerie. Even as she looked at it now, Abby felt a sense of the preternatural, a feeling that the manor didn't belong on the plane where she existed. Which was total nonsense, of course.

"Oh, come on," Nigel complained. "You don't believe in ghosts, do you?"

She laughed. "Not me. But I do remember as a kid none of us had the nerve to go near the place. All kinds of dire things were supposed to happen if you went inside." She vaguely remembered wild stories about lost children never being seen again if they ventured inside, but after so many years she'd forgotten the details that had once intrigued her growing up.

"Who is supposedly haunting the place?" Beth asked.

Abby had to think for a moment. "Beauregard's wife, was the story I heard. Some sort of a *mysterious* death. Maybe even *murder*," she said dramatically.

"Cool." Nigel grinned. "Is there any place to camp around here?"

"There are a couple of campsites along the shoreline but not up here. Day hikers come up this way but there's no water or sanitary facilities, so camping is probably discouraged."

Lifting her binoculars, she studied the old mansion. Seen up close, it was obvious that age had taken a toll. The red paint on the wooden trim had faded to a dull brown and in some places it had peeled off leaving bare wood. Many of the windows were broken. The porch steps sagged and one of the supporting posts was no longer doing its job of holding up the roof. Only the blocks of limestone remained solid.

As she scanned the structure, something caught her eye. A movement. Or maybe a reflection. Something that looked very much like a face in the tower window and then, just as quickly as she'd seen it, it was gone. A shiver crept down her spine.

"That's odd," she said. The image had come and gone so fast, she wondered if she had imagined the face.

"What?" Oscar asked.

"Oh, I thought I saw someone in the house. But it was probably my imagination." And the silly talk of ghosts had probably given her the chill.

Nigel hopped to his feet. "Come on, guys. Let's go check it out. Maybe we'll see a ghost."

"No, I don't think that's a good idea," Abby said.

"We're not afraid of any ol' ghost," Nigel insisted.

"It's not the ghost I'm thinking about. The building isn't safe."

"We'll be careful," Adam said, excited and on his feet too.

"Sorry, folks. The conservatory is responsible for your safety while you're here on the island. And I really don't want you getting hurt in that old place and having to call out the volunteer fire department to haul you down the hill to the clinic."

None of the students looked happy about her decision, but they didn't argue. Maybe they were just worried about the grade she'd give them, which was fine by her. She didn't want any of them to suffer a broken ankle falling through rotten floorboards.

But later, as they were following a slightly different path back to the van, she couldn't get the face she'd seen out of her mind. It couldn't have been a ghost.

So who could it have been? And why had he or she ducked out of sight so quickly?

CHAPTER ✿ TWO

Look at mine, Mrs. Reynolds! Look at mine!"

Mary wheeled her chair around the end of the worktable in the Little Flock Church recreation room. Wearing his harness and the blue cape that identified him as a service dog, Finnegan trotted along beside her.

There were about twenty children enrolled in the two-week vacation Bible school, and they were all busily pasting and gluing their craft projects together. Somehow that involved an enormous amount of yelling and shouting back and forth.

"That's beautiful, Laverne," Mary said. "I like what you did with the dry grass, making it look like a bird's nest."

The child's expression crumbled. "It's 'posed to be an angel's halo."

"Oh well . . ." Giving the block of wood on which the grass was pasted a half turn, Mary took a second look. "Of course, you're right. Any angel would be proud to wear such a beautiful halo."

"The grass is like gold," Laverne said. "And that's what angels' halos are made out of."

"That's certainly how humans have pictured them," Mary conceded, although she wasn't entirely sure the depictions were accurate. That was one of those things she hoped to find out when the time came for God to call her home. She was in no hurry, however, to depart her earthly form just yet.

The child beamed a glorious smile, and Mary chided herself for not remembering to let a youngster explain his or her artistic efforts before jumping to an adult conclusion. Their eyes saw things much differently and often with an innocence and creativity that grown-ups couldn't match.

As Abby had predicted, the children had managed to gather fallen cones from fir trees, leaves, seed pods and other natural products to include in their three-dimensional sculptures without a single skinned knee or stubbed toe. Mary knew she should have had more faith that God would watch out for His precious children, just as He had always protected her. How else could she have survived that dreadful car accident if He hadn't been there with her?

Another child called to her. Giving the right wheel of her chair a backward twist, she turned just as young Terry Bremmer came flying through the room pursued by P.J. Drake. Terry bashed into Mary's chair. An armful of fir tree cones popped into the air. Mary tried to grab the boy, to keep him upright, but he bounced off her chair like a rubber ball, crashing onto the floor.

"Oh my gracious!" Mary cried.

Responding to the confusion, Finnegan was on his feet in an instant, sniffing at the child and nuzzling him with his nose as if he wanted to pick up the boy and return him to Mary like an accidentally dropped hairbrush.

P.J. shouted, "I didn't do nothin'. It was him. He stole my cones!"

Josh Nicholson, the teenager who'd arrived before noon to help out at the church, came running out of the kitchen. Long and lanky, as skinny as a fence post, he reached Terry in seconds. He knelt over the boy.

"You okay?" Josh asked.

Blinking and sitting up, Terry said, "Yeah. I guess."

"Be sure, Josh," Mary urged. "He took a terrible spill." And it was over *her* wheelchair. If she'd been able to move faster like a normal person . . .

"You guys know you shouldn't be running inside," Josh said sternly. "Especially with Mrs. Reynolds here. If you'd knocked over her chair, she could have been badly hurt. You wouldn't want that, would you?"

Both boys ducked their heads. "No, Josh," they chorused.

"Okay, then." Josh helped Terry to his feet. "I think you ought to apologize to Mrs. Reynolds and then make up with each other. Can you do that?"

Josh's maturity amazed Mary. He'd fully taken control of the situation as well as any adult would have, perhaps even better because the children in the camp already held Josh in some awe. *What a sweet young man*, Mary thought. *His parents must be very proud of him.*

The boys sorted themselves out, apologized and gathered up the cones.

Mary went about her business of encouraging the young artists in her charge. Finnegan appeared to be in seventh heaven with all the children around giving him extra pets, although he had enough common sense to keep his distance from those who became overly excited.

Patricia Hale, the pastor's wife, entered the room with another group of children who had been playing outside and were now ready to start their own craft project. A striking redhead, Patricia looked more like a model than a typical preacher's wife. Indeed, she had tried her luck in Hollywood before she met her husband. Now she seemed quite content with her new life on Sparrow Island.

A child showed Mary a smiley face he'd made with seed pods for eyes, ivy vines for hair and a curved twig for a mouth; he called the result a picture of Jesus.

"He certainly looks happy," Mary said, ruffling the youngster's hair and stifling a laugh. She didn't want the boy to think she was making fun of him.

After a while she became aware that P.J. had been following her and Finnegan around the room.

"Did you want something?" she asked the youngster. He looked to be about seven and had curly blond hair and bright blue eyes.

As he gazed at her, a troubled furrow creased his forehead between his eyebrows. "How come you're in that chair all the time?"

"Because I can't walk," she answered honestly.

"Did God make you that way?"

"No. I had a car accident and hurt my back." She wasn't sure where this conversation was going. The Drake family was new to the congregation, and Mary had only seen them once or twice at Sunday morning worship services.

"I've got a little brother, Donny. He's two and he can't sit up. Mom says God made him that way. I'm afraid God will make me that way too."

"Oh, honey . . ." She opened her arms to the youngster and he stepped into her embrace, then she instinctively lifted him onto her lap. Her heart was breaking for the child's youthful worries. "God has already made you just perfect the way you are. And I bet He knew you'd be the best brother ever for Donny. Your family is lucky to have both you and your brother."

"I can run really fast."

"Yes, I saw that earlier."

"When I grow up, I'll run fast for both me and my brother."

"I know you will."

Laverne tugged on Mary's sleeve. "Mrs. Reynolds, can I have a ride too?"

"A ride?" she questioned.

"In your wheelchair."

"Well, I don't . . ." She glanced around the room. Although she didn't mind giving one child a ride, she hadn't planned to give twenty children a wheelchair ride around the room and wasn't sure it was such a good idea. Most had finished their craft projects and were getting restless now.

Fortunately, Pastor Jim Hale came striding into the room, his two-year-old, towheaded son Toby perched on his shoulders.

"Time to clean up," the pastor announced. "And then Miss Tolliver has ice cream for all of you before you go home."

A general chorus of cheers went up. Little Toby led the applause for his father's announcement. No one except Mary seemed concerned about sending the youngsters back to their parents on a sugar high. Of course, she was hoping to be first in line for ice cream and that the flavor would be chocolate, forget that her thighs didn't need the added calories.

Ida Tolliver had outdone herself earlier with the morning snack for the children. A young woman without a whole lot of money, Ida worked as a waitress at the Springhouse Café and volunteered her time and her creative talents at the church when she could. Using cookie cutters, she'd created animals out of honeydew, cantaloupe and watermelon and placed them in a watermelon shell carved like Noah's Ark. The children had loved it.

A few minutes later, the children all eating their cups of ice cream on the church's front lawn, Mary spotted Pastor Jim standing on the hillside looking pensively out to sea. With her own cup of chocolate ice cream resting on a tray in her lap and Finnegan beside her, she rolled herself along the walkway toward him.

"You're skipping the ice cream so you can keep your boyish figure?" she asked, teasing.

"Hmm?" Slowly, as though he was coming back from some faraway place, he turned. "I'm sorry?"

"I'm the one who is sorry. It looks like I interrupted you in the midst of deep thought. Is there trouble?" Although Rev. Hale could joke as well as anyone and had a grand sense of humor, he could also be quite serious.

"Not trouble, exactly. It's just that God seems determined to tempt me."

"And you were standing there telling the devil 'get thee behind me' when up I rolled."

He laughed at that. "You're on the side of the angels, Mary. I have no doubt of that. But I've had a call from a very large church in Santa Monica, California. They've invited me to apply for a position as their senior pastor. It's either a great honor or God is trying to determine just how weak I am."

Mary drew in a stunned breath. "You're leaving Little Flock Church?"

"No, I didn't say that. I've only been asked to interview, I haven't actually been offered the job."

"Well, thank the good Lord for that. The congregation would miss you terribly."

"And I'd miss them too. Every member, young and old alike. But this particular church in Santa Monica is talking about paying four or five times what I'm earning here. More importantly, they videotape the pastor's Sunday sermons and air them on public television. It would be quite an opportunity for me to spread God's Word. Plus, with a larger income, Patricia and I would have more of a chance to save money for Toby's college fund."

"Oh dear. I can see why you're tempted." Financing college in this day and age was a burden for most families, perhaps even more so on a typical preacher's salary. "But I know I speak for the entire congregation when I say we'd hate to lose you."

Nodding thoughtfully, Rev. Hale returned his gaze to the sea. "These past five years on Sparrow Island have been the happiest of our lives, Patricia's and mine. It would be very difficult for us to leave."

"I guess you'll have to ask God for guidance."

The breeze coming up the slope to the church shifted the tips of his blond hair across his forehead and he pushed it back into place. A pair of seagulls sped across the point of land beyond the church, heading out to sea.

"I've been praying since I got the phone call. As you may have noticed, sometimes God doesn't respond by overnight express mail."

"Sometimes the answer isn't obvious at all." Mary could see this was the case with Rev. Hale. He had a hard choice to make.

His lips hitched into a half smile. "You'd think a preacher would understand that, wouldn't you?"

"You're also a man with God-given free choice. You need to decide what God wants and what's best for your family. That's not easy."

"Which is why you found me staring out to sea in a stupor." He gestured to the ice cream cup in her lap. "I'm sure God intends you to eat that before it melts."

Chuckling, she popped the top off the paper cup, set it messy-side-up on her tray and used the tiny wooden spoon to taste the cold chocolate. "Abby and I will say a prayer for you tonight that you get the answer you're seeking. And we'll say another one for us that the answer is He wants you to stay right here at Little Flock Church."

"Your prayers are always welcome."

Walking around behind her, he gripped the handles of the wheelchair and, with Finnegan in the lead, pushed her back up to the lawn area where the youngsters were just finishing their afternoon treat. Parents were beginning to arrive to pick up their children, and there was much running and laughter as the youngsters related the day's activities.

Before they left, several of the children came over to tell Mary and Finnegan good-bye and that they'd see her tomorrow. Their obvious affection for her made Mary realize she shouldn't have been so fearful about leading the craft program.

Kids could adjust to almost anything if you approached them with love. She should have listened to Jesus's own words: "Let the little children come to me, and do not hinder them, for the kingdom of heaven belongs to such as these" (Matthew 19:14).

STILL WORRYING THAT PASTOR JIM might leave Sparrow Island, Mary stayed to prepare the next day's craft. She had some cutout figures for the youngsters to color that told the story of Jesus feeding the masses with just five fishes and two loaves of bread.

While she was gathering her supplies, Josh appeared from the kitchen with a push broom in his hand.

"How's it going, Mrs. Reynolds?"

"I survived the first day. And so did the children. That's a good sign. I must say, you stepped right in to help when I needed you. Thank you."

He had a cute, shy smile and a face dotted with typical adolescent acne. "They were all talking about your chair and how they wanted to ride on it."

"There are so many children, I'm not sure if that's a good idea or not."

With the broom, he reached under the worktables, dragging bits and pieces of debris out where he could gather a pile together. "I used to ride in my grandma's lap all the time. It was great." His voice held a note of nostalgia.

"Your grandmother was in a wheelchair?"

"Yeah. Almost as long as I can remember. She had MS. Multiple sclerosis."

"I'm so sorry. Where is she now?"

Josh stopped and leaned on his broom, his head down. "She died six months ago. They said we were lucky to have her as long as we did."

"But you miss her." It didn't take much intuition to recognize the boy's grief. "Are your parents vacationing here on the island?"

His head shot up. "Yeah. For the summer." He began to sweep again with renewed energy.

"Oh? How nice. Where are you staying?"

"We've, um, got one of those rental houses in Green Harbor."

"And you grew tired of hanging out with your folks so you got a job?" she guessed.

His sweet smile returned and he shrugged. "Something like that."

"Well, I for one am very glad you found Little Flock Church. I know you're an asset to Mrs. Ungar, making and serving the lunches. And to me as well."

He seemed pleased with her praise. But Mary sensed something else was troubling him. Maybe it was only his being away from his friends at home, wherever that was. Or the loss of his grandmother. In either case, she was glad such a nice, mature young man was here to help out at the church during vacation Bible school.

"I'm off for home," she said, wheeling herself toward the door. At her side, Finnegan came to his feet, always eager for the next adventure even if it was only a ride back home. "Can I give you a ride home, Josh?"

"Um, no, that's okay. I still have some cleanup to do in the kitchen."

"If you're sure."

"Yeah. See you tomorrow," Josh called after her.

Waving her hand in acknowledgment, she wheeled over to her spiffy white van with its pink pinstripe, a vehicle that had been modified with hand gears for her use. With a click of her key, the lift on the side of the van lowered. She wheeled herself onto the lift, Finnegan hopped on and she raised it again. That gave her access to the interior where she arranged her chair in the driver's position then locked the chair securely into place.

She was incredibly grateful for the independence the vehicle provided her, a gift from the Denny family whose son her parents had once helped. The customized van was the Dennys' way of thanking them and had left Mary forever in their debt. With this van, she could go anywhere on the island, including Island Blooms, the flower shop she owned in town—though much of the work at the shop was now done by her manager, Candace Grover, a very talented lady.

Mary thought again how fortunate she was to have been a part of this community all of her life and prayed she'd always be able to carry her share of the load.

Her good fortune at having so many friends reminded her that Josh lacked acquaintances his own age here on the island. She wished he had accepted her offer of a ride home. An excuse to meet his parents would have been nice. She wanted to invite them to attend church—if they were interested.

Josh's stumbling refusal of a ride seemed odd. While he might have had more work to do in the kitchen, she'd sensed that wasn't the whole reason he'd declined her offer.

She couldn't help but wonder what other reason he might have.

CHAPTER ❦ THREE

AFTER ABBY AND THE students returned to the conservatory's van, she drove them the short distance to the conservatory, an area dedicated to preserving the native plants and wildlife of Sparrow Island. Though not terribly large in size, it included rocky beaches visited by seals and sea birds, mud-flats and a marsh, as well as substantial acreage of virgin fir and cedar forest bisected by a cool, bubbling creek that drained into the ocean. During the summer, fields of wildflowers colored the landscape in a rainbow of bright blooms.

From the beginning in 1981, the conservatory had been the brain child of Hugo Baron, an internationally respected naturalist. In 1984, he built The Nature Museum on the grounds. He was the man who had cajoled Abby into accepting the position of Associate Curator, tempting her with the opportunity to set up high-tech, interactive ornithological displays and provide educational opportunities for both young people and tourists.

As an added incentive, her first assignment was to confirm a rare species, the marbled murrelet, existed on the island and develop ways to help preserve the necessary habitat to support a viable population of the special birds.

The work had brought her true joy as well as a good many challenges. Joining with Hugo in his life's work had been a good decision for her.

She parked the van in the reserved spot in The Nature Museum's lot. The students got out and walked the flower-bordered path to the main building, which took them past the giant bigleaf maple tree that was planted in the center of the circular driveway.

Hugo Baron, looking as distinguished as ever, strolled out of the two-story, stucco-and-stone building to meet the group.

Abby introduced Hugo and gave him the floor.

"Welcome, ladies and gentlemen," he said. "I trust you had a pleasant and successful outing with Ms. Stanton."

The students all nodded their assent.

"What we have here," Hugo continued, "is a small slice of our island ecosystem. The object is to preserve an area where nature, not man, is in charge. You'll find a self-guiding trail through the preserve with specimen plants identified for your information. Because this environment is fragile, we will appreciate your staying on the path rather than wandering off the trail.

"Inside the museum, you'll find displays and dioramas showing examples of animal life on the island and their natural habitats. Ms. Stanton, by the way, has provided the leadership to establish several fine displays of our feathered friends in 'The Wonderful World of Wings.' You may want to visit that area first."

He nodded appreciatively to Abby, who smiled in return. She knew he was capable of lecturing at far greater length on the need to protect and preserve the environment. But the students didn't have enough time to listen if they had any hope of seeing the museum and getting to the ferry on time.

"All right, folks," she said to the students, glancing at her watch. "You're welcome to enjoy whatever interests you, but you need to be back at the van no later than three-thirty so I can take you to the ferry. Any questions?"

Having none, the students broke into smaller groups, most of them deciding to venture inside the museum before they followed the nature trail around the preserve.

When they'd all left, Hugo held open the museum door for Abby. "How did your excursion go?"

"Quite well, I think." Hugo entered behind her as they stepped into the small lobby, situated next to a small gift shop where nature books and souvenirs were on sale.

Abby was frequently struck by what a gentleman Hugo was and how he reminded her of a British lord in both his actions and appearance, although he was American born. He was tall and slender with a full head of white hair. Instead of his usual well-tailored jacket and tie, today he was wearing khaki pants and a matching khaki shirt. He looked very much like a bwana white man traveling through the jungles of Africa, which he had indeed done more than once.

Abby had visited Africa a few times and dreamed of visiting the continent again. The many varieties of birds she'd been able to spot on each expedition had filled whole journals.

"Your concept of providing field programs for local colleges is excellent. When you have time, I hope you'll be able to expand the program."

Abby chuckled at that. "Surely I mentioned when I agreed to come to work here that I hoped to slow down a little, not work as hard as I did at Cornell."

"You may have mentioned something to that effect," he conceded. "But you're far too young and energetic to rest on your laurels."

"And you're far too smooth talking for *my* good. But, yes, I've already written to the department head at Washington State University at Vancouver to see if we can develop a joint program."

"There, you see? I was quite right about your unfailing enthusiasm."

Shaking her head in amusement, Abby said, "I'm going to see if the students have any questions. I'll check with you later."

He dipped his head in approval. "Do keep me apprised of your progress with the university."

"Of course." Smiling to herself, she made her way through the museum. The initial displays explained the geology of Sparrow Island and the San Juan Islands, and there was a wonderful holographic display of Mt. St. Helens erupting on the mainland. That was followed by a life-sized diorama showing sea life around the island, including dolphins, seals and whales. Then came displays that placed both land animals and birds in replicas of their natural habitat. And finally her Wonderful World of Wings.

Abby was quite proud of their little museum and the part she had played in its development thus far. Of course, as Hugo had implied, she had a gazillion more ideas that she'd like to implement.

So much to do and so little time.

That seemed to be the story of her life.

AFTER ABBY RETURNED her students to the ferry landing in time to catch the ferry, she stopped by The Green Grocer on Kingfisher Avenue to pick up some fresh fruits and vegetables. The only grocery store on the island, it had an amazingly wide selection of products, considering the store itself was not large. That did, however, make for narrow aisles crowded with stacked cartons, cans and jars of food stuff for sale.

The Green Grocer was also the place where you were sure to see your neighbors.

Coming across Margaret Blackstock in the produce section, Abby repeated the elementary school secretary's gesture and squeezed a head of iceberg lettuce, looking for a solid one.

"Are you enjoying your vacation from school?" Abby asked.

"Are you kidding? Ten months a year with those little sweethearts? Come summer, I'm ready to say enough already!" Even after living on Sparrow Island for a dozen years, no one had to ask if Margaret was from Brooklyn. Her accent gave her away with the first words that came out of her mouth.

Abby laughed. "I bet by September you'll be ready to go back to work though."

Margaret dropped the head of lettuce into a plastic bag and put it in her shopping cart. Her rich, brown hair always looked perfectly styled without a trace of gray—unlike Abby's that was beginning to show a few telltale signs of aging.

"I threaten to quit every June, but my Joe says I'm just yanking his chain. I'd go stir-crazy if I stayed home all the time." Margaret moved on to the bin of zucchini. "Will you get a load of these scrawny things? They're so skinny, they look like they've got that anorexia disease."

"Maybe Mr. Goodfellow didn't get a fresh shipment in today. His produce is usually top quality."

"*Humph!* He's probably got the good stuff in the back and is trying to pawn this old stuff off on the tourists." Margaret was just this side of plump and looked as though she knew a thing or two about the joy of good eating. Her figure filled out her turquoise polyester jogging suit, suggesting that jogging was not one of her regular activities.

Not quite as fussy as Margaret, Abby selected a couple of zucchini for herself. She and Mary would have to eat them tonight or they'd go bad, but she liked making a side dish of zucchini, tomatoes and a bit of onion topped with Parmesan cheese. She added the zucchini and a nice, rounded eggplant to her basket then picked up a bunch of green onions.

"How's Mary getting along lately? I keep meaning to drop by to see her."

"She's in charge of craft projects for the children in the vacation Bible school at church."

"Sounds perfect for her. And I bet you're keeping busy out at the conservatory."

"*Hmm* . . . yes." Selecting four on-the-vine tomatoes, she put them in a bag. "I took some bird-watchers up to Arrowhead Hill today."

Margaret visibly shuddered. "Stay away from Winchell Manor. It's haunted, you know."

"Oh, I don't really think—"

"Terrible things have gone on there. Why, I could tell you stories—"

"Hey, Mrs. Blackstock," Bobby McDonald, Abby's ten-year-old neighbor, interrupted. "Are you talking about Winchell Manor?"

"We were, young man," Margaret responded. "But it's rude of you to interrupt when people are having a conversation."

"Sorry." He held a loaf of bread by the tie end, swinging it back and forth like a pendulum. "I heard the woman who runs the stables out past Cedar Grove Lake tell Mr. Holloway at the hardware store there was funny things going on up at the manor."

"What kind of funny things?" Abby asked. *Faces in the tower window?*

"Stuff. Like people seeing lights on in the house at night and hearing spooky music." His intelligent hazel eyes sparkled with excitement.

"Whew." Apparently suffering a sudden hot flash, Margaret's cheeks turned red and she fanned herself with a bunch of celery. "See what the boy says? I told you that old place was haunted."

"I'm sure there's a logical explanation," Abby insisted.

"I heard some kid went up there at night," Bobby related. "The ghost caught him and threw him down an old well. Nobody ever saw him again."

"How long ago was that, Bobby?" Abby asked because it sounded a lot like some of the crazy stories she'd heard as a child.

"I dunno. Long time, I guess. Maybe when I was a little kid."

"Or maybe it was just a wild story someone made up to scare you?"

"I don't think so. Everybody knows about the ghost."

Margaret lowered her voice as though she didn't want to attract too much attention or let Bobby hear. "I've heard that on nights with a full moon you can hear a woman singing a terrible, sad song. She's supposed to be Beauregard Winchell's bride that he killed. You know, they say victims of violent death sometimes can't move on to the hereafter until their murderers are exposed."

The young woman Abby recognized as working part-time at Bayside Souvenirs, near the beach, piped up, having overheard Margaret's remark. "I thought it was Beauregard who was haunting the house because he died of a broken heart after his wife left him for another man. A pirate, I heard. I think that's so romantic."

Abby shook her head in disbelief. "Really, you can't actually believe—"

"You can doubt us all you want, Abigail Stanton," Margaret said. "But I say, where there's that much smoke there's got to be some truth to the tale. Winchell Manor is haunted. You can bet your knickers on that."

Bobby's sweet young face puckered into a frown. "Knickers?"

Margaret waved off his question. "Will you look at the price on those cherries? Gimme a break! Goodfellow must think we're turning straw into gold around this place."

Abby couldn't help but wonder if the next wild tale she heard would be about Beauregard Winchell's turning stone into gold bullion and haunting his house to protect his secret horde. After all, most rumors started with a simple misunderstood remark.

She'd had no idea the residents of Sparrow Island were so taken with the local ghost story or that they had such vivid imaginations. Of course, as a child she'd believed the tales of mysterious things going on at the manor. But somewhere between then and adulthood, she'd realized there was invariably some other explanation for ghost stories.

Still, at the moment she had no explanation for who—or

what—she'd seen at the turret window of the old mansion. *If* she'd seen anything at all.

Abby purchased her groceries and carried the bags out to the front where she'd been lucky enough to find a parking space on the street. At the conservatory, she'd traded the van for her own car, a compact gas-electric hybrid she'd recently purchased. She put the groceries in the backseat.

As she started to get behind the wheel, she spotted William Jansen, the editor of the weekly Sparrow Island newspaper *The Birdcall*, marching across the street as if he were en route to the most important late-breaking news event of his life. Which was how he always acted.

He was, however, a man who knew a lot about Sparrow Island.

"Hi, William. Have you got a minute?"

"Depends. I suppose you've got another one of your mysteries that you're about to solve."

"I don't know about that," she said with a smile as they both moved out of the street and onto the sidewalk. "I wanted to ask you about Winchell Manor."

He fingered his mustache, smoothing it over his narrow lips. "What do you want to know?"

"For starters, why does everyone still think, after all these years, that it's haunted?"

"Because the world is filled with fools. Why else would they believe in ghosts?"

Abby laughed at his blustery response. At heart, she knew he was a good man who had somehow gotten it into his head that he had to be a tough newspaper editor, even in a community as small as Sparrow Island. She suspected it was a role he played and not his real personality.

"I can tell you about the house's history," William said. "Got a file on it, of course."

Bobby came out of The Green Grocer, now swinging his loaf of bread in a plastic bag. He stopped beside Abby, curious as ever about adult conversation.

"Let's see." Thoughtfully, William buttoned the middle button of his sports jacket, then slid his hand into a side pocket, professorial style. "Beauregard was an officer in the United States Army stationed on San Juan Island during the Pig War."

"Pig War?" Bobby interjected. "Why would anybody start a war over a pig?"

Abby remembered the story, vaguely, but let William continue so Bobby could satisfy his curiosity.

"The Pig War is our big claim to fame in the San Juans—besides the beautiful scenery, that is." Playing to his young audience, William cleared his throat dramatically. "Long about 1859, an American settler got tired of a pig rooting in his garden so he shot the dang thing. Problem was, the pig belonged to a British citizen working for the Hudson's Bay Company."

"That started a war?" Bobby asked, aghast.

Smiling, Abby looped her arm around the boy's shoulder and gave him an affectionate hug.

"Seems the land here was already in dispute," William continued. "Great Britain thought they owned the San Juans, and the good' ol' U.S. of A. claimed the San Juans belonged to it. So the two sides got into a dustup over the border. Both armies moved in and stayed awhile, bored out of their gourds would be my guess."

"So it was a standoff?" Abby asked to clarify.

"Yep. Wasn't until 1872 when Kaiser Wilhelm I of

Germany settled the argument by appointing an arbitration committee. We got the San Juans. Great Britain—and eventually Canada—got Vancouver Island. A fair trade, it seems to me."

"Still sounds funny to me somebody would start a fight over a stupid pig," Bobby said.

Abby tended to agree. "Was it after the Kaiser stepped in that Beauregard built his house?"

"No, a little before that."

Bobby spotted his mother, Sandy McDonald coming out of a shop across the street. "There's my mom. I gotta go. See you later, Abby. You, too, Mr. Jansen." With only a quick check for traffic, he dashed away, the grocery bag swinging.

Abby waved to Sandy, who lifted her hand in a friendly response.

William continued as though he hadn't been interrupted. "In 1861, when the Civil War—or War Between the States, if you prefer—broke out, Beauregard resigned his commission and joined the Confederacy, like a lot of other southern lads, I might add. He was wounded a few times but made it through the war mostly in one piece. Unfortunately, his family fortunes didn't fair so well. The plantation was destroyed and there wasn't much reason for him to stay in the South. So he came back here, where he'd already bought land, started building a house and got himself a bride to come with him. That was 1867 or thereabouts."

"So why do people say the house is haunted?"

"There were always stories about his wife. Some say he killed her. Others say she left him for another man. Hard to know what the truth is, but a ghost isn't the likely answer."

"Still, it makes a fascinating story. You ought to write it up in your newspaper."

"Not me. That's old news, Abby. Nobody cares about the manor anymore. Folks now are most interested in who's getting married or what jazz band is playing Saturday night at the park."

"I don't know. History has always interested me." So did mysteries, she admitted. More than once she'd been accused of being a real-life Miss Marple.

"Tell you what, Abby. You look into Winchell Manor. You find anything newsworthy in the next week or so before D-Day, I'll print it *and* I'll take you out to dinner."

"Wow! How could I resist an offer like that?" She laughed.

Dropping back into his tough editor role, he scowled. "I don't mean an expensive dinner, you understand. There's a limit to my generosity."

"Don't worry, William. If I find out something interesting, I'll let you know. Then we'll negotiate the details."

Abby walked around to the driver's side of her car, opened the door and climbed in. She'd always been a sucker for a challenge. Or a mystery. The history of Beauregard's missing bride certainly piqued her curiosity.

Raising questions always led her to search for answers. That's why biology and science had attracted her as a career. And why she read mystery novels for relaxation. And why now she was wondering what William Jansen had meant by D-Day. She'd have to ask him the next time she saw him.

She loved putting the puzzle pieces together.

This time the pieces included a face she may or may not have seen in the upstairs window of Winchell Manor and a century's-old ghost story that she didn't believe for one minute. Except that tales handed down over the generations often had some nub of truth to them.

She wondered what parts of the story of Winchell Manor were true and which were fabricated by overactive minds.

CHAPTER ❦ FOUR

ABBY ARRIVED HOME TO find Mary in the kitchen baking date-nut muffins.

"Yum. That smells good," Abby said as she placed the grocery bags on the counter.

Mary wheeled over to the table to get out of Abby's way. "I thought we could eat a quick dinner, then run a few of these over to the folks' house."

"Sounds good to me." Abby made it a point to see her parents at least once a week, more often if possible. That was an important fringe benefit to having moved back to Sparrow Island. Taking their father the muffins he so dearly loved would be a good excuse for a visit—not that they needed one—and an added bonus for their dad.

"I bought us some fresh vegetables for supper. We were running low." She plucked the tomatoes from the bag and rinsed them under running water, setting them aside on the drain board. "So how did your day at church go?"

"Quite well, actually. At least the children seemed to enjoy their craft project, and I didn't lose any of them into the sea."

Abby heard a *but* coming.

As expected, Mary delivered. "But I did hear some troubling news about Rev. Hale."

"What's that?" Abby cut off the ends of the green onions and tossed them in the trash.

"Well, he didn't say anything about keeping what he told me confidential so I don't think I'd be violating his trust if I tell you. He's been asked to interview for a position in Santa Monica."

Eggplant in hand, Abby stopped halfway between the sink and the refrigerator. "Is he going to take it?"

"To tell you the truth, he seems torn. It sounds like it would be a beneficial move for him and his young family. But, my, how I'd hate to see him go."

"So would I. So would the whole congregation, I'm sure."

"That's what I told him. And why I'd like to go see Mom and Dad. Hand me those chicken breasts on the top shelf of the fridge while you're there, please."

Abby put the eggplant in the vegetable bin and found the chicken. "You think they could help convince Pastor Jim to stay?"

"I'm not sure it's our place to tell Jim what to do, or even try to influence him. But I have the feeling he and Patricia may not fully understand how much we all appreciate him and appreciate how much of themselves they both give to the church."

"Simply saying thank you after Sunday morning service never seems like quite enough."

"I agree. Maybe Mom or Dad can think of something appropriate to do."

"That would influence him to stay?" Abby noted her sister's contradiction between words and action.

"I did tell him we'd pray for God to help him make the right decision—then lobby God with our own prayers that he'd stay right here."

Laughing, Abby went about preparing the zucchini dish for the microwave, while Mary grilled the chicken breasts. After a few false starts, the two of them had learned to work together as a team. Now their time together in the kitchen was a comfort to them both.

Unlike Mary, Abby had lived alone for most of her adult years. In many ways, she'd enjoyed the independence and the quiet that came after a long day of work. Now she cherished the opportunity to share the day's events with her sister. Strange how she hadn't realized how lonely she'd been until she'd returned to the island.

Oh, she'd had a good many friends and colleagues. They'd gone out to dinner or to university lectures together, and had often gone camping or shared bird-watching excursions. But being with family was different.

This is where she belonged. *Thank You, Lord, for bringing me home.*

As they ate dinner, Abby told her sister about the students she'd led on the walk. "I'd guess Nigel is a first-class techno-whiz," she related after she described the young people. "He also loved to tease the women students. Fortunately, they were good sports and tolerated him."

"I used to tease my Jacob to make him laugh." A wistful

look made Mary's blue eyes sparkle. "He was always such a serious man."

"Until he married you."

"I think I was good for him. Gave him balance, you know?" Mary rested her fork on the plate.

"You were good for each other." Jacob had died of pancreatic cancer at the age of fifty-one. Abby knew there wasn't a day that went by that her sister didn't think of her husband with both a sense of love and grief, and the knowledge that she'd been fortunate to have had him for the more than twenty years they had shared together.

They finished dinner, washed the dishes then headed to Stanton Farm across the island. With Mary in a wheelchair, it was easier for her to drive her van rather than load everything, including Finnegan, into Abby's car.

The fence posts lining the road to the farmhouse cast long shadows across the narrow way, and when Mary and Abby reached the farm the lowering sun glistened off the white-washed barn. Mary drove up to the front of the house where their father, with the help of Sam Arbogast, had built a ramp to allow her easy access to the house, just one of the many accommodations they had all made following the accident.

Ellen Stanton hurried out the door to greet them.

"Hello, dears. We didn't know you were coming by this evening."

Abby was out of the van first and gave her mother a hug. "Mary was inspired to make you date-nut muffins, so we brought them over while they were still fresh."

"How sweet of you, dear. Your father will love them."

As Ellen watched Mary maneuver the van's lift and her chair, her lips pursed with the tiniest sign of sorrow but the expression was gone before Mary could notice. Ellen was very good at hiding her emotions when they could only bring grief to someone else. When Mary had been in the hospital, Ellen had often maintained God would see them through. And He had.

George Stanton appeared at the front door and waited as the women made their way inside.

"We come bearing gifts," Mary announced as Abby pushed her up the ramp, Finnegan following behind. She handed her father the basket of muffins.

"Gold and frankincense, I trust."

"Better."

George sniffed the basket and smiled. "Indeed, much better. I haven't had your mother's date-nut muffins in years."

"It hasn't been that long, George," Ellen corrected with a smile.

"It only seems that long because yours are the best in the entire country. Maybe the world. And I am more than grateful my daughter learned the culinary arts at your feet."

Having neatly complimented both his wife and daughter in one sweeping remark, he retreated into the kitchen where he'd no doubt sneak the first muffin for himself. All the women knew exactly what he was up to and laughed. Abby was perfectly happy to echo her father's praise of both Mary and her mother's cooking.

They visited awhile in the kitchen where they had always shared both good and bad news along with everyday events. The round oak table that George had made years ago was the centerpiece of the room. After all this time, the satin finish had worn thin at the places where the four of them had rested their arms on the table for so many family meals and gatherings.

Finally Mary got down to the real reason she and Abby had dropped by.

Both George and Ellen were troubled by the news that Pastor Jim might leave Sparrow Island.

"I don't know what, if anything, we should do," Mary explained, "beyond praying that God's will be done, of course."

George stood and walked across the kitchen to the refrigerator. Opening the door, he retrieved a carton of milk and poured himself a half glass. "Anyone else?" he asked.

They all shook their heads.

"Do you think Jim doesn't feel appreciated on Sparrow Island?" George asked.

"I don't think that's the case." Mary brushed some crumbs from the table and dropped them on the plate that had held her muffin. "I think he's worried about sending Toby to college— and any other children they might have, I suppose. And the temptation to be on television might be a lure too."

"Televangelists don't all have a great reputation," Ellen pointed out.

Abby said, "Jim would be a terrific TV preacher. He has such a presence about him and he's honest to the core. He'd be able to reach thousands, maybe more, with the Word of God."

"And that's probably what's tempting him, in addition to a larger salary," Mary said.

They all grew thoughtful. Abby considered that it wouldn't be fair to Jim and his family if they prevented him from following a new path, if that's what he wanted. But the thought of Little Flock Church losing their beloved pastor brought an ache to her chest. Some people were simply too special to lose.

Finally George said, "I'm reluctant to intervene at this juncture. Pastor Jim and his family have the right to make their own decisions, though I agree it would be our loss if he took that position in California."

"But you could be on the lookout for anything that comes up in the congregation that would convince Pastor Jim to stay here," Mary suggested.

He placed his hand on her shoulder. "That I can certainly do. Meanwhile, maybe we ought to pray that none of us overstep our bounds and try to get in the way of God's will."

"Absolutely," Ellen agreed.

Extending their hands around the table, the family all spent a few moments in silent prayer, asking for God's guidance, then George Stanton spoke.

"Dear Heavenly Father, we know You have a plan for us all, including Pastor Jim. Help him to search his heart and find Your plan that will bring him Your grace. And help us, O Lord, to accept Your will as well, even as we seek ways to let Jim and his family know how important they are to us. We ask this in Your name."

"Amen," the family chorused, each giving a squeeze to the hands they held.

ABBY HAD A RESTLESS NIGHT. Thoughts of the "haunted house" on Arrowhead Hill, the intriguing mystery of Beauregard's bride and the face she'd seen in the window kept her tossing and turning.

So the next morning, when Mary headed off to vacation Bible school, Abby decided to pursue her curiosity. Although she'd never had the nerve to go inside Winchell Manor when she was a child, as an adult she wasn't so hesitant. Particularly after William Jansen had challenged her to come up with something newsworthy about the old place.

In her small car, she followed the same route she had with her bird-watchers. Except, instead of parking her car, she drove up the barely visible trail left by the original occupants of Winchell Manor. Tall grass and a few shrubs grew between the grooves left by wagon wheels a hundred years ago. Sections of the land on both sides of the trail were covered with purple alfalfa blooms, probably originally planted by Beauregard Winchell for his cattle to graze and now growing wild.

She shifted down as the path steepened and wound its way up the hillside. Despite being a compact, her little vehicle could handle reasonably rugged terrain—if she was careful.

She reached the summit on the backside of the house, the opposite view of what she'd had yesterday, and saw the two additional buildings behind the manor house. One had clearly been a barn and was now crumbled and in ruins. The other building was made of the same white limestone as the manor house and might have been servants' quarters or a home for the foreman who supervised the farm.

Abby parked by the barn, found her flashlight in the glove compartment and got out to walk around the outbuildings. Startling her, a small fox broke cover from near the barn and dashed for the safety of a moss-covered woodpile. The tall grass beneath a grouping of fir trees was crushed, suggesting a deer had slept there recently. In the tallest of the fir trees, Abby noted an exceptionally large nest made of sticks and twigs, no doubt constructed by a pair of bald eagles. If the nest was still in use, the baby had already fledged. She mentally marked the spot to watch for breeding activity next spring, knowing this area was a little farther from an eagle's fishing grounds than most eagle nests on the island. This particular pair of eagles might well rely on voles or other ground animals to supplement the fish they fed their offspring.

Odd that she and her father had never included this side of Arrowhead Hill in their birding expeditions. She'd have to ask him if there was a reason.

Turning toward the smaller building, which she considered the servants' quarters, she was greeted by two small round furry faces peering out from beneath the porch steps. Their eyes were a striking shade of blue, as bright as a cornflower in midsummer.

She squatted down and held out her hand. "Well, hello there little guys."

Two yellow tiger-striped kittens cautiously tiptoed out from beneath the porch to sniff at her fingertips. They looked to be no more than six to eight weeks old.

"I bet your mommy is somewhere nearby." One kitten was braver than the other, allowing Abby to scratch him behind his ears. At various times feral cats had been a problem on the island. Families sometimes abandoned or lost their pets, and they'd gone wild. But these two kittens were adorable and appeared quite healthy. "I'm tempted to scoop you up and take you home, but I'm not sure Blossom would be pleased."

She glanced around trying to spot the mother cat. She didn't want to remove the kittens when they might not yet be weaned. But she also wanted to prevent a large population of feral cats from developing. They could play havoc with the native population of voles and other small creatures that were prey for bald eagles and the like.

"I'll come back and visit another time, little guys," she said, standing and walking onto the porch of the servants' quarters.

The door was barred, a rusty padlock hanging from the hasp. With only small, high windows, the inside was shadowed. Through a dusty pane of glass she could see a rock fireplace and a few scattered boxes. Otherwise the single large room appeared to be empty. Certainly no sign of life. Or of a ghost, she thought with a laugh.

Finally, leaving the kittens on their own, she turned her attention to the main house.

There was no reason for the flutter in her stomach, she told herself. Or the sudden clammy feeling on her palms. Ghosts did not exist—or if they did, it was only in the vivid imaginations of flesh-and-blood human beings.

She walked around the outside of the house toward the front. A couple of aluminum soda cans had been carelessly tossed aside, probably by some day hikers. The age-faded initials, A.J. + B.T., were carved on the oak newel post at the bottom of the steps to the porch.

The breeze that blew up the hillside rustled the tops of the trees, rattling first one branch and then the next as though warning that an intruder had invaded their private domain. The birds were silent; even the constant hum of insects was hushed.

Stepping over the rotten bottom riser, she gingerly made her way up the remaining four steps to the darkly stained, wooden-plank porch. It would be ironic if she injured an ankle here after warning her students away.

Wind had blown leaves and pine needles, bits of paper and other debris onto the porch where it had settled up against the limestone blocks. Several families, or maybe generations, of mud wasps had made themselves at home beneath the eaves, and it appeared a healthy colony of spiders had taken up residence in the corners of the porch roof.

The small panes of window glass that were still intact were old, rippled and grimy with so many layers of dirt it was nearly impossible to see inside. Almost expecting a ghostly face to appear staring back at her, she stood on tiptoe and peered through a broken pane. As her eyes adjusted to the dim light, she saw scattered pieces of furniture covered with white sheets as though the house had been closed up for winter, the owners expected back with the return of spring.

"Interesting," she murmured, backing away from the window.

The question now became, was she curious enough to actually go inside? Assuming she could find a way in without breaking a window or door.

Or didn't chicken out.

"Oh for heaven's sake!" She didn't believe in ghosts and therefore had no reason to be afraid of them.

Determined to see the inside of the house—and to ignore her foolish fears—she walked over to the double-wide front door, grabbed the handle, pressed down, pushed . . . and the door swung open.

She almost screeched, she was so surprised. Who knew it would be so easy?

Carefully, firmly gripping her flashlight like a policeman's baton, she stepped across the threshold. As her eyes adjusted to the interior, she drew in a soft breath.

The entry had a slate floor, a high ceiling with crown molding and a chandelier that was almost too grand for the San Juan Islands. Abby could imagine Beauregard or his bride greeting elegant guests dressed in their finery.

Admittedly the wallpaper, which had once been a floral design of bright colors, was now faded to a pale imitation of itself. And debris similar to what she'd found outside on the porch littered the floor. But there was no question that Winchell Manor had once been the home of one of the wealthiest residents in the Northwest.

Abby wondered how Beauregard had earned so much money from farming his relatively small acreage. But perhaps he had managed to preserve some of the money that his family had had before the Civil War.

To the right of the entry was a dining room large enough to hold twenty guests, although there was no longer a table in the room. Still, the floor-to-ceiling mahogany sideboard against the wall must once have been filled with enough china and silver to serve that many visitors.

In the living room on the opposite side of the entry, there was a huge fireplace made of local stone. There'd been fires laid there more recently than Beauregard's time, but from the bits of paper cups and newspapers that hadn't entirely burned, Abby once again suspected the culprits were day hikers who'd found their way inside as easily as she had.

Amazingly, Abby found several pieces of French Provincial furniture under the sheet covers. The love seat and chair looked a little moth-eaten after a hundred years of neglect. Another straight-backed chair was missing its legs, which had probably fallen victim to the fireplace.

Why hadn't anyone from town discovered this treasure trove of history? Had they all been too frightened of ghost stories to venture up here? Had only tourists made the hike? Abby found it hard to imagine.

Off the main hallway, she found what must have once been a library, its walls lined with empty bookshelves and a smaller fireplace with a raised hearth for heat. One straight-backed chair had been placed by the window. Above the fireplace was a faded oil portrait of a beautiful though fragile-appearing young woman. Beauregard's bride?

A shiver of unease raised the hair at her nape. Was that young woman the ghost of Winchell Manor? Not a very threatening visage, if she was.

Somewhere in the house, she heard a noise. The crack of wood settling—or floorboards being stepped upon. The wind rattled a window, sending a chilly breeze through the house.

Perhaps she shouldn't have come here alone.

In the opposite wing of the house, she discovered a hand pump in the kitchen. When she lifted the handle, it creaked with age and a thin dribble of water appeared. She didn't risk drinking it, however.

Off the kitchen, she found a door that she assumed was the pantry. But when she opened it, she discovered stairs leading down to a basement that was pitch black. She shone her flashlight down the steps. The stairs appeared to be intact but beyond them she could see only darkness.

Suddenly she felt like a foolish heroine in an old gothic romance. The villain was always lurking in the basement, and even though the heroine should know that, she went down anyway to her presumed doom.

"Abigail Stanton, your imagination is getting the better of you!"

She puffed out a breath and bolstered her courage. There probably wasn't much worth seeing down there, but she wasn't going to be intimidated by ghostly tales of the past.

Flashlight in one hand, she held onto the railing and cautiously walked down the steps. The air smelled stale, filled with the strong scent of dirt and age. Tension made her neck muscles ache. Her adrenaline flowed through her veins, preparing her to flee at the least sign of . . . what? she wondered.

As she reached the bottom step, the silken threads of a spider web brushed against her cheek. Startled, she stepped back, inspecting the web with her flashlight to determine if she had disturbed its maker. Not likely. Dust particles clung to the threads like miniaturized snow flakes, the web apparently unused by its owner for quite a while.

She stepped off the bottom stair and onto the hard-packed ground. Slowly she swept her flashlight around what was a relatively small room. Shelves lined one wall, and she guessed they had once held fruit and vegetables canned in the summer growing months for use during the winter. Ellen Stanton had a pantry she had filled in the same way, often with the help of her two daughters.

A second wall held floor-to-ceiling wine racks, now empty.

But it was the third wall that piqued Abby's curiosity the most. Made of brick, which was unusual in the islands, it appeared to seal off what had once been a larger room. Some of the mortar had started to crumble. Wondering what was on the other side, she ran her finger down a seam. The brick moved.

"Now look what you've done, Miss Marple!" Good grief, now she was even calling herself the fictional character.

Her heart pounding, Abby had little choice but to investigate further. After all, how could she walk away from such an enticing mystery?

Holding the flashlight between her legs, she used the fingers of both hands to jiggle the brick free. Almost immediately, one of her nails broke.

"Serves you right for fooling around down here." Not that

her fingernails ever grew very long. Her work and outdoor lifestyle saw to that.

With the one brick removed, she poked her flashlight in the opening. There wasn't much to see. Just a long tunnel dug into the hillside angling downward. But why? What was Beauregard doing that made him want to go to so much work?

Something illegal, was the answer that came to mind.

Unfortunately, the other bricks appeared to be solidly in place. As much as she scraped with her fingers, she couldn't loosen any of them, and she didn't have any tools with her that would do the job. Learning more about whatever lay behind this wall would have to wait for another day. Given the generally spooky feeling in the basement that kept tingling the back of her neck, she was ready to call her day's adventure to an end.

With another quick sweep of her flashlight around the basement room, she decided to return upstairs. She had just placed a foot on the bottom step when the door above her slammed shut.

"No!" she shouted. Panic racing through her, she ran up the stairs.

Please, God, don't let me be locked in the basement.

No one knew she was here. It would be hours before Mary returned home and later still before she sent up an alarm that Abby was missing. Perhaps days before someone thought to check the manor house. How stupid she'd been to come here by herself!

She reached the door. Her imagination running rampant, she twisted the knob.

It opened. Just like that.

Breathing hard and feeling even more foolish than she had moments ago, she stepped out into the kitchen and leaned against the counter. Her heart beat furiously in her chest. Slowly, she began to regain her composure.

She wondered why, or how, the basement door had slammed shut. She couldn't feel any breeze here in the kitchen. The house was deadly quiet, although she sensed she wasn't alone.

"Had someone been in the house all along and attempted to shut her in the basement?

She hurried to the front of the house. She checked every room but could find no sign of a human interloper. Could the door just have closed on its own?

As she passed the library again, the woman in the picture all but called to her. Her fragile appearance. The way her sad blue eyes seemed to track her movements.

Glancing furtively around, Abby walked up to the fireplace and stood in front of the portrait. Had Beauregard actually murdered his wife?

Tentatively, she ran her fingertips along the edge of the heavy wooden frame, so wide and sturdy it made the woman in the picture appear even less substantial and more lonely.

"I wish you could tell me what really happened to you."

As if in answer to her plea, Abby felt a latch click where her fingertips had rubbed against the picture frame. With a tug, the heavy painting swung away from the wall to reveal a niche about a foot and a half deep.

Inside, stacked neatly one on top of the other were three large hardbound books.

Abby stood mute, staring at the contents of the hidden recess in the wall for several long moments before she decided to act.

Slowly, almost reverently, she lifted what looked like a large family Bible from the niche and blew the dust from the cover.

It weighed several pounds, she guessed as she placed it carefully on the straight-backed chair. Opening the book to the center, she found ornately decorated pages and words indicating this was the Winchell Family Bible. The first entry was the marriage of Angus Rudolph Winchell to Regina Jane Smyth in 1779 in London, England. That was followed by lists of births, deaths and marriages of two more generations. Turning the page, she noted the final entry—the marriage of Beauregard Smyth Winchell to Theadora Montclair, 1867, Charleston, South Carolina.

"Oh my . . ." Abby whispered.

Closing the Bible, she retrieved the next book from the secret compartment. The cover was so worn from use, the pages so fragile, she could barely make out the title—*Imitation of Christ* by Thomas à Kempis. She studied the book a moment, having a vague notion this book was somehow related to one of her favorite hymns, "Amazing Grace." But for the time being, she couldn't recall the connection.

She set that book aside and picked up the third. There was no title on the leather-bound cover so she opened it to the first page. There, in an elegant cursive script, was written: *The Journal of Theadora Montclair Winchell, begun in the Year of our Lord, 1867, Sparrow Island. Washington Territory.*

"Oh my gracious . . ." Abby whispered, nearly dumbstruck and no longer concerned by ghosts or visages from the past. For here, in her hands, the past was about to come alive.

Excitement and curiosity making her tremble, Abby sat down on the raised hearth to read the journal. Slowly, word by word and page by page, she began to feel she had entered Theadora's life and was seeing it through her eyes.

CHAPTER ✣ FIVE

At last, through a curtain of mist and rain, I can see the island that is our destination, the place where my beloved Beauregard has said we will reside.

Sparrow Island rises like a shadowed specter. The landscape is indistinct. No single tree or shrub stands out. Rather the scene is a blur of gray and deep forest green, and I shiver at the cold loneliness of such a land. The warmth of Charleston, that which I have known all of my life, has seeped out of me. Now the icy fingers of the Northwest creep into my bones.

Beauregard stands beside me in the small steamer he has hired to take us from the mainland to this new shore. As the captain rounds the final point of land and enters the harbor, I see only a few scattered buildings huddled by the landing, rustic and uninviting. It is a bleak sight, but no more grim than the ruins of the Winchell Plantation or my family's own home where even my memories were torched by the onrushing Union Army.

"On a summer's day, the harbor glistens in the sunlight like it is filled with diamonds," Beau says. "You'll be able to see it from Arrowhead Hill, my love."

I close my eyes, trying to picture the scene and fail dismally. "I shall look forward to it." I slip my arm through his and hold on tight.

The journey here has been long and arduous, around Cape Horn in a ship barely larger than this steamer and then up the coast to the bustling city of Seattle. Every day at sea I had been plagued with malaise de mer. Here, at last, I can look forward to walking on firm ground once again.

Whenever Beauregard has spoken of Sparrow Island, it has been with great joy. Even before the war between the States began and his return South to join the Confederacy, Beau had planned to settle here and had purchased land to farm. "The cool air and the mighty fir trees suit me," he used to say, a wistful look in his pale blue eyes—the eyes of a poet, my mother told me.

I pray that I too will find such comfort in the land he so loves. For I am determined to be a good wife to my husband.

Men on the dock scurry about to catch the ropes of our steamer. They are strong men who wear overalls and caps, and many of them with beards to the middle of their chests. The rain seems not to bother them.

Beau closes his hand over mine. "We're home, my love. I'll take you somewhere dry and warm while I arrange transport for our goods, then hire a carriage for you."

I look up at him, a good head taller than I. The saber scar across his cheek had once frightened me. Now I see it as his badge of courage, as are his other wounds from the war.

"You will be happy here, my dearest. I promise," he whispers. His smile is crooked because of the scar, but honest and endearing.

"I wish only for your happiness, my beloved," I reply.

He takes me to a tavern near the dock, a dark ugly place where I never would have ventured in Charleston. But the men are courteous to me, doffing their caps, and the tavern owner's wife greets me with great enthusiasm.

"Land's sake!" says the woman introduced as Minerva Sutterskill, laughing a deep-throated sound that rattles through her chest. "We're glad to have a new neighbor like you and your husband. We womenfolk are anxious to hear news of any sort but mostly want to know what fashions are new. This is a terrible backwater, you know."

I surely would have guessed that from the simple skirt and blouse she wears without a corset. My poor mother would have apoplexy if I appeared in public dressed like that. Since the war, of course, I had reworked most of my old gowns to give them bustles and now wear fewer crinolines than in earlier years. I now own but a few pieces of jewelry, the most prized having been given to the Confederacy for the Cause.

During the course of our ocean journey, I have lost weight, my everyday gowns now hang on my bony figure. Surely a few months ashore with good food, my overall health and figure will be restored.

Minerva plies me with a plate of greasy mutton and turnips, and asks me all manner of questions, many of them far too personal. I did manage to learn her husband Dwain had served in the Union Army as a private and had lost an arm in the war, but held no ill will toward the South. A statement I could not in all honesty make in return toward the North. My family and friends have all lost so much.

Finally, Beau returns with a carriage and announces our goods are already en route to Winchell Manor on top of Arrowhead Hill. He has not yet seen the house he ordered built and is as excited as a child on Christmas morning.

Bidding good-bye to Minerva, Beau assists me with my cape and helps me into the carriage. He is wearing his gray greatcoat that marks him as a soldier of the South.

The rain has abated slightly, but the air is still cool and damp, the sky leaden. Beau wraps me in a coarse blanket provided by the owner of the carriage and hooks his arm around me.

"It is my fondest hope, Thea, my dearest, to provide you with everything you want and need." He brushes his lips to my temple in a kiss. "You only need tell me, my love, and your wish is my command."

"And yours mine, my darling."

CHAPTER ❧ SIX

Right before noontime on Tuesday, Mary entered the church kitchen to see how lunch was progressing while Janet Heinz, the church secretary, was taking a turn reading a Bible story to the youngsters.

Bea Ungar pulled a pan of tuna-and-noddle casserole out of the oven and placed it on the counter. Josh had already set out rolls and cups of applesauce for the children.

"That dog of yours surely is a sweetie," Bea said, returning to the oven for the second pan.

She was a heavyset woman with gray hair. The tiny, silver-rimmed glasses she wore always looked too small to go with her round face. Apparently she had an unending supply of bibbed aprons on which she had embroidered a different biblical message. She wore a different one each day and today's quote was: "Fishers of men" (Matthew 4:19). That seemed appropriate for the tuna casserole lunch menu.

Mary had a couple of similar aprons, too, which Bea had made for the church's annual bazaar and Mary had purchased.

"I had no idea I'd enjoy having a dog around," Mary said, scratching Finnegan's neck. "Now I can't imagine not having him to help me."

Bea found serving spoons in a drawer and laid them out. "My little pooch is a miniature bulldog. He's getting on in years, and Lord knows what I'll do without him for company."

Mary could understand the sentiment now that she'd learned to love Finnegan so much. She'd hate to lose him.

"Mrs. Ungar?" Standing with his head cocked to the side, Josh stared down at the casserole with a troubled expression on his face. "Would you mind if I just had a peanut butter sandwich for lunch instead of tuna?"

"Why, son, my boys used to love my tuna casserole. Won't you try a bite so my feelings won't be hurt?"

He looked less than enthusiastic. "Yes, ma'am. If you want me to."

Bea chuckled and waved off his need to please her. "Oh, fix yourself a sandwich after the children are fed. My feelings won't really be hurt."

Josh looked relieved, and he scurried out of the kitchen to let Janet Heinz know that lunch was ready.

For her part, Mary was quite sure Bea's casserole would be excellent. Her contributions to various church potlucks were always a big hit with the congregation.

Moments later, the sound of running feet and children's giggles penetrated the kitchen area as the children lined up at the doorway to be served their lunch. Josh grinned at Mary as he took his place behind the counter.

"Looks like you're first in line, Mary."

Shaking her head, she backed her wheelchair out of the way. "I'll let the children go first. They like to finish their meal in a hurry and get a little playtime outside before the afternoon session."

"In that case, I'll be sure to save you a nice big portion of the casserole," Josh told her as the first child in line stepped up to the counter with her tray.

Watching Josh interact with the younger children, laughing and calling many of them by name, Mary was struck once again that the church had been fortunate he'd applied for a job here.

She hoped his parents appreciated what a fine young man he was.

AT THE MANOR, Abby leaned back against the library fireplace, removed her glasses and rubbed her eyes. The pages of the journal fluttered closed in her lap, but the images of Beauregard bringing Theadora to Sparrow Island were vivid in her mind. Abby felt the chill fog on her arms despite the reality that outside it was sunny and that a hundred years had passed since the mistress of Winchell Manor had experienced that first wintry day on the island.

How anxious Theadora had been about moving to the Northwest. How difficult the war had been for her and for Beauregard as well. Abby's heart went out to them both across the years as she fought to bring herself back to the twenty-first century.

What a shame Theadora had not arrived at Sparrow Island on a bright, summery day. Her first impressions would have been very different.

Slipping her glasses back on, Abby stood and studied the

portrait above the fireplace with new understanding and empathy. Despite the grime that had built up over the years, muting the colors in the painting, Thea's auburn hair appeared vital and alive, the style soft around her delicate oval face and pulled back into long curls. She wore a gown in a pale yellow that accentuated her hair, although it did little to bring color to her cheeks. The low-cut bodice with cap sleeves revealed an attractive amount of décolletage and milky-white skin. A true Southern belle, Abby mused.

Glancing at her watch, Abby realized the time had slipped by and it was now past noon. Since she had the day off from work, Abby decided she should return home to study Thea's journal and the other books at her leisure.

As she carried them to her car, she paused to wonder again how or why the basement door had slammed shut on her. There was no sign of anyone nearby. The breeze had stilled, the tree branches now quiet and unmoving. From high in a fir tree, a crow cawed a hoarse croaking laugh that held no humor. Closer at hand, a red-breasted robin hopped along in a patch of gravel, unconcerned by his noisy neighbor.

It all felt so normal. Yet Abby continued to feel that prickling sensation along the back of her neck. She didn't think it was either Theadora or Beau's ghost trying to communicate with her.

But something surely had her instincts on edge. Yet she wasn't afraid. Somehow, in the hundred years that Winchell Manor had been vacant, among all the hikers who had visited the house, *she* had been the one to discover these priceless clues to the past. She could only believe God intended her to do something with this new information, the history that was such an important part of Sparrow Island.

But what?

She lowered her head and took a deep breath, then sent up a prayer asking for God to show her the way.

ALL DURING THE DAY, Mary kept her eye on Pastor Jim whenever he passed by. But she couldn't read his mood. He seemed his usual buoyant self, despite the weighty decision he had to make regarding the possible job in Santa Monica. She wished she could say or do something that would convince him to stay on Sparrow Island. Although she'd prayed for guidance, so far the good Lord's response had been silence.

Or perhaps, Mary thought, *I'm not listening hard enough*.

As the children cut and pasted mounds of paper fish and loaves of bread, Mary concentrated on praying only that God's will be done. For the most part, that took more discipline than she could muster.

As the close of the Bible school session approached, Josh came out from the kitchen and gave her a sweet smile.

"Looks like you've made it through another day," he said.

"And enjoyed it too. You don't suppose these children are becoming addictive, do you?" Seven-year-old Windy Swendson had given her a hug that morning and said she loved her. P.J. continued to be Mary's shadow and was so eager to help that when she'd dropped a pair of scissors, he'd outdone Finnegan retrieving them for her. Poor Finnegan had seemed to sulk for an hour.

Sitting on the edge of a worktable, Josh crossed one ankle over another. "The kids like you. You're not, you know, threatening."

"Because I'm in a wheelchair?"

"Maybe that's part of the reason. But mostly it's 'cause you don't yell and criticize. Kids don't like that."

Mary wondered if Josh had been yelled at more than he liked and, if so, by whom. "How are your parents entertaining themselves while they're on the island?" she asked.

He shrugged. "You know, just hanging out. They, um, do a lot of reading and stuff."

Now that would be boring for a young man like Josh. Not that she thought he wasn't intelligent. But sitting around while his parents had their noses stuck in their respective books wouldn't be much fun for any young man.

"Do they have access to a boat? The islands are very interesting to explore."

"Naw, I don't think they'd like that." He pushed himself to a standing position.

"Why don't you and your family come to church on Sunday? Better yet, you could all come to the Thursday night family dessert social this week. Maybe they'd meet some other couples they'd enjoy."

He shoved his hands into his pockets, his pants so baggy they looked large enough to hold a second Josh. "Um, I'll ask them but I don't think so. It's not, you know, what they like to do."

"Well, then, you come by yourself. There'll be lots of young people your age there. You might be able to make some friends to hang out with when you're not working."

"Maybe," he said noncommittally. "I gotta go help Ida get the afternoon snack ready. She wants to do peanut butter and jelly sandwiches cut in the shape of fish to go with the Bible story."

"How very creative of her."

He started to leave then turned back. "Say, do you like computer games?"

"Me?" The question surprised her. "I used to play a few with my son Zack when he was a teenager—at least when he couldn't find anyone else to play with." She laughed at the memory of her son *settling* to play with her. So unlike his younger years when he'd begged her to play Go Fish or Candy Land.

"Well, see, Rev. Hale has got a game on his computer that actually builds whole cities. You know, it's like whoever gets the biggest skyscraper up or builds the most schools wins. Except if redevelopment happens, you sort of crash and burn."

Mary wasn't sure she fully understood the concept. "Sounds interesting."

"Yeah. The Reverend said I could mess with it this afternoon, once I get stuff cleaned up. I thought maybe you, I don't know, would like to try it with me."

"Why, I'd be honored, Josh Nicholson. Thank you for asking."

She smiled to herself as Josh hurried back to the kitchen area. The poor kid must be desperate for friends to make a "date" with her. But the fact that he would was very flattering in a maternal way. Sometimes a boy needed someone to talk to. If he wanted to talk with her, she would be happy to listen.

Still, she felt there was something not quite right with that young man. Oh, she didn't mean he was dense or doing anything wrong. But his evasive answers about his parents were troubling. She certainly remembered Zack's avoiding questions when he knew the answers wouldn't please her. She got the same uneasy feeling about Josh. Except when he was telling her about the computer game.

He was hiding something. Without meeting and talking with his parents, though, she couldn't guess what that might be.

Perhaps she'd learn more later this afternoon.

"YOU CAN'T PUT A TUNNEL under the river," Josh explained to Mary. "It's against the rules."

"Well, it's a silly rule. There's a tunnel under the English Channel, for heaven's sake. I should be able to put one under that little bitty river."

Josh smiled at her in an understanding way, rather like he thought of her as a five-year-old, not a grown-up. "No, ma'am. The computer program won't let you."

She sighed. She was definitely more artist than computer geek. "If I don't put a tunnel under that river, then the people living in all those houses I built won't be able to get to work in the city."

"You need a bridge."

"But you own the bridgeworks and I don't have enough money to buy it from you."

"Yeah. I guess that means I win, huh?"

"Oh, you . . ." She swatted him affectionately on the arm. "You knew you'd beat the pants off of me when the game started."

He looked a bit sheepish. "Yeah, well, it's more fun for two to play than just one."

She leaned back in her chair, chuckling. The pastor's office was pleasantly decorated with a comfortable couch and chair placed near each other, their colors bright and cheerful. A vase of fresh daisies and snapdragons sat on an end table. Patricia Hale's touch, Mary imagined. The pastor's wife seemed to have a good eye. She'd make her husband's office a place where parishioners would feel at home, whether he preached here on Sparrow Island or in Southern California.

Josh fiddled some more with the computer mouse. "Someday I'd like to build a real city. Well, not all by myself, but plan it, you know? Like have lots of open space where kids could play and there'd be bike trails and stuff like that. And easy access for the handicapped."

"Sounds like a good ambition to me."

He stared at the computer screen. "To do that, I'd have to go to college."

"From what I've seen, you're certainly smart enough to go to college. Are your grades good?"

He shrugged. "They're okay."

Mary knew that shrug could mean anything from a C average to straight A's. "Well, you can always bring them up, if you need to, or go to a community college first."

"I guess. College costs a lot of money, though."

"I'm sure your parents will help you find a way to attend if that's what you want."

Without responding to her comment, he clicked off the computer and swiveled his chair around. "I gotta get going. Thanks for playing. You did pretty good for the first time."

She wasn't sure his compliment was warranted, given the way she'd lost by about ten thousand points. More importantly, she was worried about Josh. He'd gone from feeling upbeat one moment to terribly discouraged the next when they'd talked about college.

With a sigh, she wondered how she could help the boy.

Tired from her long day, she let Finnegan help pull her toward her van. But when she saw Henry Cobb, her beau, smiling and walking in her direction, her spirits lifted even as she felt the heat of pleasure color her cheeks.

MARY RETURNED HOME from vacation Bible school to find Abby in the living room curled up on the silk damask couch reading a book.

"Hi, Abby. What've you been up to today?" Mary said as she rolled across the gleaming hardwood floor.

Startled, Abby looked up from her book. "Oh! I didn't hear you come in. I had the day off from work today and was going to run errands, but I got so involved in this, I couldn't make myself stop reading."

"What are you reading?"

"You'll never believe it. This is Theadora Winchell's journal!"

"No! Beauregard's wife?"

"One and the same. It's so extraordinary. Here, let me read you the part when she first sees Winchell Manor." Adjusting her glasses, she looked down at the journal. "'To say I am disappointed in the house dearest Beau ordered built for us is an understatement. I try to smile and act pleased, but how can I when I find only four rooms? True, the exterior limestone is magnificent. It gives the structure a solid appearance worthy of a mansion. But the interior is destitute of refinement. Even with the bits of furniture we have managed to bring with us, the rooms look barren.

"'Beau assures me the workmen have already laid the foundation for additional rooms, and that I may search catalogs for decorative wallpaper and other fripperies until my heart is content. But this night, as I lie with my husband in our feather bed, I shiver beneath the weight of many quilts and my heart is heavy. Is it possible I have made a mistake by agreeing to move with Beau to this rustic land?'"

"The poor dear," Mary said when Abby looked up. "She sounded miserable. Although it seems like she should have given her husband a chance to prove himself. Then again, I don't suppose many men are as concerned about living in a nice house as women are."

"I'm hoping she'll be happy with the finished house. It's truly magnificent."

"You went there?"

Abby nodded. "This morning. That's where I found Thea's journal and these other books. In a secret hiding place, of all things. It's amazing no one else had discovered them in all these years."

"Do you think they're authentic?"

"They certainly look old enough to be authentic."

"Then maybe God intended for you to find them."

"That thought occurred to me too," Abby confessed.

Rolling her chair over to the end table, Mary examined the books her sister had indicated, astounded by Abby's discoveries. A thick family Bible and . . . "*Imitation of Christ.* Isn't that the book that inspired John Newton to compose 'Amazing Grace'?"

Abby snapped her fingers. "Of course. I knew there was a connection to the hymn but I couldn't remember what it was."

"As I recall, John Newton was a slave trader and captain of his own ship. He read the book during a particularly stormy voyage. Later he credited the author of the book and the Holy Spirit for his conversion and his acceptance of Christ as his Savior. He eventually became a pastor in the Anglican Church and wrote a good many hymns. And, of course, he gave up the slave trade."

"Yes, I vaguely remember the story now. But why do you suppose Beauregard saved this book in particular? From the number of bookshelves in his library, he must have had hundreds of volumes."

"I have no idea. It probably had some special meaning to him."

"Yes," Abby agreed. "You know, for a simple farmer, Beauregard certainly built himself an elegant mansion."

They discussed Abby's incredible find for a while and how she had discovered the hidden alcove, when Mary realized the hour was growing late.

"Henry Cobb stopped by the church this afternoon," she said. "He mentioned he was going to be on Sparrow Island all evening, so I invited him to dinner. I hope that's all right with you."

"You know our local constable is always welcome."

"Deputy sheriff," Mary corrected with a laugh. "Officially, his rank is sergeant."

"In either event, I'm always happy to have him drop by. And I'm sure you enjoy his company too." Abby gave Mary a teasing look, which she tried to ignore.

"He's a friend to *both* of us," Mary insisted.

"As we both well know, he is more than a friend to one of us, sister dearest."

"Oh, hush!" Heat rose to Mary's cheeks again—*like a silly adolescent*, she thought, embarrassed.

Laughing, Abby closed the journal and set it aside. "What can I do to help fix dinner?"

"Did I see you bought tomatoes yesterday?"

"You did. And as I recall, Henry is fond of my beef, tomato and noodle casserole."

"So am I," Mary said smiling and wheeled herself in the direction of the kitchen.

"He said he'd be here about five or five-thirty," Mary said.

ABBY PULLED THE CASSEROLE from the oven and placed it on a hot pad in the center of the dining room table. Mary had prepared the salad and warmed some dinner rolls while Henry set the table.

When they were ready to eat, Henry pushed Mary's chair up to the table. "That looks like a meal fit for a king," he said, taking the chair next to hers. "You ladies are some good cooks."

"That's what you said the last time you were here," Mary pointed out.

"Well, it got me a return invitation, didn't it?" He grinned at her.

Mary said grace and then they were ready to eat. Abby served a spoonful of hot casserole onto each plate and passed them around.

Henry was a handsome man with a fringe of white hair around his otherwise bald head. Although he might be considered stocky, he appeared to be in good physical condition, which was important given his job as a deputy sheriff. Abby suspected he'd never met a person he didn't like—except for felons, of course. But even then, Henry tried to look for redeeming characteristics in such individuals.

Henry held the serving plate of rolls for Mary to choose one first, then helped himself to two. Abby grabbed one and placed it onto her plate.

"How's the crime rate these days?" she asked.

"Pretty quiet," Henry said. "A couple of youngsters borrowed a powerboat over on Lopez last weekend and took it for a joyride. Seems like they were trying to impress some girls at Friday Harbor."

"Isn't that always the way," Mary commented. "Boys getting into trouble because of girls."

"And vice versa," Abby added. "Girls can get into a lot of mischief on their own."

"These days that's true enough. Didn't used to be though." After tasting the casserole, Henry smiled. "There's just nobody else who makes a casserole quite like this."

"It's the oregano and cheese that make the flavor," Abby said.

"Outside of that one boat incident, we're mostly getting lost tourists who don't know these waters well and go off on their own. They don't understand that from a boat's-eye-view, every island looks pretty much the same and sometimes the cove you're looking for is hidden. So we or the Coast Guard have to go searching for them and show them the way back to safe harbor."

"I remember going boating with Dad when we were young," Mary said. "The islands didn't look a thing like the map said they should from water level."

Abby added, "I thought Dad would never let me take the boat out on my own. Finally, I took it out without his permission. Sure enough, I got lost just like he said I would. Fortunately, another boat came by and led me back to Paradise Cove."

"I don't remember that," Mary said.

Abby chuckled. "That's because I never told anyone. And

don't you dare tell Dad now. I'd never hear the end of it and he'd probably ground me for the rest of my life."

They all laughed then. As they ate, the feeling of friendship and camaraderie was strong. Abby enjoyed the closeness they shared. After years of adolescent jealousy that plagued both Abby and Mary, it was good to realize *family* was far more important than childish misunderstandings.

Henry buttered a roll. "One of the problems we have every summer, I'm afraid, is petty shoplifting. It's almost as if tourists think candy bars and sodas are free for the taking here in the islands. It's mostly the kids, I think."

"Is Mr. Goodfellow having trouble at The Green Grocer?" Mary asked.

"Some. Happens every year though," Henry said.

"And he gets grumpier every year," Abby said. "I feel sorry for him because he works so hard and I'm not sure he has much to show for his efforts. He certainly doesn't seem to have much fun."

"Maybe we ought to include him in our prayers," Mary suggested.

Abby agreed and made a mental note to do just that in her evening prayers.

She noticed her sister looking pensive and asked why.

"Oh, I probably shouldn't say anything. It's just that there's a young man working at the church this summer. We're lucky to have someone willing to do some constructive work rather than getting into mischief like so many youngsters do."

"Who's the boy?" Henry asked.

"His name's Josh Nicholson. His parents have rented a house in Green Harbor for the summer. I gather he was bored so he applied to work at the church."

"A kid working at church sounds like a good thing," Henry said. "I wish more teenagers would take on responsibilities like that."

"True. And he's a sweet boy. I was playing a computer game with him in the pastor's office this afternoon. It was some sort of a city-building affair, and he said that's what he'd like to do."

"Be a city planner?" Henry asked.

"I think that's what he means. He'd like to help create handicapped- and environmentally-friendly cities."

"That sounds very mature for a teenager," Abby commented.

"Oh, he is. Mature, I mean. But lonely too."

Henry finished both his rolls, reached for another and then thought better of it. "Maybe this young Josh of yours would like to volunteer on the front desk at the sheriff's substation in Green Harbor a few hours a week. That would help him get a view from the inside about how a town is run."

"What a good idea, Henry! He could meet more people that way too." Mary's eyes sparkled with excitement. "I'll ask him tomorrow if he'd be interested."

That settled, they finished up their dinner, and Mary offered Henry coffee, which he accepted.

As Abby cleared the dinner plates, she said, "I've come up with a new mystery to investigate."

"Uh oh." Holding up his hands in a sign of surrender, Henry shook his head. "I make it a point to keep my distance from you amateur sleuths," he said jokingly.

"You'll love this one, Henry," Abby said. "It could be an old murder mystery right on Sparrow Island."

He pulled his eyebrows together. "Murder? How old?"

"More than a hundred years old."

"Oh, come on, Abby. Who was murdered?"

"Beauregard Winchell's bride perhaps." Quickly, she told him about her find at Winchell Manor and what she thought might be a secret tunnel in the basement. "I'm reading Theadora Winchell's journal now. I'm sure there will be some clues in it as to what happened to her."

Thoughtfully, Henry rubbed his palm along his chin. "Well, if you're going to discover anything interesting, it better be soon. They've condemned the building as an 'attractive hazard' and are going to start tearing down the old place a week from Thursday."

"*They're what?*" Abby gasped.

"The town council and the board of county commissioners have finally decided that old place is dangerous and a hazard to anyone who goes up there. Didn't you read about that in *The Birdcall*?"

Stunned, Abby sat down hard in her chair again. "Good grief, no. And I was just talking to William Jansen yesterday. He didn't say one word about anyone tearing down the manor." Abby just realized what Jansen meant when he said D-Day earlier—the day the manor was to be destroyed. "Granted, months ago I'd heard a rumor about tearing down the place, but I assumed nothing would come of it. How can they bring themselves to destroy such a lovely old house?"

Mary said, "I guess I hadn't noticed the final decision in the paper either. I confess, half the time *The Birdcall* goes directly from the front porch into the recycling bin."

"What are they going to do with the land?" Abby asked.

"Maybe make a hiker's shelter up there. That way folks would come to Sparrow Island and stay a couple of days. It'd be good for business, according to members of the town council—mostly Archie Goodfellow."

"They can't tear down that beautiful old mansion," Abby insisted. "It's a historic landmark. Why, it ought to be part of the National Register of Historic Places."

"Don't think that's going to happen now," Henry said. "Took 'em a long time to decide what to do with it. Now that they've made up their minds, it would take something big to sway them."

Abby was dumbstruck. Now that she'd just discovered Theadora's journal, she couldn't let all that wonderful history be wiped from the landscape in the name of so-called progress.

Somehow, some way, she would have to prove the historic value of Winchell Manor to both the town council members and the county commissioners.

And she had just a little over a week to do it.

CHAPTER ✻ SEVEN

'Twas grace that taught my heart to fear,
And grace my fears relieved;
How precious did that grace appear
The hour I first believed.

AFTER CLEANING UP THE
dinner dishes, Abby carried Theadora's journal upstairs to her
bedroom, knowing she wouldn't be able to sleep anytime soon.
She was too distressed about Winchell Manor being torn
down, too determined to find some way to save the structure
and the history it held.

When she'd moved in with her sister, Mary had insisted
Abby take the master bedroom on the second floor since Mary
could no longer climb the stairs. Abby had agreed, albeit reluc-
tantly. But the larger room provided enough space for her desk
and computer, a comfortable reading chair by the window,
plus the walnut-stained dresser and full-sized bed she'd had
shipped from her house in New York.

Unlike her sister, who preferred bright colors, Abby chose
more subdued earth tones in greens and beige. She'd decorated
the walls with her favorite watercolor paintings of endangered

birds; the top of her dresser held her small collection of porcelain birds, many of them gifts from friends and family.

Her Bible, a daily devotional book and the current mystery novel she was reading rested on the bedside table.

She changed into her nightgown and robe, then curled up in the reading chair with the journal. The thought that the county commissioners would tear down Winchell Manor before she had a chance to prove its value as a historic landmark tightened a knot in her stomach. There had to be some way to save it from the bulldozer.

She opened the journal to the spot where she had left off that afternoon. Within moments, she was once again seeing Theadora's life through the eyes of the young bride and hearing the words that were spoken within the walls of Winchell Manor.

TUESDAY, APRIL 16, 1867

For weeks I have begged Beau to find us a household servant for I fear my cooking shall poison us both before I am done. I have managed to burn all manner of food or, in turn, serve meat and vegetables so raw chewing becomes a monumental project.

I confess, my culinary efforts and the energy required to maintain a clean household have given me a deeper appreciation for my family's servants in Charleston. Before the war, I had rarely given them or their hard work a thought. Now I wonder if their hands were always as rough and worn as mine have become from washing and scrubbing all and sundry. No amount of lotion seems to soften them. Although dearest Beau continues to assure me that my touch is as soothing to him as a heavenly caress.

Construction of the second wing of Winchell Manor compounds my problems by raising dust that blows into the house through even the smallest crack. To open the windows risks a dust storm; to keep them closed on a warm, sunny day invites heatstroke. But I dare not complain. Beau is determined that we shall have a house worthy of his name.

"The living room will be large enough for the gay parties you so love," Beau tells me as we examine the drawings he has made. "In the dining room, you will reign as the most beautiful hostess in the San Juan Islands, a queen for all to admire."

The thought of cooking for a large gathering gives me heart palpitations and a queasy stomach. No doubt my guests would experience the same. "A queen who would poison her honored guests with her cooking?" I half jest.

Beau's laughter is nearly drowned out when a workman drops a big load of lumber from the back of a wagon, a delivery just arrived by steamer boat.

I adjust my straw bonnet, waiting for the racket to quiet before I speak. "Who shall we invite to these grand parties?" I ask, for I have met few people since our arrival and found none I would consider of our class. If I had just one true friend here, a woman with whom I could exchange experiences and tidbits of innocent gossip, I would be more content.

"We'll invite everyone, my love. Dignitaries from Friday Harbor and merchants from Seattle, who are even now making plans to build a railroad on the mainland. And, of course, our neighbors here on Sparrow Island."

"I shall look forward to the occasion," I promise, although I have much trepidation.

As I study the house plans, a question occurs to me. "Did you think to include a nursery, my dear?"

Although we are outside where the workmen can see us, Beau slips his arm around my waist in a gesture of affection. "I did. Here, next to what will be our bedroom." He points to a small room on the drawing. "Is it possible that you are——"

"No." I cover my burning cheeks with my hands. "I regret it is not so as yet. But I do long to present you with a son, Beauregard, and I pray it will be soon." How I ache to hold a babe of my own, and I know Beauregard yearns for a son to carry on his name. Surely soon God will bless us with a child. . .

MONDAY, JUNE 17, 1867

A housekeeper at last! Hallelujah! At Beau's behest, Nora O'Dooley—a stout Irish woman—is to serve as my household staff of one. That she arrives straddling a mule I can easily forgive if only she will take some of the burden of domestic chores from my shoulders. I conduct our initial interview in the kitchen, as is proper and the way my beloved mother taught me.

"I can only come over here two days a week, Missus," Mrs. O'Dooley announces in a voice that would have made a plantation full of servants tremble—and just as easily intimidates me. "Got me own family to watch out fer, you understand."

"Of course." Although my heart sinks at the news I am only to have help two days a week.

"Wouldn't be doing this, neither, if my old man hadn't a-broke his leg and won't be able to go a-fishing the whole season. We need the money what Mr. Winchell says he'll be paying me."

"You live here on the island?" I ask.

"North shore. Right close to Oyster Inlet, is where our cabin is. Got me four mouths to feed, three little girls and me son, Terrance. He's a dear lad."

"I'm sure he is, and I'll be grateful for your assistance, Mrs. O'Dooley. However many days you feel you can come."

"All right then! Let's get started. You give me a show around and then I'll be a-fixin' supper for you and your mister."

I have the distinct impression Mrs. O'Dooley, rather than I, will soon be running the household, if only for the two days a week she is present. I believe my mother held a firmer hand with the servants than I, but they were slaves with little choice in the matter. Times have changed almost beyond recognition.

THURSDAY, AUGUST 8, 1867

My dearest Beau is no farmer, and soldiering has prepared him poorly for such an occupation. His older brother Leopold had been groomed to inherit the Winchell plantation, but he was lost in the battle for Richmond. Beau never challenged Leopold's position in the family. Planting and harvesting cotton did not hold any interest for him then; I think he did not mourn the loss of the plantation as much as I ache for my family's home and the life I led there.

Now the effort to raise alfalfa for the animals and crops to sell at market seems almost beyond him, even with the help of Wilbur Beechum, whom he has hired as foreman.

There are days when I wonder why Beau chose to live on this remote island where agriculture is one of the few occupations available to him. Although the outdoor activity he pursues has, I think, healed many of the unseen wounds that had been dealt to his soul during the war. The frightening dreams that woke him nightly in the early months of our marriage come less frequently now. For which I give praise to God, for I am no longer awakened as he cries out for his lost comrades or flails about in an effort to find them. At those times, I could do little but hold and soothe him until the memory of the dream passed.

"I find the smells, the crowds and chaos of Seattle unsettling after living here on Sparrow Island," he tells me one evening when he returns by steamer ship from a business trip to the mainland. "Our home here is a far healthier place to live than in that city."

"Perhaps it would be less disturbing if I went with you the next time you have to go to the city," I suggest, finding the constraints of island living too limiting. I long for some measure of the excitement I left behind me in Charleston. "I could soothe your nerves."

He pats my hand as we sit at the kitchen table eating a thick beef stew, which Mrs. O'Dooley has made for us. The biscuits which I produced resemble the brown rocks that hamper Beau's farming efforts in the fields. Still, my beloved eats them as best he can, consuming my biscuits by dunking them first in the gravy.

"I would not want to expose you to the rough frontier life I observed," he tells me. "Unlike Green Harbor, there are parts of Seattle where it is unsafe for even an escorted woman to walk through the streets."

"You are most thoughtful of my welfare, my dear."

ABBY STRETCHED AND ROLLED her shoulders, almost surprised to find herself in her own bedroom rather than in the manor, an invisible companion to Theadora Winchell.

Theadora's unhappiness reached across the years clearly enough, but beyond that Abby had found no reason for the secret room in the cellar. And no clue to the mystery of Theadora's death. She seemed lost, set adrift by the trauma of both the war that had taken everything she knew away from her and her dramatic move to the Northwest. Abby hoped that time had allowed Theadora to find her way back to solid ground again.

But Abby considered it was possible the poor woman had indeed run off with another man in search of more excitement and a less arduous life.

Abby decided if she was to learn the truth about Beau and Theadora in time to save Winchell Manor she'd have to skim the journal and hope she didn't miss anything of importance.

WEDNESDAY, MAY 6, 1868

The house is complete!

Beau blindfolds me with a silk scarf and holds my hand as he leads me upstairs to the tower room. I have, of course, observed the construction from the outside but he has not allowed me to venture there until it is complete.

I giggle with excitement. My laughter echoes in the spiral stairway that rises from the second floor to the turret at the top of the house.

When we reach the landing, I feel the sun pouring in the windows. Already I can imagine making this room my hideaway where I can read or knit after my chores are done for the day.

"Are you ready?" he asks, his hands on my shoulders.

"Yes, please."

Slowly he removes the scarf and I blink in the bright sunlight. My breath stalls in my chest as I see for the first time the view to the south. Our fields of alfafa, recently planted, are a blinding green carpet that spreads down the hillside until it meets a swath of yellow and purple wildflowers that nestle beneath the broad oak trees. Firs and pine trees in their bright spring raiment rise at the borders of our land. Trees that Beau refuses to cut although the timber would provide us with a substantial income. He maintains that the migratory birds that use this route in spring need nesting places to raise their young.

For myself, I hope that these green fields of spring will be more productive and not turn brown with the lack of water as they did last year.

Below our fields I see the shingled tops of the houses in Green Harbor. And beyond the harbor the Strait of Juan de Fuca sparkles like diamonds on a cloth sea of azure blue.

"It takes my breath away." My voice is no louder than a whisper. "If I look far enough, I'll be able to see Charleston."

"Perhaps not that far, my love." Gently, he turns me so I am looking to the north. "From here you can just make out San Juan Island, our neighbor."

I strain to see the shape of land in the misty distance. But it does not matter. The view in all directions is so grand I can barely absorb its wonder.

"Thank you, my darling." Rising on tiptoe, I kiss his lips.

He pulls me closer. "When all the furniture you have ordered arrives, we will host the grand gala you have dreamed about, one more lavish than has ever been seen in the San Juan Islands."

"Are you sure? I know the harvest was poor last year and now the cost of—"

"You are not to trouble yourself over money, my dearest. One way or another, I will give you everything your heart desires. I vow that on my honor."

I could not but hope that was true. But over the winter months I have seen dearest Beau poring over his ledgers in the library. The effort has etched a permanent frown on his forehead.

I vow to do my part to conserve our financial resources until Beau finds a way to make the farm profitable.

Beau mentioned this day his regret that he has not heard word of his sister, Catherine. Since his parents did not survive the shock of losing both the war and their plantation, it is possible sweet Catherine knows not how to reach us.

SATURDAY, AUGUST 8, 1868

The party last night was a grand success. I am too exhausted to write more.

MONDAY, MAY 2, 1870

Although other farmers on the island appear to prosper, our harvest last fall was once again dismal. I know not why and I am certainly no farmer. But the slope of our fields is steeper than that of the others, and being on the east side of the island, the fields receive less rain than some. Perversely, what rain does fall quickly runs down the hillside to the harbor, or so it seems to me as I watch the gray clouds discharge their miserly gift of nourishment on our fields.

Beau traveled to Seattle again last week and returned grim but determined. I fear for our financial future. Within days of his journey, a team of men arrived and began digging into the hillside below our house. Beau refuses to explain what they are doing. And today a two-masted sailing ship anchored in Paradise Cove. Beau tells me we are the owners of the vessel and that he has hired a man to captain the ship. But he is secretive about his plans.

Is he to become a merchant? Of what, I wonder.

TUESDAY, DECEMBER 7, 1875

Rain pounds against the windows of my tower room and gray clouds scud low across the horizon. But I am content.

I have my embroidery and tatting—like an old woman—and a few friends with whom I can visit and pass the time. My one regret is that my womb has never been filled with a babe. My heart breaks at the knowledge that I may never be so blessed.

Beau is often gone for days at a time on his ship and has lost what little interest he once possessed in the farm. He does not tell me how he occupies his time while on board the Theadora II, *as he has named his vessel. I fear it is because I would not approve of his actions so I have stopped asking.*

SATURDAY, DECEMBER 25, 1875, CHRISTMAS DAY

With the first light of dawn, the tall masts of Beauregard's ship appeared in Paradise Cove. I am weak with excitement and relief that he has once again returned home safely, and hastily prepare a meal for him.

He brings with him exquisite gifts that I wonder we can afford: a jade necklace the color of a deep forest glade; a flawless blue-and-white ceramic vase from China with hand-painted village scenes; a silk gown he calls a kimono that feels as smooth as cream; and tiny vials of a dozen different perfumes.

But the gift that brings me the most pleasure is a tiny yellow-striped kitten with the brightest blue eyes I have ever seen and a purr so loud it could shake the foundation of Winchell Manor. I shall name her Victoria for she will no doubt become queen of the house.

AS SHE TURNED THE PAGE in the journal, Abby smiled to herself, wondering if the feral cats living at the manor now were direct descendants of Theadora's kitten, Victoria. Entirely possible, she thought.

MONDAY, JULY 24, 1876

Beau spoke to the members of our town council opposing the enlargement of the marina at Green Harbor. The townspeople want to attract more visitors and residents to our island in order to increase business; Beau is determined to keep Sparrow Island as natural as possible and minimize the development. Because he is the wealthiest man on the island, the local merchants are reluctant to defy him.

ABBY GLANCED AT THE CLOCK on her night table and yawned. It was past three o'clock in the morning. She felt as though she'd been cramming for a final exam but she still hadn't found the answers she needed to save Winchell Manor.

She flipped through the remaining pages of the journal to the final entry.

FRIDAY, DECEMBER 26, 1879

A note from my mother came this day. Her handwriting, once so graceful, is now nearly illegible. She says father is failing. I suspect she is not well either.

I must go home to Charleston before it is too late.

Perhaps some time away from my beloved will be for the best. I have pressed him of late to explain his long absences, and my inquiries have resulted in arguments or his withdrawal to the library, where he closes me out.

I fear the reason for his actions is that I would not approve of the answers he would provide. And I fear the anger my prodding questions generate.

I shudder at the thought that he is violating either the laws of the land or of God . . . or both.

FOR A MOMENT, Abby contemplated the dark night outside her bedroom window. At this point in Theadora's life, all had not been entirely perfect between her and Beau, and their arguments had been escalating.

A troubling thought slipped through Abby's mind. *Could their arguments have become so heated that they resulted in violence? Or worse. Could the brick wall in the basement conceal something Beauregard didn't want discovered? Something sinister?*

CHAPTER ❦ EIGHT

"COFFEE." WITH A GROAN, Abby ordered herself to find some caffeine.

Her eyes scratchy from lack of sleep, she went downstairs and headed directly for the coffeepot. As if determined to make that journey more difficult, Blossom wound her way between Abby's legs, purring for all she was worth.

"Blossom, you can't fool me. I know Mary has already fed you breakfast."

"She's just being affectionate," Mary said from her place at the kitchen table where she was eating her breakfast. "Or possibly she's spoiled."

"*Hmm.* I'll give her some attention after I get a jolt of caffeine into my system to wake me up."

"I did hear you moving around late last night. Was something wrong?"

Abby took a long sip of coffee and let the warmth steal through her. "I stayed up reading Theadora's journal for half the night."

"Did you learn anything of interest?"

Carrying her mug of coffee, Abby sat down opposite her sister. Blossom leaped into her lap and stuck her head right into Abby's face. She had no choice but to acknowledge the Persian's presence with a scratch under her chin, which only made the purring louder.

"I did find out that Beauregard ordered some digging on the hill behind the house, but Theadora didn't know why," Abby reported. "He also bought a sailing ship."

"Why would he do that?"

"I don't know. And neither did Theadora, which created some heated arguments between the two of them. Apparently Beau would shut himself off in the library when she pressed the issue. He wasn't very forthcoming about his business activities."

"That's not good for a marriage. Keeping secrets, I mean. Jacob was awfully good about confiding in me. He always told me we were a team, bless his heart."

"You got one of the good ones, all right." Still a little punchy from her late night, she watched Mary spoon a few bites of cereal into her mouth. "There was no indication that Theadora was about to run away with another man, as some of the stories about her suggest. But her last entry in the journal said she wanted to go home to Charleston. Her parents were ill. She also wanted a little time away from her husband."

"It must have been difficult for everyone who moved out West and were so far from their families. I'm not even sure there were telegraphs here on the island then."

"I'm not sure either but probably not. How could they have strung the wires across the water? But there was mail service. She received a letter from her mother, though there's no telling how long that letter took to reach her. The entry was dated shortly before Theadora is said to have died. Or gone missing."

"Or gone to Charleston."

"That's possible," Abby conceded. "Maybe she didn't come back for some reason. But she did seem to truly love Beau and it sounded like she had finally adjusted to island living. I don't think she would have deserted him."

Mary downed the last of her glass of orange juice and set it aside.

"Then again," Abby said, half in jest, "maybe their arguments escalated, and Beauregard was upset that she wanted to go home and locked her in that tower room she was so fond of. Or a more troubling possibility is that he actually could have killed her and buried her in the basement."

"Gracious! That sounds barbaric. He wouldn't have done that, would he?"

"Beyond the fact that they were having some marital problems, I have no idea. And I didn't even get to the second floor of the tower when I was in the house to see if there were any clues to Theadora's life there." Abby intended to revisit the house and search for clues at her first opportunity. "And I certainly haven't come up with any big revelation that would convince the town council or anyone else to save the manor house from being torn down. Although I did discover Beau was an early environmentalist here on Sparrow Island." Abby had developed an affinity for the former Confederate soldier and local landowner—all the more reason to save Winchell Manor as a historic site.

Assuming he wasn't also a murderer.

"Dearest sister, whenever you've had a mystery to solve or a cause to further, you've never given up. I'm confident you won't this time, either." Smiling her encouragement, Mary rolled her chair back from the table and carried her bowl and glass to the counter.

Finnegan stood, stretched and gave himself a shake that jingled his dog tags together.

Abby hoped her sister was right. But there wasn't a whole lot of time left. And she couldn't skip another day at work to investigate further. A deadline was looming for a grant request she was working on to fund visits to The Nature Center and the conservatory by sixth grade students from all of the neighboring islands. She wanted the field trips to become a part of the school science and ecology curriculum.

She just hoped the Washington Community Foundation would see her project as a worthwhile cause. If Beauregard Winchell were around, she imagined he'd support the concept.

MARY LEFT FOR VACATION BIBLE SCHOOL, taking Finnegan with her. Blossom paced into the living room, hopped up onto the chair by the fireplace and curled herself into a comfortable ball, apparently planning to spend her day that way.

Abby didn't have that option. After eating her breakfast, she went upstairs to shower and get dressed.

By the time she was ready to leave for work, she felt a bit more alert. The morning temperature was a comfortable sixty-two degrees and a few scattered clouds drifted in the pale-blue sky. By afternoon it would reach the mid-seventies, another perfect God-given day in the San Juans.

Thank You, Lord.

As Abby pulled out of the garage, she turned to see Bobby

McDonald jogging over from his house next door. How he never seemed to trip over his untied shoelaces was nothing less than a miracle.

She waited with the engine idling until he drew closer.

"Hi, Abby. Where you goin'?"

"To the conservatory. I have to work today."

"Oh. I was hoping you were gonna investigate the ghost at Winchell Manor. I thought maybe I could come with you."

"Sorry, buddy. I can't today. Why did you want to see the manor?"

"Well, see, I was talking to my mom and she says they're gonna tear down that old place."

"So I've heard. As a matter of fact, apparently I was the last to hear."

"Anyway, I got this idea. I went to the library yesterday and Mrs. Yardley helped me find a whole bunch of neat books on ghosts. They've even got pictures and stuff of *real* ghosts. Mom says I can borrow her camera, if I want. But she says I can't go up there alone. So I thought maybe, you know, that you'd go with me."

"Bobby, I'm really too busy today . . ."

"But if we got a picture we could *sell* it to Mr. Jansen for *The Birdcall.*"

Smiling, she reached out the window and patted the boy's arm. "Honey, ghosts aren't real."

Bobby squared his jaw and squinted his hazel eyes in determination. "But everybody says Winchell Manor is haunted."

"Then it's a good lesson for you to learn that just because everyone *says* something, it doesn't necessarily make it true."

"I suppose." He didn't look convinced.

"I'm also glad your mother won't let you go up there by

yourself. Old buildings can be dangerous." She could just imagine Bobby falling down those stairs to the cellar and hurting himself. "You stay away, okay? Promise me."

"Okay. . . I just thought—"

"I know. You wanted to be a ghost hunter."

"I just wanted to make some money. It's not easy for a ten-year-old kid to get a job, you know."

She stifled a grin. "I'll tell you what. I'll ask Mary if maybe there are some odd jobs that need to be done around here that a really smart ten-year-old kid could do. How's that?"

He brightened considerably. "Okay. But it'd still be cool if I could get a picture of a real ghost some day."

"Very cool," she conceded with a laugh.

WHEN HUGO ARRIVED IN HER OFFICE, Abby was at her computer. One part of her brain was working on the grant request she needed to submit to the Washington Community Foundation. The other, and perhaps larger portion of her intellect, was working on how to save Winchell Manor. Maybe it was as simple as Bobby had suggested. If only they could snap a picture of a *real* ghost, everyone would get excited about the Manor house. Historic value counted for much less in this technological society than phony supernatural phenomenon. And sometimes the same people who embraced ghost stories refused to admit the spirit of God into their lives because they couldn't "see" Him.

There was simply no understanding human nature.

"How is it going, Abby?" Hugo asked.

She glanced up and smiled. He was wearing a dark-blue jacket with a spiffy maroon cravat. In his mature way, he was dazzlingly handsome.

"I think we've got a good shot at the grant request for sixth graders. For the rest of it . . ." She shrugged.

"There's trouble in paradise?"

Saving the computer file, she leaned back in her chair. "What do you know about Beauregard Winchell and the manor house he built?"

"Probably no more than most people here on the island. Wealthy southerner. Brought his bride West after the Civil War. Her mysterious disappearance." A nonchalant lift of his shoulders suggested there was nothing else to tell.

"Have you ever visited the manor house?"

"I did take a hike up there shortly after I arrived on the island. It seemed quite a mansion for its time, but I've had no reason to return."

"It must have been exquisite in its day, almost posh." Unable to resist, she described the elegance of the mansion, the incredible coving in the entry, the library that must have held hundreds of books. And Theadora's journal. "There's a cellar. I think I've found a secret room or passage down there. I have no idea where it leads. Or what, if anything, is hidden there."

Hugo rested his hip on the edge of her desk. "A secret room, eh? Now that's something I didn't discover on exploration of the old place."

"They're going to tear it down in a week. I have the dreadful feeling that house, and its history, is something that should be preserved. But I can't find a persuasive argument that would convince our town council, much less the county commissioners, to lift a finger to stop the demolition."

Stroking his chin, Hugo said, "Yes, I know. In spite of the efforts of myself and the local historical society to persuade them otherwise, some of the local merchants feel the manor is actually a deterrent to tourists. It's dangerous. There's nowhere for hikers to camp up on the hill. They're talking about replacing the house with a shelter for campers. They think it will bring business to Green Harbor."

Abby groaned, despite the fact she approved of hikers—those who did no harm to the environment—visiting Sparrow Island.

"But nobody seems to care about the historic importance of—"

"You know what? You should visit Lillian Trumble. She knows more about this island than anyone else I know. If you have questions about Winchell Manor or anything else on this island, she's likely to know the answer."

Abby shook her head. She'd been away from the island so long, she didn't know half the residents and then some. "Who's Lillian Trumble?"

"She lives in a cabin up near Oyster Inlet. I'd guess, from what I know of her, that she's nearly a hundred years old. Perhaps older. And a good deal of her life she's lived right here on Sparrow Island."

"She lives alone up there?"

"I think it's safe to describe her as one independent lady. She also has a memory like a steel trap. Over the past few years, I've had some wonderful chats with her. We should all be so alert when we reach her age. Quite admirable."

Abby couldn't argue with Hugo's conclusion. And she did want to follow his advice. As soon as she got a minute to herself, she'd go up to Oyster Inlet to visit Lillian Trumble.

But for now, she desperately needed to finish the grant request. Foundations frowned on requests that came in two minutes too late. They simply wouldn't consider them. There were far too many worthy projects these days that deserved funding.

Winchell Manor and assorted ghostly tales would simply have to wait.

BY THREE O'CLOCK, she'd completed the grant request, made the required six copies and was ready to overnight the package to the foundation along with letters of support from all the school principals involved.

En route to the post office, she decided that after she mailed the package she would still have enough time to stop by the library before it closed. She should have thought of Naomi Yardley earlier; the head librarian of Sparrow Island Library might be a good source of information. Her talk with Bobby had sparked the idea.

The Sparrow Island Library was housed in a small building on Municipal Street, quite close to both the post office and the school. Though not large, it had a nice collection of children's books, especially research material related to schoolwork, and a good selection of recent best-selling fiction. If you couldn't find what you wanted, Naomi or her assistant, Beverly Coxswain, were always glad to order it for you from the library in Friday Harbor, or even from the state system.

Like all libraries, it had a distinctive smell, which Abby attributed to a combination of ink, paper and bindery glue as well as the dust of many years. This afternoon there were a half dozen students doing summer school homework at the two long tables in the center of the room. Naomi was working behind the checkout counter.

Looking up from her computer screen, the librarian smiled. "Hello, Abby. It's good to see you."

"Hello, Naomi. How are you?"

"I'm well, thank you," the woman in her mid-forties said. "What brings you here?"

"I thought you might have some information about Winchell Manor."

"Ah. With the demise of the manor imminent, I pulled together what little we have on the subject. More's the pity, I couldn't find anything that would stop Archie Goodfellow and his cronies from tearing it down."

"You tried to stop the demolition? I'd heard the rumor they were thinking about it, but I was so wrapped up in expanding the bird exhibit at the museum, I wasn't paying close attention to what was happening." Abby decided she really needed to read *The Birdcall* more often if she wanted to keep up with local issues.

"The Sparrow Island Historical Society lobbied as hard as we could to save the place, but to no avail. The society made an effort to locate grant money to restore the structure, but they came up empty. It appears both the county and the town council consider it an attractive nuisance and are afraid someone will get hurt and sue the pants off of whomever they can find."

"I guess that would be a worry."

"Since the property has been abandoned for so long and there are no known heirs, responsibility and de facto ownership falls to whatever government has jurisdiction. The town and the county have been fighting over that for years and what to do with it once they settled ownership."

Coming out from behind the counter, Naomi led Abby to a display case near the front door. "If our historical society had the funds, we'd restore the old place and move our little museum out of my garage and up there. But the cost would be prohibitive."

Putting on the reading glasses that had been dangling on a chain around her neck, Naomi used a key to open the case. "The material we have in our museum mostly dates from World War I—uniforms, letters home and so forth. Truth is, we don't know much about Winchell Manor at all. Our best information about the Winchell property is the 1870 census record." She picked up a slender book and opened it. "Both Beauregard and his wife Theadora are listed along with six head of cattle, two pigs and an unnamed number of chickens."

"Really?" Excited, Abby took the book and scanned down the age-yellowed page, turned to the next entries and found Nora O'Dooley and Minerva Sutterskill and their families listed. "Look at this. Theadora mentioned in her journal that Mrs. Sutterskill had served her her first meal when she arrived on the island. And Nora O'Dooley was her housekeeper."

"Journal?"

The surprise in Naomi's voice caused Abby to look up. "Yes. I found Theadora's journal and the Winchell family Bible."

"Why, bless the good Lord! How did you find them? Where?"

Abby provided a brief account of her activities, concluding with the regret that she hadn't yet found anything that would convince the town council to spare the manor house. Still, Naomi looked absolutely ecstatic with her find.

"Both of those records are so important from a historical perspective," Naomi said. "They're invaluable. Worth more than gold to scholars of the period, I assure you. We must preserve them for future generations."

Abby quite agreed, although she hadn't planned that far ahead as yet. "I'll keep them safe, I promise. Then, at the very least, I'll know the papers will find a good home with the historical society."

Holding her hand against her heart, Naomi said, "More than a good home. A place of honor."

Smiling, Abby turned her attention to the contents of the display cabinet. Most of the remaining material Naomi had gathered related to the general history of the San Juan Islands. There were, however, a few fairly recent articles clipped from *The Birdcall* describing emergency rescues made of hikers who had hurt themselves on Arrowhead Hill, one of whom was so badly injured after a fall he had to be evacuated by helicopter. The story indicated a sinkhole had opened up on the backside of the hill, swallowing the poor man and half burying him alive. It took several hours before volunteers were able to dig him out.

Little wonder Archie Goodfellow was afraid he and the town leaders might be sued.

From Abby's perspective, the situation looked bleak. The beautiful old mansion with its hidden secrets and amazing history seemed doomed—with or without its ghost.

Mentally lifting her chin, Abby vowed she wasn't going to give up her effort to save the old place. She still had Lillian Trumble to see. Perhaps she would provide the inspiration Abby needed.

CHAPTER ❦ NINE

W HEN ABBY GOT HOME from work Thursday, Mary was all set to go. Abby had completely forgotten that the monthly dessert social at church was scheduled for that evening. She arrived home later than usual so she changed quickly from her casual working clothes into a comfortable skirt and blouse. Mary had tossed together a chicken salad for a light dinner since there would no doubt be plenty of delicious homemade food at the social.

When they arrived at church the parking lot was nearly full. Mary pulled into the last handicapped spot.

"Praise the Lord. There are some advantages to this wheelchair business," Mary said as she switched off the engine.

With a weak smile, Abby nodded in agreement. She knew full well her sister would happily give up her handicapped parking permit even if it meant walking a mile. But there wasn't any way Mary could redo that disastrous day when she had swerved to avoid hitting a deer and ended up in a ravine.

Mary maneuvered herself out of the van with ease. Finnegan

hopped down next to her, and the three of them headed toward the church.

Children were playing outside on the lawn, running and tumbling and having a great time. Three of the little girls broke ranks and ran to Mary.

"Mrs. Reynolds! Mrs. Reynolds! Can we pet Finnegan? Pleeeease," they chorused.

Mary ordered Finnegan to sit. "Remember to be gentle," she warned the girls.

"He's so pretty," a little blonde crooned.

"I wish I could have a dog like him," a redhead said wistfully.

Abby had to admit Finnegan was the picture of good behavior and looked very handsome in the blue cape that identified him as a service dog. His happily wagging tail suggested he enjoyed the children's attention as much as they loved petting him.

When the girls' friends lured them back to their games, Abby asked, "Are those girls in the day camp?"

"They are. Real sweethearts, all of them."

"It certainly seems like you and Finnegan have made a big hit with them."

"I've decided having a dog is the best thing for breaking the ice with children and making them feel at ease with me. Maybe they sense that if the dog likes me I can't be all bad— for a grown-up, of course."

"I imagine they'd figure that out without Finnegan," Abby said with a chuckle.

Inside the recreation room they found clusters of adults visiting with each other, the hum of conversation filled with laughter and the warmth of Christian fellowship. Abby spotted her mother standing near a table covered with a huge variety of desserts prepared by parishioners.

"There's Mom," she told Mary.

"I saw The Green Grocer had strawberries on sale this week. I hope she made her strawberry pie."

"Yum. I hope so too."

Abby followed her sister through the crowd. People moved aside to let Mary pass, often greeting her with a friendly, "Hello. How are you doing?" Abby received a warm welcome as well.

She gave her mother a hug. "Tell us you made your strawberry pie."

Ellen Stanton's eyes sparkled with delight. "Your father insisted. Personally, I can't wait to try one of Martin Choi's apricot tarts. I don't know how he makes the crust so flaky."

Martin Choi and his wife Terza owned The Bird Nest bed-and-breakfast in Green Harbor. Abby had been tempted more than once to stay there overnight just so she could enjoy the couple's wonderful cooking and their gracious hospitality too.

"Perhaps you could bribe him for the recipe," Mary suggested.

"I've thought of that," Ellen said. "But then I'd have to bake them myself, and it's so much nicer to eat someone else's cooking."

Laughing, Abby asked, "Where's Dad?"

"He's meeting with some of the members of the congregation, I think. Probably in the pastor's office. The past couple of days, he's been busily plotting something with the church leaders. I think it's about the problem you two girls mentioned."

Glancing around the room, Abby noticed a good many familiar faces. And a few new people. A surprising number of visitors to the island made Little Flock Church their church home for the summer. Both the pastor and the congregation made it a point to extend a warm welcome to all who joined the congregation, whether it was for one service or the entire season.

The children began filtering in from their outdoor play. George Stanton appeared along with the group of church leaders, many of them community leaders as well.

Sensing it was time to begin, Rev. Hale called for everyone's attention.

"Thank you all for coming this evening to share both fellowship and an enormous number of calories." The crowd chuckled. "If what I see on the table is any indication, I'll expect all of you to join me jogging tomorrow morning at six o'clock. I know I'll have to go at least an extra mile to make up for what I plan to eat tonight."

"It'll take about ten miles for me, preacher," someone shouted out. "Margaret brought her New York cheesecake and I'm going to get the first piece."

They all laughed at that and Abby was sorely tempted to race the gentleman in question to that first slice of cheesecake.

"With that said," Pastor Jim continued, "please join me in saying grace before there's a stampede to the dessert table." He raised his hand for silence and closed his eyes.

"Dear Heavenly Father, we thank You for the blessing of good friends and family joining together in Thy presence. Let Your bounty of love and goodwill fill us with joy and reverence for Your goodness. Bless these gifts that we share, make the hearts whole of those who are troubled and lift up the spirits of those who struggle to know You and accept Your will. We ask this in Your name. Amen."

"Amen," the group echoed.

He was about to invite everyone to partake of the desserts when Abby's father stepped forward.

"Pastor Jim, before we begin I have something to announce that needs to be said in front of the entire congregation." A low murmur of surprise rippled through the room. "First of all, the members of the congregation want you to know how much we appreciate your leadership here at Little Flock. And the significant contribution Patricia makes to church life, as well." With a nod, he acknowledged the pastor's wife, who was standing nearby with little Toby in her arms.

"No amount of money would ever be enough to compensate for what you both give to us every single day you are here, and we want you to know you have our gratitude beyond what any words can convey.

"However, after carefully reviewing the church budget and our personal pledges, we believe there is something we can do that may make it clear how important you and your family are in our lives.

"As of tomorrow morning, Little Flock Church will open a college fund for Toby and any other children you may have in the future."

Patricia's hand flew to her mouth and tears suddenly welled in her eyes, making them shine. Looking equally surprised, Jim looped his arm around his wife's shoulders.

"Each year the church members pledge to contribute to that fund while you are our pastor. We want you to know that the balance of the fund will be in your name to do with as you desire, should God call you to serve another pulpit. Although it's difficult to predict how much college will cost by the time Toby is ready, our goal is to invest the money wisely and we expect the final amount to defray a large part of the expense.

"What we're doing, Jim, is bribing you to stay at Little Flock. We hope you don't mind."

There was a moment of silence while Jim tried to find his voice. "Patricia and I, we're very grateful. Not just for your thinking of a college fund for Toby, but more importantly, for your love." The depth of his emotions showing, he glanced around the room then cleared his throat. "I thought we all came here to eat. How about we get started."

Everyone applauded, and Abby could tell the members of the congregation were as moved by the pastor's love and gratitude as she was.

LATER, WHEN MARY SAW JOSH standing alone by the windows, his plate piled high with desserts, she wheeled her chair over to him.

"I'm so glad you decided to come tonight," she said.

He chewed vigorously, trying to down a big forkful of strawberry pie he'd just put in his mouth. "This is great," he mumbled. "Really good."

"Did your parents come too?"

"Um, they had something else they wanted to do." He popped a chocolate chip cookie into his mouth.

He ate like the proverbial teenage boy trying to fill his hollow leg. Mary remembered Zack being the same way when he was in the middle of one of his adolescent growth spurts—something that lasted for years, as she recalled.

"Well, maybe they'll come next time. Tell them they'd be more than welcome. How about the idea of volunteering at the sheriff's station a few hours a week? Have you had a chance to ask them about that yet?"

He licked some chocolate off his finger. "I decided, you

know, I'm not real interested. Police work isn't what I had in mind. But thanks anyway."

"Of course." Searching for some better way to involve him in the community, she glanced around the room. "Have you had a chance to meet any young people your age?"

"Not really."

"I'd be happy to introduce you."

"Naw. I'm okay." He wiped a few crumbs from his mouth with the back of his hand. "I think maybe I'll have another cookie or two, and then I'll split."

"Whatever you'd like. I'll see you tomorrow."

"Yes, ma'am." He scooted past her and headed directly for the dessert table one more time.

Mary couldn't help but smile despite the fact that she was worried about the shy young man. She really wished she'd had a chance to meet his parents. That might reassure her that Josh was in good hands.

Pastor Jim sneaked up beside Mary and squatted down by her chair, resting his hand on her arm. "I have a feeling you're the one behind Toby's new college fund."

"I confess I told Dad about your upcoming interview in California. I hope you don't feel I violated your privacy."

"No, not at all. It isn't a secret that Patricia, Toby and I are flying down there this weekend to talk with the church leadership. But I was absolutely stunned by your father's . . . well, really, this church's generosity. So was Patricia. And very grateful."

"I imagine they thought lifting one worry from your shoulders would help, whatever decision you eventually make."

"Well, whoever came up with the idea, we can't say how much we appreciate your thoughtfulness."

"You and your family deserve whatever we can provide."

"Sometimes even a minister can get so wrapped up in worrying about providing for his family that he forgets God's promise in Matthew 6:26. 'Look at the birds of the air; they do not sow or reap or store away in barns, and yet your heavenly Father feeds them. Are you not much more valuable than they?' I know those words as well as I know my own name. But isn't it strange how easily we forget to apply them to our own lives?"

Mary palmed his cheek as she would her own son's. "You're a good man, James Hale. Don't you doubt that for a single moment."

Jim stood as another man joined them. "Mary, you know Steven Jarvis, the bank manager here on the island, don't you? Steven, this is Mary Reynolds."

Mary extended her hand to the man who was wearing a business suit, starched white shirt and a conservative navy-blue tie, far more formally dressed than the rest of the men attending the dessert social. "Fortunately, I haven't had any bad checks bounce, so we haven't had many dealings."

He took her hand, his smile was both confident and reassuring. "I promise, if one of your checks should bounce for some reason, I'll cover it myself and give you a personal call."

"I hope that doesn't happen any time soon," she responded. "But I certainly appreciate the thought. Nice to know our local banker is looking out for me."

"I do my best, Mrs. Reynolds. For all the folks on Sparrow Island."

"Steven is in charge of managing Toby's college fund for us," Jim explained. "They tell me he's something of a genius at investments."

"I wouldn't go quite that far," he replied modestly.

Although he appeared to be in his mid-thirties, he was totally bald, having shaved off what little hair he had left. His size and broad shoulders made him look more like a football player than a banker. But his mannerisms were all top-drawer business, and Mary had no doubt he would take good care of Toby's money. And hers, for that matter.

"Maybe I should give you some of my savings to invest too," she said.

"I'd be happy to open a special account for you, Mrs. Reynolds."

"Why don't you call me Mary? Otherwise you'll make me feel *really* old."

"From what I hear from Pastor Jim, you're a woman who will always be young at heart."

Chuckling, Mary decided this man was so polished and intelligent, it wouldn't be long before he was the bank president. And quite a lady-killer, too, she imagined. He almost made her wish she were twenty years younger. Almost, that is. Maturity had its own rewards. And she had Henry.

As she and Abby were leaving, they caught up with their parents who were also en route to the parking lot.

"You did good, Dad," Mary said, wheeling up beside him. "I never would have thought to start a college fund for Toby, but it was the perfect answer to at least one of the problems that's been worrying Pastor Jim."

"You two girls planted the seed," he said, grasping one handle of her wheelchair. "My job was to make the problem known to others and see if they could come up with an answer. With God's help, of course."

Ellen caught her husband's free hand and laced her fingers

through his. "In this case, I hope the answer will be enough to encourage Pastor Jim to stay here on Sparrow Island."

"Amen to that," Mary agreed.

IT WASN'T UNTIL THE WEEKEND that Abby had a chance to visit Lillian Trumble, who lived near Oyster Inlet on the north shore of the island. She hoped Hugo was right that Lillian might have information about Beauregard Winchell and his wife.

The road to the north shore was under repair, so Abby opted for traveling by boat. She could have taken her dad's fishing boat that he kept in the Green Harbor marina, but that would mean motoring around the point where the ferry arrived, then all the way up the east coast of the island. It would be a shorter trip to start at Paradise Cove.

So, making sure she knew how to get to Lillian's cabin, she arranged to borrow Stuart Lynch's outboard motorboat. Long-time family friends, the Lynches had a summer home with a private dock at Paradise Cove, near the north end of the con-servatory property. They'd given the Stanton family a standing invitation to use the boat whenever they wanted. The sixteen-foot aluminum craft was easy for one person to maneuver and had plenty of horsepower.

After finding the key to the boathouse in its not-so-secret hiding spot above the metal door, Abby helped herself to a life jacket and oars, which she put into the boat along with her backpack containing snacks, bottled water and of course, her binoculars.

In upstate New York where she'd lived for so many years, there'd been few opportunities to study shore birds. Abby appreciated the chance she had now and hoped to devote not only more of her own free time to the endeavor but also to expand the displays at The Nature Museum.

Here in Paradise Cove there was no shortage of species to enjoy.

A pair of sea ducks floated lazily on the slowly undulating water at the end of the dock. At the shallow end of the cove where eelgrass grew, a solitary great blue heron stalked its prey. Across the cove, a group of western sandpipers played tag with the two-inch-high waves that rolled onto the sandy beach, snatching bits of food as the waves departed again.

Untying the lines, she gingerly climbed into the boat and sat down at the stern by the outboard motor. She checked to make sure she had plenty of gas for the round-trip. Then, with one press of the starter, the motor came alive with a hearty growl. She idled the engine for a moment before easing away from the dock.

The sea ducks scampered out of her path to the relative safety of the far side of the dock.

Slowly she navigated toward the mouth of the cove. As she reached the entrance, a flight of cormorants skimmed along the top of the open water heading north, their long necks extended as though they were determined to reach their hunting grounds as quickly as possible.

Although she was anxious to learn more about Beauregard, Abby intended to make hers a more leisurely trip. Setting her course, she reached into her backpack, plucked out her binoculars and placed the strap around her neck.

A mixed forest of fir and spruce rose up along the shoreline on this side of the island. Periodically a break occurred, revealing a summer cabin nestled in the woods with its own private dock at water level. Some of those cabins, she noted, were as large as Mary's house and had a wall of windows that provided a full view of the water.

A pair of porpoises overtook her. They sped out in front of her boat, leaped into the air and showed off with a somersault. Wheeling around, they came back alongside the boat as though asking for her approval, then cavorted over and under the wake of her boat.

Laughing, she applauded. "Nicely done, gentlemen. I'm sorry I don't have any fish for you. Maybe next time."

The larger of the two acknowledged her promise, or so she thought, by making another graceful arc through the air. Then the two of them swam off, bounding along in a perfectly synchronized water ballet. Using her binoculars, Abby watched them until they were out of sight.

As she rounded the next point, she waved to the occupants of a twenty-foot cabin cruiser going by in the opposite direction, a Canadian flag flapping from its fantail. Moments later the cruiser's wake gently rocked her boat. The sea in every direction appeared to be dotted with weekend sailors enjoying a bright, sunny day

As she scanned the shore again, she spotted a mother deer and her two fawns grazing on clumps of grass above the high tide mark. Not far from them a cow was placidly chewing her cud while her calf nursed.

Smiling, Abby let Genesis 1:24 run through her head. "And God said, 'Let the land produce living creatures according to their kinds: livestock, creatures that move along the ground, and wild animals, each according to its kind.' And it was so."

"Thank you, Lord, for this beautiful day," she said aloud, feeling almost giddy with the fullness of His love, thankful for the path in her life that had brought her home to Sparrow Island.

CHAPTER ❦ TEN

Through many dangers, toils and snares,
I have already come;
'Tis grace hath brought me safe thus far,
And grace will lead me home.

ABBY THROTTLED BACK as she reached the area near Oyster Inlet that Hugo had described. Sandy spits stretched out into the water, piled high in places with a tangle of old, water-smoothed logs and other debris. Boulders lined the shore where the pounding of the sea had cut away the hillside leaving a six-foot-high berm.

There were fewer houses along this stretch of the island. Poorer access to the sea and the distance to Green Harbor made it less attractive to summer visitors and impossible for most permanent residents to manage.

Except Lillian Trumble.

Abby cruised slowly by the inlet, well offshore so she wouldn't get snagged on an old, water-soaked log or run aground on a submerged rock. Hugo had told her Lillian's home was located on the eastern side of the inlet, which meant she'd missed it on her first pass.

Turning the boat around, she headed back, this time staying in closer to shore. The entire area seemed untouched by human hands, left the way God had intended it to be. A rock strewn shoreline in the foreground, a mature forest of pine and fir trees as a backdrop. Abby wouldn't mind spending a few days here herself, communing with nature and enjoying the wilderness.

On her third pass by the area, Abby finally spotted what she hoped was Lillian's log cabin behind two huge boulders that protected it from the winds that could sweep down from the Arctic regions. The roof was sod, and a thin trail of smoke drifted up from a pipe chimney. Evidently, Lillian was something of a recluse.

Beaching her boat on a sandbar and securing a line around a heavy log, Abby took off her life vest and hooked her backpack over her shoulder. She walked up what appeared to be a path toward the cabin. In a slender inlet on the sheltered side of the spit, she saw a small boat with an outboard motor tied up to a rickety old dock. Apparently the boat was Lillian's mode of transportation if she needed to visit civilization.

Struggling up a few steps cut into the side of the hillside, Abby reached the top breathing hard. And there, standing on the front porch of a cabin that looked like it had been built using a grand set of Lincoln Logs, stood a woman with a shotgun in her hand . . . pointed at Abby!

Oh dear . . .

"Chances are real good you're lost, Missy. I suggest you get yourself on back to your boat, or however you got here, and head south. I don't abide trespassers."

Abby suspected as much. "Are you Lillian Trumble?"

The woman, who was a tiny thing with thinning white hair, and probably weighed less than a hundred pounds, lowered the shotgun an inch but no more. "I am."

"Hugo Baron sent me. I wanted to ask you some questions about Beauregard Winchell and his wife."

"Well, for pity's sake, why didn't you say so, girl? Hugo called to say you might drop by. Come on up here where I can get a good look at you."

"Yes, ma'am." Swallowing hard, Abby did as she'd been told. And as she drew closer to the log structure, she realized it was far larger than she'd imagined, with rooms added on to what she guessed had originally been a one-room cabin.

Fortunately, the owner of the cabin propped the shotgun against the porch railing, which reassured Abby. "I'm sorry I showed up without calling. Hugo didn't mention you had a phone and for some reason I assumed—"

"I don't give out my number to most folks, and Hugo knows that. People are always calling just to stick their noses in your business. Don't need any of that. But Hugo, there's a true gentleman. More's the pity I didn't find a man like that when I still was young enough to care."

Desperately trying to suppress a smile, Abby nodded in agreement. "He's a fine man. I'm working with him now at the Sparrow Island Nature Conservatory. I'm the Associate Curator."

"Well, don't that beat all." She motioned Abby up onto the porch. "Come on in, girl. I'll give you a glass of my special root beer."

"Root beer?"

"My own recipe. I make it by boiling bark. It tastes purely dreadful but it keeps the ol' juices flowing, I'll tell you that."

With a shake of her head, Abby followed the woman inside. While the place was rustic, and the furniture in need of reupholstering, it was the shelves upon shelves of books that impressed Abby the most. Volumes spilled out onto the floor and were piled on top of every horizontal surface in sight. The collection rivaled the Sparrow Island Library.

"Come into the kitchen, girl. There's more room there. Hugo mentioned your name but I've forgotten. Old age, you know."

"It's Abby. Abby Stanton."

The woman halted so abruptly, Abby almost ran into her. "Any relation to Elizabeth Cady Stanton?" she asked.

"The suffragette? Not that I know of."

"Fine woman, Elizabeth was. My mother was real fond of her and told me all about her." Lillian proceeded into the kitchen, which had a makeshift counter and a small propane stove. More books were stacked on the table. "You from around here?"

"I grew up on Sparrow Island. My father is George Stanton. He used to run a charter boat service here in the islands."

"Heard of him, maybe. Don't know him personally though. I was born here but didn't live here my whole life. Had other things I wanted to do. Came and went over the years, then came back here permanently maybe twenty years ago. Haven't left since. No reason to."

"I see." She didn't really. But she certainly didn't want to argue. This lady was one powerhouse of a woman despite the slight hump of her back from osteoporosis and fingers mis-shapened by arthritis.

"Your mother was involved in the suffragette movement?" Abby asked.

"That she was. As I got old enough, she took me along too." She laughed an amazingly hearty laugh for her size. "Now, didn't we just show those boys a thing or two in the old days. They didn't know what hit 'em when we showed up waving our banners and marching around."

"It must have been a fascinating experience for you."

"We made history, that we did." Opening a small refrigerator, she retrieved an old milk bottle containing a dark liquid. "Now then, you ready to give my root beer a try?"

Abby tried not to grimace. "Actually, I'm not thirsty. But thank you for offering."

She barked another laugh. "Smart girl. Maybe you'd like some sun tea. Make that myself too."

"As long as it's not made from trees, I'd like that."

Finding two mismatched glasses in a cupboard, Lillian poured the tea out of a pretty cut glass pitcher that looked like it might be antique. They sat down opposite each other at the kitchen table. Through the window, Abby could see her borrowed boat on the beach and the water beyond. She could barely make out the low silhouette of San Juan Island in the misty distance.

"I've never spent much time exploring the north shore," Abby said. "It's quite lovely in its way."

"My Grandfather O'Dooley built this cabin more than a hundred and thirty years ago, and my mother was born right here. 'Course, the place was much smaller then and didn't have fancy stuff like a propane stove. Imagine my grandpa would think I'm slothful, not chopping my own wood to cook and heat with. But I like my creature comforts, I do." Nodding at the thought, the older woman took a long sip of tea.

Barely able to believe her ears, Abby stared at her hostess in amazement. "Was your grandmother Nora O'Dooley?"

"Yep, one and the same."

"And she worked as housekeeper for Beauregard and Theadora Winchell?"

"That's the truth, all right. But how did you know?"

"I've read Theadora's journal. This is the most incredible thing. I had no idea . . ." Hastily, between swallows of tea so her mouth wouldn't go dry, she told Lillian about finding the journal and how the county was going to tear down the manor house in less than a week.

"Over my dead body they'll tear down Winchell Manor!" Lillian said when Abby had brought her up-to-date on the situation. "Don't those fools understand anything about the history of that place?"

"Apparently they are more concerned about getting sued if someone seriously hurts himself on the property. I'd desperately like to find some way to save and restore the manor. What I know of the history makes me think it's an important landmark, but I don't have enough evidence of its value to convince the town council, much less the county commissioners at Friday Harbor, to save it. The only thing the merchants in town want to do is find a way to use the property to attract tourists so they'll spend money in their shops."

For a few moments, Lillian's blue-gray eyes glazed over and she seemed to draw into herself, looking backward through time. Abby waited patiently.

Outside, a crow cawed a warning to his flock, and a dozen of his friends took to the air in a flurry of black wings. Almost immediately an eagle soared past the sand spit where Abby's boat was beached, perhaps in search of an easy lunch of crow. *Better luck next time, fellow*, Abby thought.

Lillian shoved her chair back. "I think I may know of something that will help. My grandmother, and my mother in her time, became fast friends with Beauregard. Both of them kept diaries. I've done the same for most of my life." She got up from her chair. "Come this way."

Excited, Abby followed her into the living room.

"Most of the books you see belonged to Winchell. After he died, Mother didn't know what to do with them. Grandma O'Dooley was dead by then. So mother brought them over here so thieves and vandals wouldn't get 'em, and here they've sat ever since."

Looking more closely at the spines, Abby realized the volumes were quite old, many of them books on philosophy, religion and science. Naomi Yardley at the library would be in seventh heaven to get her hands on these for the Sparrow Island Historical Society.

"Here's what I was lookin' for," Lillian announced, tugging a book from a tightly packed shelf. "Grandmother's diary from about that time. Haven't looked at it in years, but seems to me she had a lot to say about Beau. I know she described the whole layout of the manor in great detail. She was quite taken with the place, don't you know. She even described the velvet drapes Theadora ordered specially made and the Turkish carpets." She cleared a stack of books from an easy chair and sat down, opening the diary in her lap.

"Does it say what happened to Theadora?" Abby asked. "There are so many rumors."

"My mama was never a hundred-percent sure about that. According to Beau's story, Theadora was washed overboard on his sailing vessel in a wicked-wild storm in 1880 or there-abouts. They were somewhere en route between here and the mainland, Seattle likely."

"On her way back to visit her family in South Carolina?"

"Don't know about that. Mama told me the man was so dis-traught, he didn't like to talk about what happened to Theadora. Which, according to Mama, meant he was keeping some sort of a secret."

"So it's possible he did murder Theadora? And that's why people think she's haunting the manor?"

"Is that what they're sayin' in town? Here, let me find the entry for you." She flipped through the pages, finally coming to a stop near the middle of the diary. "It's dated Tuesday, March 15, 1881. My own mother would have been less than a year old then."

Finding a pair of reading glasses among the clutter of books on the end table, Lillian put them on and began to read from the diary.

Beauregard came to see me this afternoon. I had not seen him in weeks and barely recognized him now. His body was gaunt, his cheeks and eyes sunken, his hair long and stringy and unkempt. His clothes looked as though he had worn them for weeks without change, either day or night. I drew him into the house and asked if he was ill. He told me a terrible tale, which I will try to relate in as much detail as I can recall, although there were moments when Beauregard became so distressed during the telling I could not be sure what was fact and what were the ravings of a man on the edge of madness.

"I have lost her. My beautiful Theadora. She is gone to Heaven."

"What happened?" I asked, shaken that the woman who had become my friend has met her Maker.

"It is my fault. I should have known a storm was coming. But she was anxious to leave and upset with me and my ventures. I thought surely with time apart she would come to understand what I had done was for her. For us. And she would forgive me.

"But God sent down His heavy hand upon me and struck me to my soul. He let the waves rise up higher than my ship, clear to the Heavens before crashing down on us. We took on water. I knew we would sink. I rushed to Theadora's side below decks in our cabin and brought her topside. She was the first into the dingy, I made sure of that, and brooked no argument from my men.

"But then God's hand swept her over the side. Without a thought, I went in after her. I swear I did."

At this point in his tale, he began pacing about the room, muttering to himself, "Take me, Lord. I deserve the fires of hell for what I have done. Take me . . ."

At this point, I tried to calm Beaugard and offered him a cup of tea. When he finally returned to his senses, I asked him to continue. He looked as pale as death itself.

"Once in my struggle to reach Theadora, I closed my hand around her gown, to save her, but she was torn from me and could not swim. And then she was gone. Forever.

"I should have died. I prayed to God that He would take me too. But He did not answer my prayer."

The poor man wept in my arms for hours, and I held him as I would one of my own babes. I have never known a man to be so bereft over the loss of his wife. I am heartsick as well and grieve for them both. Though the entire truth we may never know.

LILLIAN LEANED BACK IN HER CHAIR. "There you have it. According to Beau, Theadora Winchell was lost at sea."

"Although your grandmother did harbor some doubts."

"She did. Yet their friendship continued until his death, so she must not have feared for her own life."

After reading Theadora's journal, Abby couldn't imagine Beau killing his wife or her running off with another man. "But what happened to him after Theadora died?"

"My mother used to tell me how he'd show up at odd intervals, sort of an eccentric uncle figure in her life. Other than our family, he had little contact with the outside world."

"A recluse," Abby concluded.

"As Mother grew older, she and Beau developed something of a friendship. And when Grandmother passed on, he consoled her."

"Did she ever learn why Theadora was angry at Beau?"

"Not that I heard about. Grandmother had related the two of them had some arguments, but she didn't hold with being too nosy about their private business. Particularly since she worked for 'em."

"It's true enough that he'd lost his ship, so he didn't go sailing off anymore. And then in his grief, he all but became a monk, studying the Bible almost every waking hour and searching for forgiveness. He carried a terrible burden of guilt."

Tenting her fingers in front of her chin, Abby thoughtfully considered what she'd learned of Beau and his life. "I think he may have found salvation and had his life changed the same way John Newton, the author of 'Amazing Grace,' did."

"How's that?"

"Newton experienced his conversion and found Christ after a disastrous storm, just like Beau. Among other things, Newton credited the book, *Imitation of Christ*, for his personal acceptance of Christ as his Savior." Abby paused a moment because she could hardly believe that she'd discovered the key to the final years of Beau's life. *What an amazing story.* "I found that book hidden along with Theodora's journal."

Abby had been perched on the edge of the couch, which was covered with books. Still struggling to put the puzzle pieces together, she pushed herself up and paced to the window, looking outside. The sun had circled to the south, which cast most of the northern shoreline in shadows.

"The history of the Winchells is incredibly fascinating, but I'm still not seeing how it will help me save the manor house."

"Well, horse feathers! If nothing else, the town council could turn it into a tourist attraction as a haunted house. That ought to draw folks up there, and they have to eat somewhere. It'd be a regular amusement-park attraction for the island."

"Except it isn't really haunted. Although a young friend of mine had pretty much the same idea, making it a haunted house. Still . . ." She didn't think that's what God had in mind when He led her to find Theodora's journal and now Nora O'Dooley's diary that described Beauregard's grief over the loss of his wife. There had to be some larger, more important reason. Something to do with the history of the area. Or perhaps Beauregard's religious conversion.

"There might be one other person who could give you some help," Lillian said.

Abby raised her brows. "Who?"

"A fisherman by the name of Bryant Pettigrew might know something I don't. His daddy, and his granddaddy before that, ran the old lighthouse up 'til the time a new one was built, and later it was automated. They might have passed down stories about Beauregard's sailing ship and what he was up to."

"Where would I find this Mr. Pettigrew?"

"The ol' coot has his smelly ol' boat tied up at the marina. It leaks like a sieve, as near as I can tell, but he fusses around her day and night like she was a fancy fifty-foot yacht belonging to the Queen of England or somebody just as snooty."

"In that case, I'll make it a point to visit him at the marina as soon as I can."

"Well, if he can't come up with anything that'll stop the authorities from tearing down the manor, we can always hold off the demolition with a protest. You know, pickets and banners and such. I could lash myself to a pillar or something 'til they back off. Did that in one demonstration in Albany, New York, and they had to haul both me and my mother off to jail, the dern pillar included. It was a sight to see, I'll tell you that. We made headlines that day!"

"I imagine you did," Abby said with a laugh. "If it comes to that, I'll certainly keep you in mind, along with Naomi Yardley and the members of the historical society."

"You do that, girl. It'd take me no more than a half hour to get to Arrowhead Hill. We'll show 'em."

Abby cocked her head. "It must have taken me two hours to motor here in my boat. How on earth could you—"

"Honey, I got me a sweet little ATV—all-terrain vehicle— a four-wheel baby that can take me up the old trail my grandma used to take to the manor when she was working there. Of course, she rode a mule."

Abby laughed out loud. "Lillian Trumble, I can't tell you how glad I am to have met you. You are one incredible woman!" Even if they couldn't save the manor, knowing Lillian was worth a lot.

Lillian extended both of her arthritic hands to Abby and

held hers. "Sweetie, you need me to and I'll round up half the folks on Sparrow Island. I have a little influence still even if I don't go to town often. We'll have ourselves a protest like them ol' boys here have never seen the likes of."

Abby didn't doubt her word for a minute. But the question remained, what could or should be done with Winchell Manor if they didn't tear it down?

IT WAS MID-AFTERNOON when Abby returned to Paradise Cove and secured Stuart Lynch's boat to the dock. The placid waters of the cove held new meaning for her now, the image of Beauregard's sailing ship vivid in her mind.

Looking up toward Arrowhead Hill, she imagined Theadora impatiently waiting in the tower room for the first sign of the ship's masts and Beau's return from his latest adventure. Abby knew she was past due to see that view for herself, but her further investigation would have to wait until she made a quick stop for gas.

Although Abby's hybrid car was very fuel efficient and economical to drive, periodically she did need to fill it with gasoline. Given the downward angle of the needle on her dashboard and the red Empty mark, Abby decided now— before she drove up Arrowhead Hill—would be a wise time to get gas at the one station on the island, which was Al's Garage on Municipal Street.

She pulled up to a pump and got out to serve herself. Just as she'd inserted the nozzle in the tank and started the pump going, a man approached her. Probably in his mid-twenties, he was tall and slender, with dark brown hair pulled back in a ponytail and a scruffy beard. His jeans and lightweight jacket looked as though he'd slept in them for weeks. Only his white running shoes looked reasonably new.

"I'm sorry to bother you, ma'am," he said. "Somebody stole my wallet when I was sleeping on the beach last night."

"Goodness. Did you report it to the sheriff's office?"

"Yes, ma'am, I did, but they couldn't be much help. See, the thing is, I'm trying to put together enough money so I could ride the ferry to the mainland. My mom's been sick. Once I'm on the mainland, I could hitchhike home. I haven't had anything to eat except peanut butter sandwiches for days and now that's run out. If you could see your way clear to give me a couple of bucks, that'd be a real help, ma'am."

"I see." Abby knew a panhandler when she met one, and based on her experience, this young man probably had more money in his pocket than she did. "Tell you what, I'll give you directions to Little Flock Church. It's not a long walk from here. Pastor Jim or the church secretary can give your mother a call. I'm sure she'd be willing to wire you some money for ferry and bus fare home plus some spending money for food."

The young man's pleasant expression evaporated. "Look, lady, all I'm asking for is a couple of bucks. It's no big deal."

"Which is why I'm confident the church would be more than willing to contact your family."

The panhandler said something unpleasant under his breath, wheeled around and stalked away.

Shaking her head, Abby finished filling her car with gas. As she got behind the wheel again, she noticed the panhandler talking to a middle-aged couple who were strolling up the street. The gentleman handed the young man a bill from his wallet, then the couple continued on their way while the panhandler shoved the money in his jacket pocket, turned and approached the next couple he spotted.

Abby believed in helping those in need, and she tried not to be judgmental. But this kid, who appeared to be perfectly able-bodied, looked like he was taking advantage of other people's generosity instead of finding himself a job.

She admitted it was possible she was wrong, however. She didn't want to get the young man in trouble with the law for violating the anti-panhandling ordinance.

For now, she'd leave it alone. Perhaps later she'd have a chance to ask Henry Cobb what he thought of the panhandler's story, including whether the missing wallet had been reported.

Pulling out of the gas station, she drove down Municipal Street to Primrose Lane, the road that went past Stanton Farm, and headed toward Arrowhead Hill.

When she got to the manor, she parked behind the house. The two little kittens tumbled out from their hiding place under the smaller building's porch. Curious, they came right up to her without coaxing.

She knelt to pet them, noting again how very blue their eyes were. *Are you descendants of Theadora's cat Victoria?* All these years, yet it seemed so right. "I'm going to have to do something about you two kiddos."

The way things were going, she'd have to write herself a note about the kittens or she'd forget again. *Apparently, Lillian Trumble wasn't the only one with short-term memory problems,* she thought with a self-deprecating smile.

Entering the house through the front door as she had the first time, she first walked through the downstairs looking for signs of recent visitors. All appeared in order until she reached the kitchen. An empty can of tuna that hadn't been there during her prior visit now sat on the counter by the stained sink.

"I don't imagine tuna fish is a favorite with ghosts," she muttered. But it did make an easy meal for someone living out of a backpack. She'd done it herself on a few back-country trips but had always packed the empty can back to civilization.

Trying to ignore the uneasy sensation that gnawed at her stomach she climbed the stairs to the second floor. Along the hallway were several empty bedrooms. The layer of dust on the floor appeared as though it had been undisturbed for years.

But on the steps that led to the tower room she found footprints. Several of them. Some with the telltale tread marks of contemporary running shoes. No ghost would leave a trail like that. But the panhandler in town could have, she realized with a start.

She swallowed hard. "Hello! Anyone up there?" Her voice echoed through the empty house.

Cautiously, her flashlight in hand, she climbed the spiral staircase to the top of the turret. Her dry mouth forced her to swallow again and lick her lips.

When her head reached the floor level, she quickly looked around then edged up the remaining stairs. On one side of the room, beneath the windows, was a daybed of sorts with a wadded blanket at its foot. A duffel bag was open on the floor beside the bed. Squatting down, she examined the bag without touching it.

No name tag. Masculine clothing. A slight smell that hinted of gym clothes, old locker rooms and too few baths. Nothing at all sinister or ghost-like.

These probably belonged to either the panhandler or another man, a hiker, she guessed. Someone who wanted to stay on the island but couldn't afford any of the accommodations in town. Or preferred to stay here away from the crowds of tourists.

Maybe she had indeed misjudged the man she'd met. Although if his story about an ill mother was true, he would have jumped at the chance to get some real help from a church.

Standing again, she looked out the windows. Except that Green Harbor had grown in the past hundred years, the breathtaking view was exactly as Theadora had described it. The ferry was departing the harbor, passengers leaning on the railing as they watched the dock slip away. The marina for private boats was undoubtedly larger than it had been in Theadora's day. The tall masts on sailing yachts formed a forest of spires, and the protective canvas over the boat cabins and decks accented the scene with splashes of bright blue.

To the east, Paradise Cove stood with the open arms of a safe harbor awaiting the return of Beauregard's ship.

Her gaze fell again on the daybed where some visitor to the island had slept. *Whomever he is, there should be somewhere safe and clean for him to stay without trespassing on private property, abandoned or not, and at a price he could afford. A place where college-age biology majors and adult bird-watchers could stay while they study the migration patterns of birds that call Sparrow Island home for a span of days or weeks. And learn about birds who nest here and are year-round residents.*

Her gaze settled on the small but sturdy building behind the manor and realization struck her like a lightning bolt.

Dear Lord, You answered my prayer a week ago by leading me here, but I wasn't listening to You. Forgive me. I should have realized simply by 'wishing' for a place for students to stay that You would provide a place for them. And you have. Thank You, Lord. Help me now to glorify Your name and reach the hearts of those who learn of Your Works. Amen.

Abby was so excited, she could barely breathe. The manor could be restored as a testament to Beauregard's life and his conversion to Christ. Assuming she could talk Lillian into it, all of the books Beauregard had treasured would be returned to the shelves in the manor library. *Imitation of Christ* would be in a place of honor as well as Theadora's journal and the Winchells' family Bible. The history of the island and its people would be on display. And the building in back would house students as a youth hostel. A safe place to stay and study.

She hurried down the stairs, her hiking boots loud on the steps, but when she reached the first floor, she halted. What she had in mind would cost a small fortune.

The Sparrow Island Historical Society didn't have that kind of money. And she surely didn't have a personal account that large. The funding would have to come from somewhere else.

As she left the manor, she realized the person most likely to have an answer to that problem would be Hugo, who was something of an expert on grant requests. Even if the historical society had previously explored grant opportunities, she now had more historical information that would make the request more appealing to funding sources.

Bryant Pettigrew at the marina could possibly fill in some of the blanks about Beauregard's shipping interests, and that would help too.

The town council certainly wouldn't agree to spending tax money to restore Winchell Manor even if it would bring additional tourists to the island.

She sighed and climbed behind the wheel of her compact car. Anything worth doing meant hard work, so that's what she'd have to do. And do it in a hurry.

CHAPTER ❦ ELEVEN

ALL IN ALL, I'D SAY Lillian Trumble is quite an amazing woman," Abby concluded after relating her day's experience to Mary during dinner.

"It's incredible she lives out there by herself at her age."

"Outside of some arthritis, she seems more than capable of being independent. Besides, I suspect she'd drive the management of a retirement home crazy in under a week. They'd probably take her back to Oyster Inlet themselves."

Mary chuckled at that. "I can appreciate her attitude. I'm not exactly ready for an old folks' home myself. And I'm very grateful, with your help, I still have considerable independence and can do for myself."

"And cook for me, in the process. Your fried chicken was wonderful." Using her napkin, Abby wiped her fingers. "After my visit with Lillian, I went back to Winchell Manor. There's definitely someone staying there. From the clothing I found, it's a male. He appears to be using a daybed in the tower room to sleep on, has a duffel bag with his clothing and apparently likes to eat tuna. I found an empty can in the kitchen."

"Tuna?" Mary said. "I wonder who it could be."

"Whomever is staying there has sure made himself scarce when I've been around. I did meet a young man while I was getting gasoline. He claimed he'd been sleeping on the beach and was robbed. His story didn't add up for me, particularly when I said the church would help him get back home. I took him to be a panhandler. But maybe he's also the guy squatting at Winchell Manor."

"Maybe he only sleeps there at night and the rest of the time he's out panhandling or exploring the island."

"That's a possibility. He seemed nice enough until I wouldn't give him any money, then he turned snarly. I'm not eager to hang around the manor at night on my own waiting to see if he's the one who shows up. He could be a criminal on the run or something."

Mary grimaced. "Maybe we should ask Henry to check it out. The squatter's trespassing, after all."

"Henry will probably say the problem will solve itself next week when they tear down the place, which will be true unless I can find a way to save the manor. I also have to find the funds to turn it into something else, like a historical museum."

"Goodness, won't that take millions?"

"Certainly a great deal more than I have in my bank account," Abby replied, feeling discouraged. She glanced at the kitchen clock. "I'm going to call Hugo to see if he can meet with me Monday afternoon to talk about possible funding sources. He knows more about charitable foundations than I do." Standing, she picked up both plates and carried them to the counter.

"You go call him now," Mary said. "I'll clean up here."

"But you did the cooking. I really should—"

"Go, go, Abby. If you fuss with the kitchen mess you'll just be mentally fretting about what Hugo will say. I can manage fine on my own."

Feeling a rush of affection for her sister, Abby bent down and hugged her. "How come when we were kids I didn't realize what a nice person you were?"

"Because I wasn't nice. Big sisters aren't supposed to be. They're supposed to toughen up their kid sisters by teasing and picking on them. Then the kid sister can grow up to be a world-famous ornithologist and the big sister can take all the credit."

"Oh, you . . ." Abby hugged her again, then went upstairs to her bedroom to call Hugo.

ABBY ARRANGED TO MEET HUGO at the office on Monday, then curled up in her reading chair to study *Imitation of Christ*. She'd barely heard of the book until she found it in Beauregard's secret hiding place; fifteenth-century authors had never been high on her to-be-read list. But she was convinced the book had been an inspiration to Beauregard and instrumental in his conversion and his acceptance of Christ, a process he'd needed to help him deal with his grief and guilt after he lost his wife.

The book had a musty smell to it, and the pages were flimsy and yellowed with age; smudges marked the corners where Beau had turned them. Some passages were underlined in bold, black ink as though the words had particular importance to him. She read some of those sections aloud.

It is vanity then to seek after, and to trust in, the riches that shall perish. It is vanity, too, to covet honours, and to lift up ourselves on high. It is vanity to follow the desires of the flesh and be led by them, for this shall bring misery at the last. It is vanity to desire a long life, and to have little care for a good life. It is vanity to take thought only for the life which now is, and not to look forward to the thing which shall be hereafter. It is vanity to love that which quickly passeth away, and not to hasten where eternal joy abideth.

Abby let the meaning of the passage sink in.

Apparently both the author, Thomas à Kempis, and Beauregard shared a concern that they had been too vain, too proud of their earthly possessions. Perhaps Beau had concluded he'd been wrong to build his castle—or manor, in his case—and gather riches here on earth instead of concentrating on eternal life.

Jesus taught the same lesson, she mused, admonishing His followers to store up treasures in Heaven instead of on earth and to follow Him.

Abby always left her bedroom door ajar so she could hear Mary call if she needed help. Apparently Blossom had heard Abby reading aloud and came to investigate. She tiptoed into the bedroom and stood looking at Abby with her head cocked to one side, her bright blue eyes curious.

"It's all right, Blossom. I haven't gone crazy yet." Moving

the book aside, she patted her thigh to encourage the cat to jump up.

After considerable indecision, Blossom leaped up, landing gently on her lap. The cat began to knead Abby's stomach, her paws pressing rhythmically. Smiling, Abby decided it was quite a compliment that Blossom had accepted her so easily as part of her family. Cats, she believed, adopted people, not the other way around.

"Would you be interested in fostering two little kittens?" she asked as she petted Blossom and scratched her under her chin. In response, a loud purr rumbled through Blossom's chest. "They're very playful. I'm sure I can catch the little ones, but their mommy might be too wary of people to be caught easily. If I take them away from their home, I'll have to find a good family for them. We could name them Albert and Victoria II in honor of their ancestor.

Curling up in Abby's lap, Blossom appeared to have little interest in the kittens' future.

"I thought perhaps because you were once a stray yourself that you might be a little more sympathetic," Abby teased the cat, who continued to ignore her. Abby wondered if Blossom even remembered being cold, wet and hungry before Mary took her in at the flower shop. Perhaps not, although she'd certainly made herself at home since that time.

Adjusting her position slightly to be able to read while not disturbing the cat, Abby skimmed through more pages of *Imitation of Christ* and came across another line Beau had apparently marked for emphasis. "Go forward therefore with simple and undoubting faith."

That was a message she would have to heed, too, when it

came to finding a means to restore Winchell Manor. Somehow God would lead her to find a way to save the manor.

THE RESIDENTS OF SPARROW ISLAND woke on Sunday to a cloudy day, with dark clouds scudding through the sky and the threat of a full-fledged storm promising to unleash its fury during the next day or so. Mary had heard on the news that storm warnings were up for small boats from Puget Sound north to Vancouver. Summer storms were rare, but when they came they could wallop the San Juan Islands with amazing ferocity. Living in the "rain shadow" of the Olympic Mountains didn't always help.

She pulled her van into the church parking lot only minutes before the service was supposed to begin. The lot was nearly empty.

"Looks like half the congregation was scared off by the threat of rain," Abby commented.

"No. I think it's because Pastor Jim isn't preaching this morning. Some church in Santa Monica is going to have the pleasure of hearing his sermon."

"That's right. And thousands of others will be seeing him on TV as well."

Upset that the church members had deserted the congregation because they had a substitute preacher—a retired minister who had taken the trouble to drive up from Everett, Washington at the crack of dawn and take the ferry from Anacortes—Mary maneuvered herself out of the van and said, "People should at least be considerate of someone who has gone to such effort to give us a sermon." Using Finnegan to help her, she wheeled her chair past the row of rhododendrons in full bloom, their flowers spilling over the low picket fence that set off the lawn area.

"I remember Pastor Jim talking about how a church isn't built around a particular minister or isn't a building with beautiful stained glass windows," said Abby. "It's about God and letting God into your life."

"Remind me to tell him when he gets back that he needs to do a rerun of that sermon."

"Don't get so worked up, Mary. I'm sure our visiting minister will be glad to preach to whomever shows up this morning. And I'm sure there will be a big turnout when Pastor Jim returns."

"If he does," Mary muttered.

Abby crouched down beside her. "We've prayed that Jim will find the right answer for him and his family. We have to have faith that the answer will also be best for Little Flock Church."

Mary grimaced at the reminder that her faith wasn't always as strong as she might hope. "How'd you get so smart, Abby?"

Abby grinned, then stood and took hold of the grips on the wheelchair, pushing Mary inside, Finnegan trotting along beside them. "Because I had this really smart big sister, how else?"

"*Humph!* I'll just be glad if Jim returns and tells us he hated California and is going to stay on Sparrow Island for the rest of his days."

Mary heard Abby's laughter as she positioned her wheelchair in the designated handicapped spot near the back of the sanctuary. The pianist was already playing the prelude to the service. Admonishing herself for behaving little better than those who hadn't shown up at church this morning, she bowed her head and asked the Lord for forgiveness and to grant her a whole lot more patience.

MONDAY WAS STILL CLOUDY and overcast, the threat of rain even more imminent than it had been the day before. While Mary got ready to go to the vacation Bible school, Abby took time for her morning devotions, sitting by her bedroom window where the light was best.

After she was done, she still had enough time before work to go in search of Bryant Pettigrew at the marina and ask about his forebearers, the local lighthouse keepers.

Wind snapped the flags above the boathouse and rattled the ropes against the tall masts of sailing boats in the marina, the weather keeping most of the sailors at the dock. Seagulls that normally perched on top of the masts had found sheltered spots on the shoreline out of the wind. Even so, their feathers ruffled with each gust that blew through the marina. Shivering, Abby zipped up her jacket.

She found Rick DeBow—a handyman who seemed able to fix anything from broken plumbing at the church to diesel engines—literally up to his elbows in grease.

"They certainly give you all the fun jobs," she teased.

A quick smile curled his lips and the laugh lines around his eyes crinkled. "Hey, this is a great job. I can get as dirty as I want and nobody complains. Every six-year-old boy in the country should aspire to this."

She chuckled, suspecting that was exactly how he felt about his work. "Say, do you know where I could find Bryant Pettigrew?"

"Sure. He keeps his boat at the far end of the marina. It's the *Princess Lola*." He gestured the direction with his head. "I think management insists he keep that ol' crate of his out of sight as much as possible."

"Thanks. Have fun with your project."

"I will. Stay dry. I think the storm coming will be a wet one."

She thanked him again and walked along an asphalt path until she reached the last dock. There, half grounded in the mud, she found the fishing trawler, *Princess Lola*, which looked nothing like a princess at all. Rather, she resembled a run-down lady of the sea who had seen far better days.

Sitting on the dock beside the boat was a man of indeterminate age, his face as leathery as cowhide, repairing a commercial fishing net.

"Mr. Pettigrew?" she asked.

Slowly, he raised his head. His pale blue eyes focused in on her. "Yep, that's me," he drawled. "But most folks call me Bryant. What can I do for you, miss?" His fingers were as gnarled as an old oak tree, but they worked the net with a facility born of experience.

Abby introduced herself. "I understand your father used to run the lighthouse here on Sparrow Island."

"Yep. My grandfather too. He got hired by the Coast Guard when the lighthouse weren't hardly more than a big ol' bonfire he had to keep goin' all night. Then my pa ran the new one 'til they decided weren't no need for real people to watch out for ships that were wanting to go aground. Fired him just like that." He snapped his callused thumb and forefinger together.

"That must have been difficult for your father." Since he

didn't stand, she hunkered down to his eye level. "Did your father or grandfather ever tell you stories about Beauregard Winchell, the man who owned Winchell Manor?"

"Yep."

Abby had been hoping for a little more information than a one-syllable response provided. "Do you recall if they ever told you anything about Beauregard's sailing ship or what business he was in?"

Bryant's fingers kept up a steady pace on the net, twisting and turning the heavy threads. "Yep. Biggest rumrunner in the Northwest."

Rocked back on her mental heels by Bryant's statement, Abby's jaw dropped. "Beauregard was a rumrunner?"

"Grandpa said he was one slick operator. Brought in a bunch of fancy ceramics and whatnot from the Orient too. It weren't necessarily legal, I'm thinking."

"No, perhaps not." Abby had read somewhere that rumrunning was a frequent occupation during the late 1800s. She simply hadn't considered that Beauregard might be involved. She could see why his wife would object, which no doubt led to their arguments. "Do you know if, after his wife died, he continued with his illicit trade?"

He took a few more tucks in the net. "Don't see how. His ship went down in a winter storm. Lost half of his crew, and lucky to survive himself, according to my grandpa."

"Was his wife lost at sea as well?"

His fingers halted their busywork and he lifted his gaze. "Why you askin' all this stuff?"

"Because they're going to tear down Winchell Manor and I'd like to save it. If I can, I'd like to prevent the demolition from happening, which means I need to know everything about Beauregard and his wife."

Silent, Bryant looked off into the distance. The wind whipped at his thinning hair, blowing the gray strands almost upright.

"My grandpa said Beauregard's wife was one fine lady. Given the chance, I think he would have married her hisself. To hear Daddy tell the tale, Grandpa grieved almost as much as Beauregard did when Theadora went down with the ship. She must've been something special."

"Yes, I think she was." With two accounts of Theadora's death at sea—plus the evidence in Theadora's journal of her love for her husband—it seemed unreasonable to believe Beau had murdered her. In this case, Abby was more than happy to conclude the evidence suggested Beauregard was innocent of any wrongdoing toward his wife. The fact that he and Theadora argued over his rum-running only showed marital discord—not murderous intent.

Abby stood. "Thank you for you help, Bryant."

"Weren't no trouble."

Smiling, she wished him a good day and hurried back to her car. She was anxious to get to work. In the afternoon, she'd meet with Hugo and enlist his aid to find funding to restore Winchell Manor. Both the incredible beauty of the mansion and the stories that it held demanded it not be lost to a bulldozer.

THE MORNING WENT BRISKLY for Abby as she finished some museum paperwork she had to get out of the way before her afternoon meeting with Hugo. The rain started just as Abby arrived at The Nature Museum. Glad that she'd worn her rain jacket, she hopped out of her car and hurried inside.

Given the marginal weather, a good many local families as well as tourists had decided The Nature Museum was the place to spend a rainy afternoon. Kids scurried around checking out the exhibits. The Mount St. Helens hologram had drawn a big crowd. At the mammal display, a five-year-old girl had begun to name the stuffed animals. "You can be Bernard," she informed a red fox. "And you're Eddy because he's small too," she told a white-footed mouse. "You better run lickety split or Bernard will eat you up."

Stifling a laugh, Abby proceeded to the back of the building where the offices and workroom were located. The workroom contained stacks of boxes and the materials for new and rotating exhibits.

In contrast to the workroom, Hugo's office was incredibly neat.

Looking up from a book he was reading, Hugo greeted her with a smile. "I gather you found Lillian Trumble an interesting woman."

"I did. And now that I know more about Beauregard, I'm more determined than ever to save Winchell Manor."

"Well, let's see what we can do." Standing, Hugo pulled open a file drawer, each blue folder tabbed with its own neat plastic label. "I have here summaries of the requirements and areas of interest of various charitable foundations. In addition to the fact the Sparrow Island Historical Society had previously approached some of these foundations for support, I think your problem is going to be their respective deadlines. In order to save the manor, you need a funding source that can make instant decisions. That's not generally how they operate."

"But this is an emergency." There were only days to go before the wrecking ball showed up. After that, her efforts would be pointless.

"Well, let's take a look." Lifting several files from the cabinet, he laid them on a conference table. "Maybe we can find some circumstances that will allow us to apply for an emergency grant."

Abby certainly hoped so.

As she poured through foundation mission statements and grant histories, the rain outside grew heavier, blowing against the windows. Drops formed on the window panes and streamed down in rivulets to the sill. Occasionally a burst of childish laughter could be heard coming from inside The Nature Museum.

Both Hugo and Abby stayed with the search for a suitable foundation until after closing time. Outside, it had grown prematurely dark and the security floodlights had automatically turned on.

Inside, the overhead lights flickered and a few moments later Abby heard the rumble of thunder in the distance.

She took off her glasses and rubbed her eyes. "Have you had any luck?"

"Not much," Hugo conceded. "Given enough time, our own little Sparrow Island Historical Society might be able to raise some money locally. But even that would need to be supplemented by an outside source."

"I'll talk to Naomi at the library. I've been reading the material on the Washington Island Preservation Trust. I think they're my best bet."

"The Washington Community Foundation is a possibility. But generally they provide funds for educational or community development undertakings like your sixth grade program, not historical projects. I'm not optimistic about them." He passed the file across the table to her.

Taking the file, Abby put it with the Washington Island Preservation Trust material. "I'll call them both first thing in the morning. If I could just get a commitment from one of them, I could probably convince the town council to hold off for a while."

The lights dimmed again and thunder followed.

"Is there anything unique about the manor we haven't considered?" Hugo asked. "You mentioned something about a cellar."

"Of course!" Abby came to her feet. "We've got to check out what's behind that false wall. I know there's a secret passage of some sort. Do you have a sledgehammer or a pick?"

He appeared startled by the question. "Here at the conservatory?"

She headed toward the door. "There must be some tools in the conservatory building out by the nature trail. We can get them and drive up to the manor house now. Then, whatever we discover, I can tell the foundations about it in the morning."

"Abby! Are you talking about going there now? It's almost dark."

She glanced back over her shoulder. "That doesn't matter. It's always dark in the cellar. Besides, what happened to your spirit of adventure?"

Shaking his head, he said, "I fear I may regret this decision but, as a gentleman, I cannot let you go alone. I would never be able to forgive myself if the 'spirit' of Winchell Manor did you harm."

She grinned at him. "Bring the biggest flashlight you can find."

LIGHTNING FLASHED ACROSS THE SKY. The windshield wipers on Abby's car worked frantically to clear the rain—a losing battle. The headlights barely pierced the downpour, making it difficult to make out the old wagon trail that wound its way up Arrowhead Hill to Winchell Manor.

"We might have picked a worse day for this little adventure," Hugo commented, "but offhand, I can't think what it would have entailed. An unexpected blizzard, perhaps."

Abby's lips twitched with a hint of a smile. "I'll plan something special for you the next time the weatherman predicts snow." That was an unlikely forecast in the San Juans.

"Please do. I recall the time I was in the Himalayas. Dangerous place, that. Nearly froze my fingers off making snowballs. The village children had ganged up on our hiking party. We went down in terrible defeat only to be rescued by the elders with cups of warm horse's milk. Amazing restorative powers, that horse's milk."

Without taking her eyes off the trail, Abby laughed. "It seems unlikely we'll need to take such drastic action tonight." Her tires slipped sideways on a muddy spot and she began to wonder if she might need more than a cup of horse's milk to rescue her from this escapade. If her car lost traction, she'd need a tow truck to get her up the hill—assuming she didn't slide all the way back down again. She would have been wiser to borrow her father's pickup.

Reaching the summit, she drove around to the front of the mansion instead of parking in the back where she usually did.

She wanted to minimize the distance she and Hugo would have to run through the storm, shovels and hammers over their shoulders.

As she pulled up, a flash of lightning zigzagged from the dark clouds directly overhead to the iron lightning rod on top of the house. The entire tower room lit up with an eerie white light. Almost instantly, thunder bombarded the top of the hill along with the bitter smell of ozone.

Abby cried out. Or maybe that was someone else's scream she heard. Instinctively, she covered her ears and ducked down on the seat. In an equally spontaneous move, Hugo used his body to shield hers. As the thunder continued to reverberate across the hilltop, Abby became aware of the rapid beating of her heart and the reassuring caress of Hugo's hand on her back.

"Easy now," he murmured. "We'll be all right."

Slowly, her pulse rate returned to normal and the only sound she heard was the steady beat of rain on the car's roof. She lifted her head as Hugo eased his protective embrace. She'd been on her own for so many years, it had been a long time since a man had sheltered her in his arms.

Licking her lips, she tried to steady herself. "I think that's the closest I've ever been to being struck by lightning."

"Makes you realize how puny man is compared to nature's power."

She exhaled in relief. "Amen to that."

"I don't supposed you'd consider waiting until the morning to continue this little adventure."

Looking up at the tower room, it appeared perfectly normal with no flames or smoke shooting out of the windows. Thank goodness. She would have hated for the house to be destroyed by nature's fury before she had a chance to save it and discover what other secrets it held.

A distant bolt of lightning appeared well off to the east. The thunder that she knew would follow didn't reach her ears.

"I think the storm's moving on now. So as long as we're here, we might as well get it done." Grabbing her flashlight, she opened her door, pulled the hood of her rain jacket over her head and climbed out. Hugo did the same on his side and they both picked up tools from the trunk of the car.

The rain had lessened considerably, but there was a lingering scent of ozone in the air as they reached the front porch. Abby opened the door.

"We just let ourselves in?" Hugo asked.

"That's what I've done before. So have periodic hikers, based on what I've seen."

She shone her flashlight around the entryway and stepped inside.

"Impressive," Hugo commented, following her, his flashlight playing around the entry and the chandelier overhead.

"Worth saving."

This time she walked to the foot of the stairs that led to the second floor. She didn't want to come upon the panhandler from the ferry unexpectedly. She'd sensed in him a temper that he didn't always keep in check, and if he was the man camped out upstairs, he could well consider the manor his private domain.

"Hello! Anyone up there?" Considering the crack of lightning she'd heard, someone sleeping in the tower room would have gotten a rude awakening. She hoped whoever had been staying there had had enough sense to be somewhere else when the storm started.

Hearing no response to her call, she headed for the kitchen and the door to the cellar. Curiously, the empty can of tuna was gone from the kitchen counter. In its place was a commercial-size jar of peanut butter and an empty bread wrapper. Just what the panhandler said he'd been eating.

The screech of old, rusty hinges startled Abby. She took a step back, bumping into Hugo. He steadied her so she wouldn't fall.

"Not to worry," he said. "It's only the wind blowing open the back door."

"Odd. I thought that door was bolted shut from the inside. Unless you think Beauregard unlocked it," Abby said with a nervous laugh.

"I think perhaps the storm drove off Beauregard's ghost."

Abby didn't really think the ghost had anything to do with the back door. But perhaps, between the storm and the visitors arriving, the resident hiker had thought better of hanging around and had left it unlocked. She pulled the door shut to keep out the rain and threw the bolt. "Let's go downstairs while our shy trespasser is elsewhere."

The cellar was as dark and musty smelling as it had been on her first visit, and the eerie sensation that crept along the back of her neck was just as potent. She was very glad to have Hugo there to back her up.

She loosened the brick again and let Hugo peer inside.

"Can't see much from this angle," he commented.

"Well, there must have been something in there at one time or there wouldn't be any reason to seal it off."

"Maybe we're dealing with the Winchell equivalent of the Edgar Allan Poe story, 'The Cask of Amontillado,' where the unfortunate character Fortunato was mortared into a secret room and left to die."

Abby shuddered at the thought of someone being bricked up behind that wall while he, or she, was still alive. "Let's hope not. From what I've learned about Beauregard, I've gained a certain amount of respect for the man. I wouldn't like to think of him as having a cellar full of skeletons."

"Very well. You hold the light and I'll see what I can do about uncovering the secrets of the past."

Hugo struck the brick next to the missing one with his hammer three times before a corner of it broke off. The rest remained firmly in place.

"I'd say whoever built this wall did a very journeyman-like job," he commented. "And used quality materials. This is going to take a while."

Watching as he pounded away on the bricks, Abby had to agree. The wall had been built to last a long time. She wondered if archaeologists digging around in ancient Egyptian tombs got the same impression and were as excited as she was about uncovering long-lost mysteries. She wished she'd thought to bring her camera to document their findings, whatever they might be.

After Hugo chipped away at the bricks for a half hour, Abby relieved him and gave it a try herself. A sledgehammer would have worked much better, or a small stick of dynamite, she thought as the hammer bounced off a particularly stubborn brick, doing it little damage.

She lost track of time. The shovel they'd brought along was useless, so they took turns with the hammer, first one and then the other. The constant ring of the hammer against brick dulled her senses.

Finally, Hugo stepped away from the wall, a fine sheen of sweat on his forehead. "I think the hole is big enough for you to get through now. If you're up to it, why don't you give it a try?"

Swallowing hard, her flashlight in her hand, Abby squeezed through the irregular opening.

CHAPTER ❦ TWELVE

The Lord has promised good to me,
His Word my hope secures;
He will my Shield and Portion be,
As long as life endures.

I ANYTHING, THE ROOM she'd entered was darker than the cellar she'd just left. The blackness pressed against her face, almost as though the very atoms in the air were themselves larger than normal particles, expanded by the weight of carrying more than a century of secrets within them.

Slowly, using her flashlight, Abby scanned the area in front of her. Not a room, a tunnel. There, no more than ten feet away, the passage was blocked by a sheer wall of dirt carved from the hillside and braced with wooden pilings. But the tunnel was empty.

Disappointment slammed into her chest like a fist. She'd been so confident that more secrets were hidden here beneath the house. But there was nothing.

Hoping that what she saw was somehow an optical illusion, she walked forward and touched the wall. The dirt felt cool to her fingertips and very solid. Turning slowly, the bitter taste of defeat in her mouth, she let the light play over the walls of the empty passageway until, to her right, the light shot past the wall and beamed down a longer tunnel.

"Hugo, the passage turns here. I'm going to follow it."

"Wait for me, Abby. I don't want you in there alone. It could be dangerous."

She heard him start to pound on the bricks again to widen the opening. Her excitement building once more, she peered cautiously into the passage. The sides and ceiling, braced with wooden cross bars, reminded her of old gold mines she'd visited in the California foothills of the Sierra Mountains.

Within a matter of feet, the tunnel widened slightly and the wall on the right became brick, the same deep red color of the wall that had separated the cellar from the passageway. But this wall had a massive oak door.

Puzzles within puzzles, she thought. A bold crucifix was carved into the door as though it was the entrance to a cathedral. Or a tomb.

With Hugo still pounding at the bricks, Abby could wait no longer. She entered the tunnel and headed for the door. She ran her fingers across the fine-grained wood. Gripping the handle, she pulled the door toward her, straining against the weight and the years of disuse. Slowly, with a protesting groan, the door released its hold on the past and swung open.

Air as dry and stale as a desert and tinged with the faint scent of pine oil escaped from its century-old confinement.

She swept the light around a room that was twice the size of the living room upstairs, so deep her flashlight could barely penetrate to the darkest corners. The ceiling was high enough that it was beyond her reach and looked to be whitewashed;

the solid floor was made of paving stones placed closely together so no dampness could creep up from the soil.

And everywhere, ghostly pillars rose like macabre spirits from another world or giant gravestones in dusty gray marble. There were rows of them, stretching back as far as the beam of light could reach.

"Hugo?" Her voice was barely above a whisper. She tried harder, filling her lungs with the dry, stale air before she called him again. "Can you come back here?"

A moment later, a second light appeared. "I'm here," he said breathlessly. "What . . ."

"You tell me."

They stood there a moment, both of them playing their flashlights around this strange, hidden room trying to decipher what they were seeing.

Apparently less dumbstruck than Abby, Hugo stepped forward and gingerly touched the first. . . whatever it was.

"I believe it's a sheet of some sort." He lifted what was now obviously fabric and pulled it away from the first object.

Not a pillar or a gravestone but a lovely rococo dresser, a woman's piece in layered rosewood. The mirror had silvered, the reflection dulled with age, but the clusters of exquisitely carved fruits and flowers around the mirror and on the dresser itself were intact.

Abby drew in an amazed breath.

"I'm not an expert on furniture," Hugo said, "but I'd guess this is pre-Civil War."

"Theodora's dresser. I'd stake next month's paycheck on it. She may have brought it with her all the way from South Carolina." With a loving touch, Abby ran her fingertips across the polished top that had been unchanged since the day

Theadora left her home for the last time. The dry air and the absence of termites had protected the wood, although the finish looked worn by years of use. A tiny stain appeared on one corner. A spill of perfume? Something as simple as a splash from a cup of coffee or tea? There was no way for Abby to tell.

Turning, more confident now, Hugo whisked the cover off another piece of furniture. It was a clock that stood five feet tall and resembled gothic clock towers in England or France. The hands stood frozen at ten minutes past ten. Abby couldn't help wondering if that was the hour Beauregard lost his beloved wife.

"Incredible," Hugo murmured.

The next piece he uncovered was so large it could only have gone in the grand living room upstairs. The decoration was reminiscent of an Egyptian sphinx surrounded by animal paws and birdlike wings. Abby had no idea what utilitarian purpose it might have served or how Beauregard got it through the wooden door. But it was certainly impressive.

"I think Theadora may have gone overboard trying to impress her neighbors," Abby commented. "There couldn't have been anything else quite like this in all the San Juans."

"Perhaps Robert Moran's home on Orcas Island and his Rosario Resort, but that was in the early 1900s. Other than Moran, no one I can think of would have had furniture like this. Certainly no one on Sparrow Island."

Fascinated, they explored further, lifting the covers on two rococo occasional chairs and a lovely hall table with a marquetry design of contrasting woods on the top and ornately carved legs. It was like Christmas morning with more presents under the tree than Abby ever could have imagined.

As she looked around, she realized this had been

Beauregard's way of protecting this storehouse of priceless antiquities from any dampness that might creep up from the ground. He'd turned this room into a monument to his wife and what she had loved—a shrine to her memory that he never intended to visit again after sealing up the passageway.

"I think we need to get an expert on antique furniture out here," Abby said. "I know all of these pieces must be incredibly valuable. The total worth could go into the thousands."

"Perhaps more." Hugo raised a sheet that had been covering a mahogany desk. On top of the desk was a blue-and-white porcelain urn with a distinctly Oriental design.

Removing another covering, Hugo revealed a wooden packing crate that was open at one end. He rummaged through the contents, finally showing Abby a daguerreotype he'd found.

"It's labeled Winchell Plantation, South Carolina, 1850," he said.

It was hard to see the details with only a flashlight, but Abby could make out a stately manor house with Ionic columns across the porch. Two huge magnolia trees framed the house.

"From Theadora's journal, it sounded like Winchell Plantation was in total ruin after the Union Army got through with it."

"Dreadful loss of both the historic beauty of the countryside and the men who gave their lives for one side or the other."

"If only they'd found some other way to end slavery," she said.

"There are more pictures here," Hugo said as he shifted through the artifacts in the crate. "And this." He riffled through the pages then showed Abby a small book. "Looks like a Civil War diary."

"What an incredible treasure trove we've found." Letting her fingers trail across the marquetry table, Abby considered what she knew of Beau's life, particularly after he lost Theadora.

"I think, in Beauregard's grief over his wife's death, he drew more and more into himself, studying his books and becoming a religious recluse. In order to rid himself of all his worldly treasures, he brought them down here and sealed them off so he'd never see them or be tempted by them again. He wanted only to store up his treasures in heaven but he couldn't entirely let go of his wife.

"My guess is the tower room became his monk's cell, perhaps in part so he would feel closer to Theadora. And to God. He retained only enough furniture in the house to maintain a minimalist existence." She shook her head in amazement. "Incredible."

"You may well be correct in your assumptions. Stranger things have happened after the loss of a loved one," Hugo agreed.

"Wouldn't it be wonderful," she mused, "if we could restore the old house and put all this furniture back where it once was. Naomi Yardley would be in seventh heaven."

"I can think of a good many museums that would count themselves fortunate to own this collection."

Deciding further investigation would require a great deal of time and much better lighting, Abby stepped outside the room, taking a moment to study the brick wall. She'd never seen bricks laid with such precision, the mortar lines so carefully drawn the wall was almost too perfect.

"Beauregard was a man obsessed," she commented.

"Which was fortunate for us." Hugo helped her to close the heavy door. "His obsession is what protected his treasures by keeping it bone dry all these years. Quite an amazing accomplishment."

"Rather like the tombs of Egyptian rulers."

"I have the feeling somewhere in this room we'll find a compound, something similar to packing materials used these days, that absorbs moisture. Beauregard would have needed that to keep his possessions so pristine."

"You could well be right." Abby started to go back to the cellar, then realized there was more to see. She hadn't yet reached the end of the tunnel. She turned to the right to explore farther.

The floor of the passageway angled downward. Being so far underground, Abby didn't know which direction she was heading. She suspected the tunnel led to the back of Arrowhead Hill, and was the product of the digging project Theadora had been so curious about.

Not entirely to her surprise, after a short distance the beam of her light picked up a stack of wooden barrels along one side of the tunnel. RUM was stencilled on each barrel.

"Well! Looks like we can confirm Beauregard's rum-running activities." Rapping her knuckles on a barrel, she heard the deep thud that told her there was still liquid inside.

Turning her flashlight down the tunnel again, she realized they'd reached the end of the line. "I thought for sure we'd come to a door or gate that would open up near Paradise Cove. That's where Beau brought in his booty to store here. Or at least, I think that was probably the case."

"He certainly didn't have all of this dug out and the dirt carried back up through the house. I think . . ." Moving closer, Hugo examined the end of their road. "This looks like there's been a cave-in. There are some broken supports." He flashed his light on the end of a broken beam. "And this dirt looks loose compared to the rest of the tunnel."

Frowning, Abby said, "I read an article in an old issue of *The Birdcall* about a hiker falling in a sinkhole on the back side of Arrowhead Hill. I bet this is it, but nobody figured out it was a cave-in, not a sinkhole that had opened up."

"An amazing amount of history here, Abby. You've certainly made a grand discovery."

"Surely with all of this, the town council and county commissioners will decide to save the manor and restore it for others to enjoy. It would be quite a tourist attraction."

By mutual agreement, they both started walking back toward the cellar.

"There's still the issue of money," Hugo pointed out. "You might be able to convince Archie Goodfellow to restore the place if you were willing to sell off the furniture and other artifacts to finance the project."

"That would be close to criminal. To sell all those valuable pieces? They belong upstairs where visitors can enjoy them, not in a museum in South Carolina or somewhere else. Everything we've found—as well as the accounts of Beauregard's and Theodora's lives—are part of *our* history right here on Sparrow Island."

She was getting herself worked up. That persistent streak of stubbornness she'd always battled was raising its head.

"Besides," she said, "if we can restore the manor, then we can use the structure in the back as a hostel for students and bird-watchers who come to the island. That alone would create extra business for the good Mr. Goodfellow." She edged her way through the opening into the cellar.

Ducking, Hugo followed her. "Talk to him. If anyone can persuade Archie and the others, you can."

"That's exactly what I plan to do."

The rain had turned to a light mist as Abby and Hugo drove away from Winchell Manor, and a few scattered stars had appeared in the sky.

When they reached the conservatory, Abby pulled her car up beside Hugo's in the parking lot.

"I can't thank you enough for going with me tonight, Hugo. I never would have been able to break through that wall by myself."

Affectionately, he patted her arm. "As always, it was a grand adventure. I'll look forward to the next one we share."

She smiled as he got out and walked the few paces to his car. She sincerely liked Hugo. Not in a romantic way, she hastened to remind herself. But he was a wonderful boss, caring and concerned about everything she did. She could have done far worse in making her move back to Sparrow Island. All in all, she was grateful for his presence in her life.

BY THE TIME ABBY GOT HOME, Mary had already gone to bed. She was sorely tempted to wake her sister to tell her about their wonderful discoveries, but she thought better of it since the hour was so late.

Since she'd missed dinner, Abby opened the refrigerator in the hope of finding something to snack on. Bless Mary's heart, she'd made her a meatloaf sandwich and had it sitting right on the top shelf. After quickly washing dirt and hundred-year-old dust from her hands, Abby poured herself a glass of milk and sat down at the table to eat and contemplate her next steps.

Blossom, having heard activity in the kitchen, tiptoed out of Mary's bedroom to find out what was going on. She sat patiently on the floor staring up at Abby, blinking her big, blue eyes. But when it became obvious she wasn't going to get an extra snack—forbidden by Mary so as not to spoil Blossom any more than she was already—the cat did an about-face and returned to Mary's room where she usually slept.

Even as Abby rinsed off her dishes and put them away, she was quite sure that getting to sleep this night would be all but impossible. Her head was spinning with the calls she needed to make and the people she needed to contact in person.

There were only days left to achieve her goal and an incredible amount to be accomplished if she was to be successful.

Once upstairs, she prepared for bed and put on her nightgown. Desperate for God's help and guidance, she knelt beside her bed as she had throughout much of her childhood and prayed.

Dear Lord, let me be Your servant and help me to convince others that Beauregard's life is not only a special part of our history here on the island, but that it is also a testament to Your saving grace. Let my heart be pure and my word true. In Your holy name, Your will be done. Amen.

Turning off the bed light, she slipped under the covers and looked up toward the ceiling of her bedroom. The eaves outside still dripped from the heavy rainfall. Only darkness shone through the blinds on her window.

And then, almost miraculously, a light appeared as bright as daylight, rays streaming onto her bed. The moon had sliced its way through the cloud cover and was, Abby imagined, smiling down on her.

Although she didn't believe in omens, she smiled. Tomorrow she'd do God's work as she understood it and hope for the best.

THE NEXT MORNING, Abby did her usual devotionals, beginning her day in prayer. When she went downstairs, she discovered Mary had already left for Bible school. Abby grabbed a cup of coffee from the pot on the counter and after a quick breakfast, she headed for the conservatory.

She decided to start her search for funding right away. The first phone call she made was discouraging, to say the least.

"I'm sorry, ma'am. The Washington Community Foundation doesn't fund museums." Mitsy-Sue Richman, secretary to the executive director, had a honey-sweet accent and the key to an iron gate that separated callers from her boss. The original Miss Steel Magnolia. "It is not part of our mission, y'all need to know that."

"Could you at least pass on the information to Mr. Pratson? The situation is really quite urgent."

"You're welcome to submit a grant request, ma'am. The information you'll need is on our Web site. I'm sure you'll find everything you need there. Our response time is generally six to nine months."

Mentally, Abby groaned. This wasn't getting her anywhere. "Thank you for your time, Ms. Richman. Good-bye."

"You take care now, you hear?"

Disconnecting, she closed that file and opened the one for the Washington Island Preservation Trust, punching in their phone number. It rang three times before it picked up with a recording.

"Hello. You have reached the Washington Island

Preservation Trust, dedicated to maintaining the natural, historical and environmental integrity of the beautiful San Juan Islands of Washington State. We appreciate . . ."

Numbly, Abby waited for the tone before leaving an urgent message. Surely the Preservation Trust would be excited about the prospect of saving Winchell Manor from a wrecking ball or the jaws of a backhoe.

She had one other idea. Finding that number, she called the Washington Heritage Museum in Olympia, Washington.

After she explained the situation, the head curator said, "That sounds very exciting, Ms. Stanton. I'm sure our furniture specialist, Kendrick Kerstan, will be eager to take a look at what you've discovered."

"I think the house itself has the potential to become a regional museum under your direction. The manor and its furnishings look to be very representative of the territorial era." Abby knew the Heritage Museum had a special exhibit reflective of that era and hoped to tempt the curator with a bit of delicious bait.

There was a long pause before he said, "An interesting idea. However, as you may be aware, funding for our museum has been severely restricted by the legislature in recent years, and private fund-raising is always a struggle. I have difficulty imagining the board of directors approving an expansion of that sort. I will ask our Mr. Kerstan to visit you at his earliest convenience."

"I know it's short notice, but he'll have to come today or tomorrow at the latest."

"I don't believe that would be possible. Mr. Kerstan is in the midst of taping an antiques television show for public televsion and will be out of the office all week."

Abby momentarily thought that maybe she could get the entire TV crew to tape the show here on Sparrow Island. Even to Abby, that idea sounded like pie-in-the-sky. "Well, thank you very much. If you'd have Mr. Kerstan call me when he's available, I'd appreciate it." And she hoped it wouldn't be too late.

Having struck out—for the moment—Abby decided her next step had to be talking with members of the town council. If she could at least get them to delay the demolition, she'd have the time to take a serious run at rounding up funding for the restoration.

After checking in with Hugo, she headed into town. Archie Goodfellow was the chairman of the town council as well as an influential merchant. He wasn't an easy man to talk to but she needed him on her side. She'd have to be her most persuasive to succeed.

CHAPTER ❧ THIRTEEN

Dcvvv

D URING THE MORNING snack period the next day, Mary saw Pastor Jim walking across the lawn. She wheeled down the sidewalk toward him, anxious to know what had happened in Santa Monica. The storm had passed during the night but there was still a quickening breeze, cool enough that she was glad for the jacket she wore.

"You're back already," she said. "I thought you might stay a few extra days in sunny Southern California."

He smiled warmly at her and reached down to scratch Finnegan between his ears. "I admit we were tempted. Toby loved wading in the ocean, which is something he doesn't have many chances to do here. The water's too cold most of the year."

Mary sincerely hoped the pastor's sunny beach trip wouldn't weigh too heavily in the final decision to move south.

"But despite the temptation, we flew back to Seattle last night and came in on the first ferry this morning."

"I don't mean to be nosy. . . well, I do, of course," she admitted a bit shamefacedly. "Did they offer you the job?"

He knelt beside her. "Mary, I know you've been worried. But they are still interviewing candidates. No decision has been made yet."

"I'm surprised they didn't offer you the job on the spot. I'm sure you're the best man they'll find." *How shortsighted those church leaders must be*, she thought in a huff on his behalf.

Pastor Jim chuckled at her outrage. "It sounds like you *want* me to accept the position if they offer it."

"Oh, gracious me, no!" She felt her cheeks warm. "I just think that . . . well . . ."

He patted her hand. "I know, Mary. And I appreciate your support. But things will work out whatever happens. God will take care of us all."

"You're right, of course."

Standing, he said, "I was about to enjoy some of Ida Tolliver's gingerbread cookies. Would you like to join me?"

"I would. Ida's so clever, I don't know where she comes up with her ideas. Today's cookies are shaped like camels and angels. The children are loving snack time."

"I think Ida's enjoying it too. It's her way of finding her path to God. For each of us the journey is different."

"And sometimes filled with a few potholes," Mary added wryly.

Laughing, the pastor gripped her chair and pushed her toward the excited crowd of children gathered around Ida, vying for their share of cookies and individual boxes of apple juice.

"After I have my daily cookie allowance," he said, "I'm going to go help Bea in the kitchen. For some reason, Josh didn't show up for work today."

"Oh, I hope he isn't ill." Mary had been working with the

children to press dried flowers into bookmarks and hadn't noticed Josh was missing.

"I tried to call the number he put on his job application but it's not in service. If he doesn't call or come in tomorrow, I may go around to see if there's a problem."

"He told me his parents had rented a house in Green Harbor for the summer."

"Yes. On Myrtle Street. Number thirty-six, I think it was."

"Let's hope his parents wanted him to go to the mainland for some reason and he didn't think to call here. He seems like such a responsible young man, I don't think he'd simply skip work."

"We'll get to the bottom of it."

When they reached the table where the cookies were being served, Mary looked up at Rev. Hale. "I'm still hoping you'll stay with us."

"I know." Picking up a cookie, he bit off the gingerbread angel's head and grinned like a mischievous little boy. "My favorite. I doubt that Santa Monica has anything that would top this."

AFTER SNACK, when Mary wheeled herself back to the recreation room via the kitchen, she found Bea in a dither. Every cupboard door was open and most of the drawers too.

Ordering Finnegan to stop, she brought her wheelchair to a halt. "Bea, is there something wrong?"

"I'm going senile, that's what." The cook climbed onto a step stool, stood on tiptoe and peered into the highest shelf above the refrigerator. "I thought for sure I had some peanut butter left from my last order but I'll be a one-footed tap dancer if I can find it. Could be I didn't even order the stuff, that's how batty I'm getting." Her gray hair was in disarray, the ends coming loose from the clips that held it back, and her face was flushed.

"I'm sure you placed the order. You had a very complete list. Maybe something went wrong and it wasn't delivered. Do you need the peanut butter for today's lunch?"

"No, thank the good Lord. We're having spaghetti and carrot sticks today." Climbing down, Bea pushed her hair back into place. "But tomorrow I was going back to sandwiches. That's what the kids like the best."

"Can't you call now and order another jar from your supplier to be delivered tomorrow? Or you could buy some from The Green Grocer."

Bea exhaled deeply. "I guess I'll have to do something. But I hate to waste the church's money when I'm so *sure* there was another jar of peanut butter here when I left last Friday."

"Maybe the Sunday school folks used it for some reason."

That gave Bea a moment's pause. "Do you think that's it?"

"I wouldn't want to blame them without knowing for sure, but it does seem possible someone needed the peanut butter and didn't realize you'd need it for the Bible school lunches."

"You could be right, you know."

"I think the best thing is for you to order whatever you need and I'm sure it will all be sorted out later."

Looking relieved, Bea nodded. "I do hope you're right. I've been forgetting things lately, but I thought it was because I've been terribly busy. And then today when I couldn't find the peanut butter . . ."

"You're not going senile, Bea. At least no more than I am." Mary laughed. "Of course, now that I think about it, that news may not be all that encouraging."

Bea joined her with a chuckle. "I guess if the worst we have to worry about is being a little forgetful, then we're doing fine for a couple of old gals who've traveled a lot of miles."

Mostly good miles, Mary thought. Ever since her accident, she'd had good times and had gained a better understanding of herself. And by working at the Bible school she'd learned she still had a lot to share with young people. It was nice to feel needed and appreciated. The children had given her that very special gift.

She'd have to thank Pastor Jim for cajoling her into helping out . . . and God for putting the idea into his head.

ABBY FOUND ARCHIE GOODFELLOW behind The Green Grocer helping to unload crates of produce from a delivery truck. A big man—in all directions—he handled the heavy boxes with ease. His royal-green butcher apron had a caricature sketch of him stencilled on the front with the words THE GREEN GROCER beneath it.

"Hi, Archie. Have you got a minute?"

Scowling, he glanced in her direction. "You'd think I had all day the way my delivery service shows up two hours late. They aren't the ones who get lambasted for shriveled zucchini and wilted lettuce."

Remembering Margaret Blackstock's complaints, Abby grimaced. "I'm sure most of your customers understand it's hard to get produce shipped in by ferry."

"Huh." Hefting a cardboard box marked BANANAS out of the back of the delivery truck, he lifted it to his shoulder and marched from the platform to the backroom. Although the air was still cool after the storm had passed over the island, sweat beaded his forehead. "What's on your mind, Abby?"

"Winchell Manor."

"An eyesore, as far as I'm concerned, and an open invitation to getting Green Harbor and Sparrow Island, as well as the county, sued for every dime some jokster can find."

"It's a historic building, Archie. Beauregard and Theadora Winchell were early settlers here. If we handle the manor properly, it could be a real tourist attraction and bring in a lot of money to the community."

He dropped the bananas with a thud. "How's that?"

At least she had his attention now. "I've been doing a little investigation—"

"Another one of your mysteries to solve?"

"Well, sort of. But the fact is, I've found Theadora's original journal that tells about her time here on the island. And Lillian Trumble out at Oyster Inlet—"

"She's a nutcase, if you ask me."

"Well, she has her grandmother's journal that reveals a great deal about Beauregard. The history of both the manor and those two people is incredible."

"Great. I'm sure that will make Mrs. Yardley's day," he said sarcastically. Ripping open the carton with his hands, he pulled out a plastic bag full of bananas that were so fresh they were still tipped with green. "I gotta get these out where people will buy 'em. They won't make me any money back here."

She followed him into the store. Since it was Tuesday and most of the weekend vacationers had gone back to the mainland, there weren't many customers around.

"Archie, I found an amazing treasure trove of furniture and artifacts in the manor's cellar. We can't tear down that building until we know just exactly what's there."

The bunch of bananas he held looked almost small compared to the breadth of his hand. "Treasure?"

Abby lowered her voice. "I don't think we should spread that around until we can provide some security for the manor house and its contents. I really don't want treasure seekers or vandals to get word of what we've found."

"What are we talking about? Gold? Silver?"

She shook her head. "Period furniture. Some early imports from the Orient, probably made in the 1800s. Pictures, a diary from the Civil War era. It's an extraordinary find, Archie. Trust me on this."

His scowl deepened. "I thought you were into birds and stuff like that."

"I am. But . . ." How could she explain? "Archie, I would consider it an enormous favor if you would call a meeting of the town council tonight. I'll describe what I've found. If the council decides they want to delay the demolition of Winchell Manor, then I can go to the county commissioners and get them to wait until I can find a way to fund the restoration of the structure."

"Restoration? Shoot, Abby, we've been trying to get rid of that nuisance for years. We can't stop now."

"Please, Archie," she pleaded. "Give me a chance. You and the other council members won't be sorry. Particularly when you realize what a great tourist draw Winchell Manor could be as a Civil War and territorial era museum. It could actually draw lots of tourists to our island—as many as the American Camps and all the Pig War memorabilia bring to San Juan Island."

Archie didn't look entirely convinced, but finally he nodded. "Okay, but for it to be legal I'll have to get William Jansen at *The Birdcall* to post an official notice and he'll have to get somebody to hand out flyers around town. We can't hold secret meetings, you know."

Thinking that Bobby McDonald would be perfect for that job, Abby quickly agreed. If necessary, she'd even deliver the flyers herself.

She only hoped the notice wouldn't alert any unsavory characters who would take advantage of the situation and plunder the treasure of Winchell Manor.

ABBY HAD A QUICK BITE of lunch at Springhouse Café, then spent the rest of the afternoon at the conservatory rounding up her supporters by phone for the five o'clock town council meeting. Since the town of Green Harbor wasn't incorporated, the council was more of an advisory body to the county commissioners than a decision-making group. Still, some of the discussions could get pretty heated.

She made it back home in time to tell Mary about what she and Hugo had discovered the prior evening.

"That's amazing," Mary said. "All these years and no one had any idea the cellar was full of Beauregard's things."

"I'm convinced that God led me to the discovery for His own reasons. But now I have to convince the town council to petition the county commissioners to hold off until I can find the funding for restoration."

"That may not be an easy sell. Once the council members make up their minds . . ." Mary shrugged. "Sometimes people feel they'll lose face if they change their point of view."

"I know."

Mary drove them to Green Harbor Public School where the council meetings were held in the multipurpose room. They arrived a few minutes early and were met by William Jansen in his ace reporter mode, notebook in hand and pencil stuck behind his ear.

"So what's going on, Abby?" he asked. "Why the emergency meeting?"

"After you hear what Hugo and I found at Winchell Manor, I think you're going to be happy to buy me dinner. Maybe even steak and lobster at Winifred's."

His eyebrows shot up. "Don't tell me you actually saw the ghost." Taking the pencil from behind his ear, he prepared to take notes.

"No." She laughed. "But I believe a spiritual conversion took place there and that Beauregard was the first environmentalist on the island. It would be tragic to tear down the manor and wipe away so much of our local history. The demolition that's planned for Thursday would also destroy some priceless antiques we found in the cellar. It has to be stopped."

"That'll be some trick if you can pull it off at this eleventh hour."

"I know. But I have to try."

He nodded toward the front of the room where the council members had taken their seats. In addition to Archie Goodfellow, who chaired the council, there was Ed Willoughby, the local pharmacist and soda fountain owner. Rarely seen far from his drugstore, he was a real sweetheart of a man who Abby thought she could influence with reason.

The owner of the hardward store, Frank Holloway, might be a harder nut to crack. Since his grandson had started to work for him, she suspected Frank was considering retirement. However, he did know the views of virtually everyone in town since most of the local men tended to hang out on the front porch of his store discussing earth-shattering issues such as the Mariners' baseball schedule and the best way to repair a leaky faucet.

Abby had always respected Ana Dominguez, who owned In Stitches craft shop, had been elected and was the only woman on the council. She'd surprised the men more than once by standing up to them when she felt strongly about something.

Rounding out the council membership was Keith Gordon. After years of experience in the hospitality business worldwide, he'd purchased The Dorset, the most upscale hotel on the island. His Scottish burr made him a delight to listen to, but Abby had no idea which way he might vote on restoring Winchell Manor.

Archie banged his gavel. "Okay, let's get going so we can all get home for dinner. Abby, you've got the floor."

She hurried to the front of the room. About a dozen people were in the audience, most of them people she had contacted about the meeting, including her parents, Hugo, Naomi Yardley and, of course, Mary, who had parked herself next to their mother. Abby gave them all a smile, then faced the council members. Before she spoke, she took a deep breath and sent up a quick prayer to ask for God's help.

First, she thanked them for giving her the opportunity to speak to them. Then she went through a brief history of Beauregard and Theadora, as she had recently discovered it.

Frank Holloway spoke up. "I don't see where we're going with this, Abby. We decided months ago that the place was a hazard and needed to be torn down for everyone's safety. All we need is some kid to get hurt there and we'd all be in trouble."

"I understand that. Really I do. But once my curiosity was piqued, I had to find out as much about the manor as I could. Hugo Baron and I discovered a wealth of treasures down in the cellar from Beauregard's days."

A murmur of interest went up from the council members

and the spectators. Archie banged his gavel again. "We had county inspectors go through that whole place. They didn't find anything of value there except a couple of old sticks of furniture."

How Abby wished she'd taken pictures of what she and Hugo had found. "There is a secret room and a passageway that has been sealed off for more than a hundred years. Beauregard stored all of his worldly goods there and became a recluse. There are thousands and thousands of dollars' worth of antiques in that cellar."

Now they were all speaking at once and had no interest in Archie bringing them back to order.

In a pleasantly firm voice, Ana penetrated the commotion. "What is it you want us to do, Abby?"

"I want you to recommend to the county that the demolition should be delayed long enough to explore the possibility of restoring Winchell Manor and turning it into a museum." For now, she wouldn't present her idea of a hostel for students. Getting the demolition stopped was her first priority.

"Oh for goodness sake," Frank grumbled. "We've been all through this more than once. You'd need a structural engineer to tell you if it would be economically feasible to restore that old place. And then where on earth would you find the money to do it, assuming it was worthwhile in the first place?"

"Do you have any idea how much money it would take to restore the manor?" Archie asked.

"No, not yet. But I do know if we tear it down there won't be any amount of money that would rebuild it into what it once was," Abby said

Keith Gordon cleared his throat. "If we're considering other uses for the Winchell Manor, you might want to be thinking about turning it into a hotel. I imagine, from what you've said, that the rooms would be spacious and the view would certainly lend itself to fine dining and entertaining. In time it might pay for itself, although not initially. The demand for the use of our wedding facilities at The Dorset has gone up appreciably in recent years. The island could sustain a second facility, possibly operated under the same umbrella organization."

Abby hadn't thought of that. Though she wasn't willing yet to give up her museum concept, turning it into a hotel might be better than tearing it down.

"Given enough time, we could develop several alternative plans for the property," she said.

"Enough time!" Archie barked. "The place has been abandoned for a hundred years. If there was a good use for that old pile of stone, don't you think someone would have thought of it before tonight?"

"But with this new information—" Abby said.

"I move we get someone to haul the furniture and stuff out of there tomorrow, then tear the place down, just like we planned," Archie said. "We can sell the stuff and turn a profit for a change."

Abby's heart sank.

"No!" Naomi Yardley shouted from the audience. "You can't treat antiques so cavalierly. It's unthinkable."

"I agree with Mrs. Yardley," Hugo said, standing. "Abby and I didn't find *stuff* in the cellar, but priceless heirlooms. They must be treated with the utmost care and not sold off simply to gain a profit."

"After all these years, what's your hurry to tear down the place?" Sandy McDonald, Bobby's mother, said. "Whatever's down in the basement is part of all of our children's heritage.

So is the manor. A few more days, or even weeks, won't matter if it gives us an opportunity to provide our children with a history lesson they'll never forget."

Knowing Sandy taught English at Green Harbor Public School, Abby suspected she was already planning field trips to Winchell Manor with lengthy reports to follow.

Sandy's husband Neil, who worked on the ferry, stood. "My wife is right. I didn't much like history when I was in school." He smiled sheepishly and brushed his sun-streaked hair back off his forehead. "But now I can see how important it is for kids to learn about what happened before they got here. It's a continuity thing, you know?"

Archie looked taken aback by the vehement support of Abby's idea from the audience. No one seconded his motion.

"*Por favor*," Ana said, slipping into her native Spanish as she sometimes did. "Please. I would like to make a motion that we ask the county to delay the breaking down of Winchell Manor long enough for us to study this new situation."

"Second," Ed Willoughby said, speaking for the first time.

"Now wait a minute," Archie said. "We can't—"

"There's a motion on the floor and it's been seconded," Keith calmly pointed out. "I suggest we vote the motion up or down, and then we can all go home."

Archie didn't look thrilled about either ending the discussion or the possiblity of being on the losing side of the vote. But he shrugged and said, "All right, all those in favor of the motion, raise your hand."

Ana, Keith and Ed Willoughby raised their hands. Only Frank and Archie were opposed to delaying demolition.

"That's wonderful." Abby was ecstatic. At least now she had a chance to make her dream come true. "Thank you so much.

All of you. I'll go over to San Juan Island and talk with the commissioners first thing in the morning. Would it be possible for one of you to fax the result of your vote to the commissioners so they'll have that when I arrive?"

Scowling, Archie said, "I'll take care of it. Though you can bet the commissioners won't be any happier about the idea than I am. Chances are good you won't find a way to fund your grand scheme and we'll be right back where we started, tearing down the old place."

Abby hoped that wouldn't be the case.

As the meeting broke up, Abby's mother was the first to congratulate her. "You were wonderful, dear. And how exciting that you uncovered so much of the Winchell history. Dad and I are very proud of you."

"Thanks, Mom. It's been a couple of busy days for me." She hugged her mother, then her dad stepped up to give her an embrace too.

"Sorry to interrupt this love fest," William Jansen said with a firm grip on both his notebook and sharpened pencil. "But if you're going to earn your dinner on me, I need a lot more details. How many pieces of furniture did you find? What era are we talking about and what's the condition of these pieces? I'm working on a deadline, you know. As it is, I've already put tomorrow's paper to bed. I'll have to redo the entire front page. I wish you'd given a heads-up. Newspapers don't write themselves, you know."

"We didn't count every piece of furniture. We didn't even look at everything in the storage area. Most of what we did see was probably Civil War era or shortly thereafter. But William, can you hold off printing this news until next week's edition?"

His head jerked up. "You're kidding, right?"

"No, I'm not. We've got to get some security up there before the general public hears about what we found. A twenty-four hour guard, some fencing. Right now, anyone could walk into the house and help themselves." Including the panhandler or whoever was already squatting there. He could stumble on the entrance to the secret passage she and Hugo had left gaping open. "It would be a terrible tragedy if all the antiques and artifacts walked off and there was nothing left for the museum.

"You don't have a museum yet, Abby. And I have an obligation to my readers. This is big news."

Abby sighed. "Please. I'm begging you. I'm even willing to skip the dinner if you'll hold off for a few days until we get things sorted out. Maybe you could publish a special edition after security is in place."

She could tell her appeal to his thrifty nature tempted him, but he finally shook his head. "Sorry, Abby. I have my journalistic ethics to consider. Holding back on a story of this magnitude wouldn't conform with my principles of the public's right to know. I just can't do it."

She had an urge to tell William to forget his ethics this one time, but that wouldn't be right. He had a job to do. So did she. And she'd do it if she had to stand guard over Winchell Manor all by herself.

"I understand, William. And I'm sure you'll understand if I don't fill you in on all the details just yet."

"I can develop other sources, you know."

She glanced around the group of friends, including Hugo, who was talking with her parents. She knew Hugo would keep her confidence until it was time to reveal all they had discovered.

"You're welcome to try, William."

Frowning, he jotted a note on his pad. "I've got to put something in the paper tomorrow. If I don't have the whole story, so be it. But you can bet all the treasures in the cellar that for next week's issue, I'm going to dig deep and make it the lead article, all of it above the fold with a big headline. It may not get me a Pulitzer, but it'll be the best story I ever write."

"I'm sure it will be a wonderful article, William. Maybe you'll get a whole series out of the story of Winchell Manor and it will be picked up by some dailies. Certainly the Seattle papers would be interested. Perhaps the newspaper in Winchell's hometown of Charleston, too."

He brightened at the thought. "Yeah, you're right."

Abby could only hope she could block the demolition and secure the property before hordes of both reporters and opportunists descended on Sparrow Island.

CHAPTER ❧ FOURTEEN

Yea, when this flesh and heart shall fail,
And mortal life shall cease,
I shall possess, within the veil,
A life of joy and peace.

THE NEXT MORNING, Abby took the early ferry to Friday Harbor on San Juan Island. It might not be the fastest way to get there—a speedboat could cross the distance in half the time—but it was convenient. Besides, she knew the county commissioners didn't convene their meetings until at least nine o'clock. She'd have plenty of time to talk to their deputy and get her concerns on the agenda, particularly if Archie Goodfellow had faxed the motion passed by the town council to the powers that be, as he had promised. Given the new circumstances, surely the commissioners would agree to hold off on demolition, at least for a few days.

Feeling optimistic about the day's outcome, she climbed the steps to the main deck on the ferry.

Abby walked out onto the outside deck to watch the lines being cast off from the dock. She couldn't help but remember Theadora's first impressions when she arrived at Green Harbor.

Some things simply didn't change.

The increasing beat of the engines throbbed through the soles of her shoes and rumbled in her midsection. The light breeze picked up, carrying with it the scent of sea salt, and feathered her short hair around her face.

Slowly the ferry edged away from the dock, a behemoth moving with grace through the still harbor water. A sleek motorboat ran parallel with the ferry, but its wake was puny compared to the larger vessel. Hundreds of cars and trucks, even a moving van, were stowed below deck. Some vehicles carried merchandise, others belonged to tourists or business travelers. All of them sailing on an ocean highway connecting one island to another, the lifeline of the San Juans.

Abby found a bench on the leeward side of the boat and sat down to enjoy the scenery. Placing her slender briefcase beside her, she wrapped her suit jacket more snugly around her against the cool morning air. For the meeting she had in mind, she'd worn her dress-for-success outfit—a navy-blue suit with low pumps. Not her favorite attire or her most comfortable, but one that set the tone for what she wanted to accomplish.

She was Dr. Abigail Stanton, someone worth listening to. Despite her general optimism, her stomach was churning with anxiety and knotted on the fear of failure.

THE PUBLIC MARINA at Friday Harbor was much larger than the one at Green Harbor and was filled with all kinds of boats. More visitors bustled along the streets of the town of Friday Harbor than they did on all of the roads of Sparrow Island, which was why Abby preferred her hometown.

However, she always enjoyed a trip here. And this was the seat of county business.

She disembarked and walked the short distance up the hill to the courthouse. Inside, she found a door labeled Board of County Commissioners and entered.

The middle-aged clerk behind the counter didn't bother to look up from his project of stapling two sheets of paper together, setting them aside in a neat stack, then selecting two more to staple. Each time he pounded the stapler with so much authority, Abby had to wonder if he was imagining hitting something—or someone—else.

"Excuse me," she said, directing her words to the top of the clerk's head. "I have an item I'd like to get on today's agenda for the county commissioner's meeting."

"They're not meeting today."

The news confused Abby for a moment. She thought the commissioners always met on Wednesdays. "Why not?"

The clerk took aim on his stapler again. "They're all in Olympia for a seminar." *Whack.*

"Will they be back tomorrow?"

Whack. "Yep."

"Will they have a meeting tomorrow?"

"Unless they decide otherwise." *Whack.*

It would not be good politics for Abby to *whack* the clerk, but she was sorely tempted. She prayed for patience. "If they do meet tomorrow, would it be possible to get my item on the agenda?" Hopefully the first item after the flag salute.

He raised his fist to hit the stapler again. Having not been granted an iota of additional patience, Abby reached across the counter and snatched the stapler away.

His head snapped up. He scowled at her with eyes so droopy she wondered if he had gotten any sleep last night.

In response to his scowl, she smiled sweetly. Or at least as sweetly as her sudden dip in mood would allow.

"That would be up to the deputy," the clerk said.

"Would it be possible for me to talk to her?"

"It's a *he*. And he's in Olympia with the commissioners."

Abby did a mental eye roll. "Sir, it's very important that I talk with the commissioners as soon as possible. A historic building on Sparrow Island is scheduled to be torn down tomorrow by the county. I want the commissioners to hold off for a few days until I can develop funding to restore the place."

"Have the commissioners already approved a bid to have it torn down and authorized the money be spent?"

"I assume so, yes."

The clerk snatched the stapler back from her, smirking in satisfaction. "Then they aren't going to cancel the contract. They'd have to pay for the work anyway, and they sure aren't going to spend taxpayer's money and have nothing to show for it."

"But you don't understand. New information has come to light. If the commissioners had known—"

Whack.

Placing her briefcase on the counter, she retrieved the material she had printed out the prior evening. "I've made copies of a statement I was going to read to the commissioners. Could you arrange for them to receive this statement as soon as they return from Olympia?"

Amazingly, the clerk had finished whatever it was he'd been collating. With great care, he evened the stack of papers, placing them squarely in the center of the counter. "I can put the statement in their mailboxes, if that's what you want, but I can't guarantee when they'll read them."

"I understand. And that is what I want. Please." She handed him the copies for the commissioners.

For a moment, he looked befuddled, not quite sure where he should place the papers on the otherwise occupied counter. He finally chose the top shelf of the In-basket.

"This really is important," she emphasized.

"Everything that comes into this office is important to somebody, or so they claim."

"I imagine that's true." She snapped her briefcase closed. "I do appreciate your help, Mr. . . . ?"

"Jones. Excalibur Jones. My friends call me Ex. My mother was particularly fond of King Arthur stories."

Finding herself totally speechless, Abby could only smile and nod. Mr. Excalibur Jones didn't resemble any heroic character she recalled from King Arthur's court.

Exiting the office, Abby realized this trip to Friday Harbor hadn't gone at all as she had expected, or as she had hoped. Now unless something extraordinary happened, she'd have to face the real possibility that the wrecking crew would show up at Winchell Manor tomorrow morning and she wouldn't be able to stop them.

Reaching the sidewalk, she halted and looked around at the bustle of tourists. She felt lost and alone, lacking direction.

The only possibility that remained was to get Lillian Trumble to help her lead a protest at the manor and chain themselves to the rickety porch posts. But that would only delay the inevitable for a short time. And she might well get both herself and Lillian thrown in jail.

Neither Sergeant Henry Cobb nor Abby's family would be thrilled at that prospect.

With a sigh, she thought of Psalm 25:4–5. The words brought her surprising comfort.

"O LORD. . . guide me in your truth and teach me, for you are God my Savior, and my hope is in you all day lomg."

Lord, I'm at the end of my rope. I don't know what else to do to save Winchell Manor, and I'm sure that's why you led me there and to the stories of the two people who lived in that old house. What do I do now?

WHEN ABBY ARRIVED HOME late that afternoon, she found Mary thoroughly agitated.

"Josh didn't come to work again today," Mary blurted out, wheeling her chair around to meet Abby at the door to the attached garage.

Abby set her briefcase on the table in the kitchen. "Do you think something happened to him?"

"He didn't come in yesterday, either. And didn't phone in sick. Pastor Jim was going to visit him at home, but he was called down to the medical center. Mrs. Tuttle—she's been a member of Little Flock for ages—has taken a turn for the worse." Mary's hands flew around, fidgeting with the buttons on her bright rose sweater, then smoothing her skirt. "Dr. Randolph was going to transfer her by helicopter to Harborview in Seattle and asked if Jim could ride along with the poor dear. It's congestive heart failure, you know. Of course, Jim said he would."

"Of course." Although Abby only knew Mrs. Tuttle as an acquaintance, she was confident Pastor Jim would do whatever he could to help a member of his congregation. Or anyone, for that matter.

"Would you go with me to Josh's house?" Mary asked. "I'm so concerned."

Abby could see that. "Give me a chance to change into something more comfortable and I'll be right with you."

"How did it go at Friday Harbor?" Mary called as Abby went up the stairs.

"Not well. I'll tell you about it later." Abby was sure Mary was in no condition to listen to her woes. In fact, she hadn't yet decided how she should proceed since the county commissioners might not even read her statement until after the wrecking ball had done its dirty work.

Hanging up her suit, she pulled on a comfortable pair of jeans and a knit top. Once in the van, Mary drove them into a quiet residential area of town with narrow streets, tidy sidewalks, and houses fronted with small, well-kept lawns and flower beds that were in full bloom. She parked in front of 36 Myrtle Street and they both got out, as did Finnegan.

"I don't see any sign of teenagers living in the neighborhood," Abby commented. "No basketball hoops mounted above garage doors. No skateboards lying around waiting for the unwary to trip over them."

"I think that's why he came to work at the church. He was lonely and bored."

Both sides of the walkway to the house were lined with alternating beds of pansies and marigolds, and on either side of the small porch were mature rhododendron bushes. The yard and the house were both so well kept, Abby had a hard time believing it was a rental.

Abby rang the doorbell while Mary waited below the steps on the walkway.

A woman opened the door partway. "Can I help you?"

"We're looking for Josh Nicholson," Abby said. "Is he at home?"

"I'm sorry," the woman replied, looking puzzled. "You must have the wrong house. There isn't any Josh here."

"Perhaps we got the street number wrong," Abby said.

"Maybe you've seen him in the neighborhood," Mary added from the walk. "He's a tall, slender boy, about seventeen, I think. Longish blond hair and some acne on his face. His parents are renting a house for the summer."

The woman shook her head. "We've lived here for about three years. My husband wanted to get out of the city after he retired. I don't think any of the houses on this street are summer rentals. They're all owner occupied. And there aren't many teenagers nearby. It's a very quiet area."

She called her husband to the door, where they conferred.

"I'm sorry," she said. "I don't think we can help you."

Thanking the couple for their time, Abby walked with Mary back to the van.

"Where could he be?" Mary asked.

Abby waited while Mary lowered the lift. "I don't know. But it certainly looks like he lied about his address."

"But why?" Mary asked.

Abby didn't have a good answer for that. In fact, it seemed to be a day that hadn't provided any of the answers she'd been looking for.

AS THEY DROVE HOME through Green Harbor, Abby spotted Henry Cobb's tan-and-green cruiser in front of the sheriff's substation. Mary pulled in and parked.

"What are we doing?" Abby asked.

"I, um, thought maybe Henry could suggest. . . I don't know. I'm just worried about Josh."

Appreciating Mary's concern, Abby followed her sister into the sheriff's station, which had been modified some years ago with a concrete ramp to accommodate the handicapped.

When asked, the deputy at the front desk called Henry on the intercom. Moments later, he appeared.

"Hey." His smile was broad and friendly, and directed mostly toward Mary. "I was thinking about calling you tonight."

She flushed slightly. "Do you take missing persons reports?"

Henry's eager expression turned professional. "Who's missing?"

"Well, I'm not sure. I mean . . ." Mary fidgeted with the hem of her sweater, then looked up at Henry. "The young man who's been working at the church the past week didn't come in the last two days. That's not like him. He's very responsible. And now, well, it turns out the address he gave on his job application is phony. The couple living there has never heard of him."

Henry stepped behind Mary's wheelchair. "Let's go into my office. We'll talk there."

He pushed Mary's wheelchair and Abby followed. Finnegan, in his harness and blue service-dog cape, trotted along beside them.

Henry's small, private office was less cluttered than most movie detectives' offices. Still, there was a sense of urgency in every scrap of paper and the air held a certain scent of machismo mixed with the residual aroma of gun oil. Definitely the lair of a cop, Abby mused.

Taking his seat behind a metal desk, Henry said, "Now, tell me who this Josh kid is."

"Josh Nicholson," Mary said. "He's been working at the church as a helper at our vacation Bible school. Remember you offered him a job at the station."

"Yes, I do. He's supposed to live here on Sparrow Island?"

"With his family. He said they'd rented a house for the summer."

"But the address is no good," Abby said.

Henry appeared to ponder that for a moment. "Did he say where they live the rest of the year?"

Slowly, Mary shook her head. "I don't think I ever asked him, and he never said. I really should have—"

Henry waived off her comment. "You're a good woman and you accepted this kid at face value. You didn't want to pry."

"In this case, I should have."

"Maybe." He shrugged, then shuffled through a pile of papers on his desk, pulling one from the stack. "We got this missing person flyer a couple of days ago. One Joshua Walker from Idaho." He turned the faxed flyer around so Mary and Abby could take a look. "Could this be the kid you're looking for?"

With Abby looking over her shoulder, Mary studied the description of the runaway adolescent and his picture, which was blurry and ill-defined, a poor representation. Abby suspected the sheriff's fax machine needed an overhaul or the sender's did.

"I can't be sure," she said, shaking her head. "It could be the same boy. I simply can't tell from this picture."

"That's okay, Mary. First thing in the morning I'll see if I can get a better photo. Meanwhile, let's assume Josh is still on the island. Where would he be now?"

"Since the address he gave is bogus, I simply don't know, Henry. I'm sorry. Maybe one of the beach campgrounds?"

He glanced at Abby to see if she had anything to add.

"I'm afraid I haven't even met the young man," Abby said. "I meant to help out at the Bible school, but my schedule has been too full." And she'd been so distracted by the potential demise of Winchell Manor, she'd barely been able to think about anything else.

"I guess we're not much help," Mary said.

Standing, Henry walked around his desk and rested his hand on Mary's shoulder in an encouraging way. "We'll find your Josh, Mary. Likely as not, he's here or on one of the other islands. I'll alert the deputies. They'll keep an eye out for him."

Mary covered Henry's hand with hers. "Thank you. I'm just so worried."

"He was working at church, so he sounds like he's a good kid. With luck, we'll find him before he can get himself into too much trouble."

Their eyes met, and Abby envied the affection she saw pass between them. Mary was a lucky woman to have a man like Henry interested in her. Not that wedding bells were going to chime soon. But maybe someday . . .

Abby thought she'd be pleased if her sister ever did decide to marry Henry. Mary was meant to be a part of a pair.

The three of them went to dinner together at the Springhouse Café on Shoreline Drive—Henry's treat, he insisted. Ida Tolliver was waiting tables that evening.

Abby went over and gave her young friend a quick hug. "I hear your snacks at church camp have been a big hit."

Ida smiled and shrugged. "Making up silly things the kids will like and that go with the day's Bible story has been kind of fun. A challenge, I guess you'd say."

"You are a multitalented young woman, Ida. Don't you forget it."

"The guy at table six is going to think I'm a doofus if I don't get him his clam chowder pretty soon." She grinned and scurried back behind the counter to dish up a bowl of soup for her customer.

Abby was ever so pleased with how much Ida had matured lately. Ida was even planning to go to college, a goal she hadn't imagined only a year or two ago.

Joining Mary and Henry at their table, Abby picked up a menu. Abby wasn't that hungry. A turkey sandwich on whole-wheat would do her just fine. Her hope of saving Winchell Manor appeared to be slipping further away by the minute, and she was fresh out of ideas. Apparently her appetite had taken a hike too.

"Oh, I meant to ask you, Henry," Abby said, "did a young man recently report that his wallet had been stolen at the beach by the ferry dock?"

Henry looked up from his menu and frowned in thought. "I don't recall anyone reporting a missing wallet. Why?"

"A young man approached me while I was getting gas, asking for a handout. That was the story he gave me, but I suspected he was panhandling."

"At Al's Garage?" Mary asked.

"That's right. After I refused to give him money—and suggested instead that he drop by Little Flock Church to ask for help—he went off in a huff. Later I saw him talking to couples walking on Municipal Street and them giving him some money."

"You're right. Sounds like a panhandler to me." Henry closed his menu. "I'll have my men keep an eye out for him in town."

Glancing out the window, Abby thoughtfully considered

the pedestrians walking by, most of them tourists. "You know, that panhandler may also be the one who's squatting in Winchell Manor and not staying at the beach at all."

"If he is," Henry said, "that problem will solve itself in a hurry—when the building is torn down."

That was exactly the response Abby had expected and what she was afraid of.

WHEN THEY RETURNED HOME, Abby checked her mail and found nothing of interest. Mary turned on the TV, with the same result.

"I think I'll go on to bed," Mary said. "Maybe if I read awhile I can stop worrying about Josh."

"You need any help?"

"No, I'm fine. Frankly, I've turned into a real whiz on that trapeze above my bed. I'm thinking of taking my show on the road with the circus."

"You'd be a sensation, I'm sure. Barnum & Bailey would never be the same." Bending down, her heart aching for Mary's loss and her courage, Abby gave her sister a kiss on her cheek. "I love you."

"Likewise, Abby. I love you too."

Abby waited until Mary had wheeled herself into her room, then slowly walked upstairs. Her heart felt so heavy. Tomorrow, a large part of the history of Beauregard's and Theadora's lives would vanish from the face of the earth. There seemed to be nothing she could do to stop it.

In her bedroom, Abby changed into her nightgown, then sat down heavily in her chair. Idly, she fingered the elaborate design on the cover of the Winchell family Bible. Although the colors had faded over time, it was still a beautiful edition, an heirloom Beauregard had carried from South Carolina to his new home in the San Juan Islands. He must have been a very proud man and one who had loved his bride beyond his vows of "until death do us part."

Except for a quick glance at the birth and death records, Abby hadn't perused Beauregard's Bible in any depth. Now she opened the heavy tome, riffling through the pages decorated with colorful designs in the margins and at the beginning of each chapter.

As she turned the pages an envelope yellowed with age slipped out of the book and fell to the floor. As she picked it up, her fingers tingled as though it was charged with some electrical power. Carefully, she opened the envelope and spread out sheets of paper covered with wildly scrawled handwriting. Slowly, she began to decipher the antiquated cursive writing.

This is the last will and testament of Beauregard Smyth Winchell, saved by the blessings of Christ, in the Year of our Lord, 1892.

Abby's eyes widened as she quickly read through the will. There was no question about what Beauregard had intended. And as far as she knew or could tell, nothing had happened since Beauregard's death to alter the provisions of his will.

Her first impulse was to call . . . someone. But who?

The county offices certainly weren't open at this late hour. The town council members could do nothing at this point. And it was too late for her to call anyone to ask for help.

This night, she suspected, could well be the longest in her life. But she had hope again. And a piece of paper from the past that could well change the future of Winchell Manor.

CHAPTER ✿ FIFTEEN

ABBY WOKE WELL BEFORE six o'clock, surprised she had slept at all. When she'd gone to bed, her mind had been whirling with all she had to do this morning.

Dressing quickly, she hurried downstairs, carrying the Winchell Bible and Beauregard's will. Blossom came trotting out of Mary's bedroom to see what was going on so early in the day.

"Sorry, Blossom," she said, popping a piece of bread into the toaster. "I'm really in a rush. Mary will get your breakfast for you. I promise."

Just then the phone on the kitchen table rang. Abby grabbed for it before the second ring in the hope it wouldn't wake Mary. "Hello."

"Abby?" the caller asked. "This is Sandy McDonald. I'm sorry to call so early."

"It's all right. I was up. Is something wrong?" All that Abby could think was that something had happened to Bobby, and her heart constricted.

"I'm not sure if I needed to call or not. Were you able to get the county commissioners to stop the demolition of Winchell Manor?"

"No, but I think I've found a way—"

"Neil worked his regular shift on the late ferry last night. He just told me now at breakfast that a bulldozer and a huge dump truck came over from San Juan Island on that run. He thinks it's probably the contractor who's going to tear down the old house on Arrowhead Hill."

Abby's breath caught. She'd hoped she'd have a few hours to get back to Friday Harbor and present this latest information to a friend of her father's, Judge Daniel Swink, before the demolition actually started. She wanted Judge Swink to issue a temporary injunction, which would give her time to sort out who was the rightful owner of the Winchell property.

"You have to stop them Abby," Sandy pleaded. "All that heavy equipment could already be up on Arrowhead Hill. And who knows what they'll bring over this morning. Once they start—"

"I know." Abby's thoughts spun as she tried to decide what to do first. She couldn't fail now, not when she was so close to success. "Sandy, I need you to do me a favor."

"Of course, anything."

"Call Naomi Yardley. Tell her to contact all the members of the historical society that she can reach. Get them all up to Winchell Manor as soon as possible to stop that bulldozer. I'm going to call Lillian Trumble. She'll tell everyone what to do."

"Okay. I'll get a hold of Naomi. What are you going to do?"

"Get myself to Friday Harbor as fast as I can. And pray for a miracle."

Hastily thanking Sandy for letting her know about the

arrival of the heavy equipment, Abby disconnected, then dialed Lillian's number.

"It's time for Operation Suffragette, Lillian," she said when the woman answered. "They're about to start tearing down the manor house."

"Ha! Not on my watch, they won't."

"I've got a friend rounding up some volunteers for you. But you'll have to hurry."

"We'll stop 'em, missy. I still got my chains and a good ol' padlock it takes a diamond-tipped saw to cut through. I figured this might happen when you told me what was goin' on, so I made me up some fine picket signs and a banner too."

Abby almost laughed. "Bless you, Lillian."

"You call the TV folks yet?"

"Television?"

"Sure. You don't think a protest does diddly without some high-powered media coverage, do you? You gotta get the public on your side. Make the commissioners the bad guys. Big government and all that. The worker bees are just pawns of all those greedy government types."

"I hadn't thought of that."

"That's why you've got me around. I'll get the media here for you. Expect they'll come running when they hear from me. Probably by helicopter, would be my guess. Not just little Willie Jansen at *The Birdcall*, either. No siree, they'll be showing up from Seattle too. The networks will hop on board, you can count on it. Nothing like an old broad like me tying herself to a bit of history to make good video."

"You're a marvel," Abby said sincerely, smiling in spite of her concerns. Maybe Lillian was the miracle she'd been hoping for.

When she hung up, she found Mary had wheeled into the

kitchen. She was still in her nightgown and robe, her silver hair uncharacteristically mussed.

"What's all the excitement about?" she asked.

Abby explained that the equipment to tear down the manor was already on the island. "More importantly, I found Beauregard's last will and testament last night. He made his sister his heir, and if she has no descendants, he wanted his estate to go for 'some good and valued purpose on Sparrow Island.' Which means the manor and its contents are private property until a court rules differently. The county commissioners can't destroy or dispose of it simply on their own say-so."

"That's incredible. But how would we find any descendants of his sister?"

"I'll worry about that later. Right now I have to get an injunction to stop the contractor from damaging anything. Then I'll have to talk to the current branch manager of Green Harbor Bank."

"You mean Steven Jarvis?"

"His predecessor, several generations back, was named executor of Beauregard's will. I'm hoping the bank still has some records that will verify ownership of the estate."

"Goodness. You must have been up half the night figuring all of that out." Wheeling around, Mary went to the counter to start a fresh pot of coffee.

"I was. Now I have to call Dad and get him to call Judge Swink for me."

As Abby reached for the phone again, Mary said, "I didn't sleep well either, thinking about Josh. I'm terribly afraid he's been camping out somewhere on the island and is sick or has hurt himself. Or worse, he's gotten involved with someone like that panhandler you told Henry about. Bea told me the other day that a big jar of peanut butter was missing from the church's pantry. That, after she couldn't find all the tuna she'd bought. But I didn't think the culprit could have been Josh. So I just don't know what to think now."

Abby had only been half listening when Mary mentioned the jar of peanut butter—a large one like she'd seen on the kitchen counter at the manor. Thoughtfully, she stopped dialing her dad's number and watched as Blossom circled her dish, looking for all the world as though she'd accept nothing less than a big serving of tuna fish for her breakfast.

Something, some awareness, niggled at the back of her mind like an irritating buzz she couldn't quite decipher. Why on earth would she connect the panhandler, peanut butter and tuna? The combination sounded revolting.

Except the connection was about a sandwich.

Tuna. The favorite of full-grown cats and little kittens alike. Not necessarily to Josh's taste. Which is why she hadn't considered Josh might be the one who was sleeping in the tower room.

But the feral kittens at Winchell Manor would have considered tuna a special treat indeed. For a bite or two of tuna, the kittens would have lost their shyness and eagerly greeted anyone who they hoped had a handout for them.

Like Abby.

Or Josh.

Not something the panhandler would think to do—share his treats with two little kittens.

The pieces of one puzzle came together with a mental snap. *Of course . . .*

"Josh is the person staying in the tower at Winchell Manor," she announced.

Surprised, Mary glanced over her shoulder. "But you said—"

"I'm betting that Josh, the sweet young man you've described, is so kindhearted that he's been feeding a family of feral cats the tuna he took from the church kitchen. And he's been eating the peanut butter himself."

Mary's eyes widened. "But that means he might still be there. If he is, we have to get to him now before those workmen start knocking down the walls. Or blowing them up with dynamite," she said with a gasp. "He could be hurt!"

"You're right." Making sure a young man was safe took priority over saving a building from the wreckers, even a historic one. Abby could only hope she'd be able to do both. "I'm going to take my car and see if I can find Josh. I'll call Dad on my cell about Judge Swink along the way. You follow me in your van after you get dressed. Then I'll head for Friday Harbor."

The timing couldn't be more tight. She didn't know how long Lillian and her crew of protesters would be able keep the workmen at bay, and she wasn't sure a single piece of paper from a judge would carry much weight without any authority figure to enforce the injunction.

"Mary, call Henry before you leave. Tell him I'm trying to get a temporary injunction. I'll call when I get it and I'll want him to stop all demolition activities on the spot. And ask him, please, not to arrest Lillian Trumble or any of the protestors. He can arrest me later if he needs to lock someone up." Which Abby sincerely hoped wouldn't be necessary.

Mary agreed to call Henry, and Abby hurried out to her car. For the moment, she'd forgotten all about her toast or the coffee Mary was brewing.

She had far more important things to attend to than eating breakfast.

AS SHE DROVE AWAY from the house, Abby called her father. Like most farmers, he was already awake. She quickly explained what was happening and why she needed him to reach Judge Swink.

"I'll call him right away," her father said. "Good luck up at Arrowhead Hill."

"Thanks, Dad. Pray for me."

"I always do, honey."

At this early hour, few pedestrians were out on the streets of Green Harbor and there was almost no traffic. Abby sped through town, only slowing for stop signs, then zipping through the intersections when she saw they were clear. Turning onto Primrose Lane, she raced past the Stanton Farm, catching the scent of the lavender her father raised for Mary's flower shop.

When she finally reached the dirt track that led up to Arrowhead Hill, she had to slow down because of the rougher terrain. The sight of marks made by tractor treads digging into the soft soil sent a chill up her spine. The bulldozer was already at Winchell Manor.

She spotted the bulldozer and dump truck parked behind the mansion, but there was no sign of the drivers. Maybe the men had stayed in town overnight and wouldn't start work until later. *Much* later, she hoped.

Her tires sliding on a patch of gravel, she rounded the house and came to a stop by the front porch. She hopped out. Jumping over the broken step, she jogged up to the door and opened it.

After the bright sunshine outside, the interior of the house was dim. And silent.

"Hello!" she called. "Anybody here?"

Glancing first toward the kitchen, she proceeded to the foot of the stairs. "Hello! Josh, are you up there?"

Slowly she began to climb. The railing felt cool to the touch, the steps solid beneath her feet. At the first landing, a column of sunlight from a broken window had snared dust motes dancing in the air.

Somewhere in the house, someone coughed once, then coughed again.

She swallowed hard. "Josh. I'm Abby Stanton, Mary's sister. From church. I'm coming up."

Hearing no response, she continued up the stairs. When she reached the landing in the tower room, she looked around. The duffel bag was still on the floor but the day-bed was empty.

Frantically, she looked around, then squatted down to peer under the bed. No one. Yet she'd heard *someone* in the house.

One of the workmen? But where?

Snatching up the duffel bag, she hurried back down the stairs to the second floor. Moving as quickly as she could, she checked all of the bedrooms, even the small room off the master suite that Theadora had hoped would one day be a nursery.

Every single room was empty, with not a stick of furniture, much less Josh . . . or the panhandler.

She'd been so sure . . .

Her shoes loud on the stairs, she went down to the first floor. If she didn't find Josh or someone there, the cellar would be her next stop—and she hadn't brought her flashlight inside.

The main living room was vacant. She turned, about to step into the library, when she spotted a blanket spread over a form on the floor in front of the fireplace. A human form.

She approached cautiously and the lump under the blanket moved, one foot appearing.

"Is that you, Josh?" she asked softly.

"Yeah." He coughed, a thick congested sound and pulled back the cover from his face. His eyes looked bloodshot, his cheeks flushed.

The poor kid. It appeared the "ghost" of Winchell Manor had caught a terrible cold.

Crossing the room, Abby sat down beside the boy. Instinctively, she placed the back of her hand on the teenager's forehead. He was burning hot.

"Why are you sleeping here instead of upstairs?" she asked.

"Lightning." He coughed. "Scared me."

No wondered he'd vacated the tower room if he'd been there the night of the storm. "Mary's been worried about you, Josh."

"I'm sorry. I should've called or somethin'." Turning his face away, he coughed again. "I didn't want to give the kids my cold, you know?"

"I know." She tucked the thin blanket around his narrow shoulders. "Your name is Josh Walker, isn't it?"

His eyes widened momentarily before he gave a dejected nod. "How'd you know?"

"Your parents are worried about you too. They filed a missing person's report."

A spark of panic appeared in his eyes. "Are they here now?"

"No. They don't have any idea where you are. Mary and I just figured it out this morning."

He seemed relieved at that. "I don't want to go home," he said rather mulishly, given he was so ill.

"We'll talk about that later, okay? Do you think you can walk on your own if I help you?"

"I guess."

"Good, then this is what we're going to do. Mary's going to

be here in a few minutes with her van. I'll get you outside on the porch, and she'll take you to our house." It seemed the best thing to do under the circumstances. The youngster was far too sick to be out on his own. "She'll get you something for your cough and your fever, and find a warm place for you to rest and be comfortable. Later, we'll figure out what we should do next."

"Are you gonna call my folks?"

"Not until we talk, I promise." Abby had no idea why the boy had run away from home. If he'd been brutalized by his parents, she had no desire to send him back to his abusers. But knowing that he'd been so devoted to his job at the church and had been such a respectful adolescent, she suspected the problem at home was something less traumatic than being an abused child.

"Can you sit up?" she asked.

Slowly, and a little unsteadily, he eased himself to a sitting position. Except for his shoes, he'd been sleeping in his clothes, which were thoroughly wrinkled. She helped him put on his running shoes, helped him to stand, then grabbed his duffel bag.

Hearing some noise outside, Abby looked out the window. A pickup with an extended cab and a contractor's logo on the door was just coming up the hill. Mary's van was right behind the truck. And just appearing over the crest of the hill was a giant backhoe with a huge claw at the end of its folded mechanical arm, a piece of equipment that must have arrived on the early ferry.

Abby's stomach clenched. Time was running out.

She looped the blanket over Josh's shoulders. "Okay, let's get you outside. Mary will be here in a minute."

"I'm sorry to put you and Mary—Mrs. Reynolds—to so much trouble. I mean, I'll be okay in a couple of—" Another cough rattled through his chest. The young man never should have been staying out here alone. He needed to be at home with his family.

"Mary makes an exceptional bowl of chicken soup, Josh. She'll have you feeling better in no time and be glad to do it."

The effort of walking had Josh breathing hard, and he started to cough again. It's possible Mary would have to take the boy to the medical center to see Dr. Randolph. Abby would let her sister decide that later. Certainly Mary had a lot more experience nursing children back to health than Abby did.

They reached the front door and stepped out onto the porch.

"Hey!" a big, burly man wearing a hard hat shouted at them. "What are you guys up to? You shouldn't be in there. We're gonna tear down the place today."

Not if I can help it. "Good morning, sir," Abby called to him. "Lovely day, isn't it?"

Mary pulled her van up near the porch and rolled down the window. "Josh! Thank heaven Abby found you."

"Lady, you can't park there. This is a construction zone." The man, who was apparently the foreman for the job, stomped toward the van. "You gotta move that compact too. All of you have gotta clear out."

Ignoring the foreman, Abby helped Josh into the van and tossed his duffel bag into the back. "He's running a fever," she told Mary, "and has a bad cough. Take him home and feed him some of your chicken soup." Beyond his cold, Abby suspected the boy was dehydrated and undernourished as well. A steady diet of nothing but peanut butter wasn't exactly well balanced.

As she closed the door behind Josh, Mary gave the boy a quick hug. "I wish you'd told someone you were living up here, Josh. What a terrible thing."

Turning toward the workmen, Abby said, "Excuse me, sir, but do you have authorization from the owners of this property to be here?"

"Sure do, lady. The county commissioners gave us a contract to tear down this old pile of stones and haul 'em off."

Abby was playing for time. "I wonder if you could show me that authorization. You see, it's possible an error has been made."

His bushy eyebrows pulled into a straight line, and he glowered at her. He had to be well over six feet tall and two-hundred-plus pounds, mostly made up of muscle and a pot belly. From the way he was trying to bully her, Abby knew he used his size to badger people and get his own way.

"What makes this your business, lady?"

Without flinching, she held his gaze. "My name is Abigail Stanton. *Doctor* Abigail Stanton, Associate Curator of the Sparrow Island Nature Conservatory."

"So? You one of those environmentalist nutcases?"

A pulse began to throb at her temple. "No, I'm not a nutcase. But I do believe the Lord intends us to steward our natural resources, and our history, here on earth. I'm sure you'd agree with me on that."

"Not likely, lady." Using his thumb, he shoved his hard hat to the back of his head. "Now, if you'll remove yourself from the premises, along with your friend over there—" He nodded toward Mary's van. "—my men and me have got work to do."

She didn't think he'd bodily remove her, but she'd be willing to bet he wanted to.

Fortunately, she was saved by the arrival of Lillian on her ATV. She ran her four-wheel vehicle up within inches of the foreman, making him give ground, before bringing it to an abrupt stop.

"Put on your smiley face, Abby. A reporter's coming from *The Seattle Times* and a TV crew from the CBS affiliate. You can bet your bloomers the rest of the media will follow suit."

"What 'a'ya talkin' about, lady? You crazy too?"

"Like a loon," Lillian agreed gleefully. She hopped off her ATV a bit gingerly but quickly, despite her osteoporosis, looped a length of heavy chain over her shoulder, picked up a picket sign from the back of her vehicle and marched up onto the porch. The sign she waved triumphantly read: SAVE WINCHELL MANOR.

The foreman started to go after Lillian, but Abby blocked his way, ignoring the fact that he was a foot taller than she and outweighed her by a hundred pounds or so.

He looked down at her. "What the heck do you think you're doing, lady?"

"Dr. Stanton, to you, sir. And we're saving a historic building, which you intended to tear down."

He shook his head. "There's no way you're gonna—"

In the distance, Abby heard horns honking and more vehicles coming up the hill, Sandy and Naomi leading a crew of volunteers, she hoped.

The cars circled the manor house like covered wagons to ward off attackers. From her spot on the porch, the chain looped around her and a post, Lillian had the volunteers organized in no time. They strung a SAVE WINCHELL MANOR banner across the porch and took up their positions in front of the house with their own picket signs. The foreman ran from one protester to another, demanding that they come off the porch, but to no avail.

Mary wheeled her van around to leave, stopping beside Abby. "Looks like you and Lillian have everything under control. I'm going to take Josh home and put him to bed. He's really sick."

"I know. Take good care of him."

"Henry said he'd get here as soon as he can. He went back to Lopez last night."

"Thanks for calling him." Abby waved as her sister pulled away.

More cars had arrived, some with three or four people in them. This was going to be the biggest demonstration Sparrow Island had ever witnessed. If nothing else, the foreman and his two workers looked totally frustrated by all the activity.

Lillian's protesters wouldn't be able to hold the fort forever. Abby needed to get that injunction from Judge Swink as quickly as she could. It was time for Abby to leave too.

As she drove away from Winchell Manor, she heard the distinctive *whap, whap, whap* of a helicopter's rotors. She smiled to herself.

With God guiding her and with the help of Lillian Trumble, miracles could happen.

By the time she motored Stuart Lynch's powerboat out of Paradise Cove, the wind had kicked up, creating tiny whitecaps on the open water. She hunkered down at the stern of the boat as far out of the spray as she could get and navigated for Friday Harbor.

CHAPTER ❦ SIXTEEN

The earth shall soon dissolve like snow,
The sun forbear to shine;
But God, Who called me here below,
Shall be forever mine.

MARY PARKED HER VAN
in the garage at home and switched off the engine. "If you wait until I get out of the van, I'll try to help you," she said to Josh.

"I'm okay. Just a little dizzy, you know."

His color was also flushed and his skin looked dry, Mary noted. She had to get his temperature down in a hurry.

Keeping one eye on Josh, she backed her chair away from the steering wheel, picked up the boy's duffel bag and put it in her lap. She exited the van via the lift, Finnegan right beside her. By the time she was on the ground, the teenager was standing rather unsteadily next to the van, a blanket still draped over his shoulders. He looked like he might collapse at any moment.

"Grab my chair, Josh, and hold on tight. I don't want you passing out on me. We'll go into the house together."

Finnegan led the way, pulling the chair, and Mary aided him by applying her arm strength, which improved considerably after the accident. She opened the door and rolled herself inside. They made their way to the living room. The sun beaming through the sliding-glass doors in the back had warmed the house, which made the living room the perfect place for Josh to stay.

"I'm going to get a blanket and fix you up on the couch, honey. I'd let you have the guest room upstairs, but if you needed me, I couldn't get to you."

Covering his mouth, he coughed thickly and his eyes watered. "I'm sorry to be so much trouble."

"Hush, now. You're no more trouble than my own children were, and they were at it a lot longer than you've been." She shooed him over to the couch, thinking how much she missed having someone to fuss over. She realized being in a wheelchair hadn't dampened her mothering instincts one bit. "Take off your shoes. I'm going to heat up some lemonade to soothe that cough and find some decongestant for you. Are you allergic to anything?"

"No, ma'am, I don't think so." He sank wearily to the couch and toed off his running shoes. The big toe on his right foot peeked out through a hole in his socks.

Mary put his duffel bag on the floor. After she got Josh settled in and hopefully napping, she'd wash and dry his clothes. He looked like he could use a fresh set. In the next day or two, she might be able to get into town to buy him some new clothes as well.

Mary didn't know where Josh's parents might be or why he was on Sparrow Island. But those questions would have to wait until another time when the boy was feeling better.

Rounding up the medicines she needed, a spare blanket from her room and the lemonade, she wheeled back into the living room. Josh was lying down on the couch, his eyes closed.

"Josh, honey, before you go to sleep, I want you to take this medicine. You'll feel much better if you do."

With an effort, he opened his eyes and downed the pills and cough syrup, then sipped on the lemonade.

"How do you suppose you got such a dreadful cold?" Mary asked.

"I guess it was the night of the thunderstorm. A big lightning bolt hit the top of Winchell Manor where I was sleeping. Scared the, um, heck out of me. I went runnin' out of the place like the devil himself was after me." He coughed and it took a minute for him to catch his breath. "I got soaked in the rain and I was afraid to go back inside until after the storm had passed. Started feeling funny the next morning."

Nodding, Mary patted his knee. That had been a miserable storm, and to think Josh had been out in it without any shelter made her heartsick. "I wish you'd told someone you didn't have a safe place to stay."

"The old manor was great, actually. I mean, nobody bothered me or anything."

"But you were all alone. Something could have happened to you and no one would have known where to find you." In fact, that's exactly what had happened, and Mary so wished she'd known Josh was in trouble.

His narrow shoulders lifted in a shrug. "I didn't think anybody would miss me."

"I did." Smiling, she patted him again. "Here, let me take that glass. Then I want you to take off your shirt and pants. I'll wash them while you're napping."

"You don't need to do that."

"Indulge an old woman, would you? People took care of me for months after my accident. I miss having someone I can take care of." She wheeled a few feet away. "Just toss your things on the floor. Finnegan will pick them up for me."

She wheeled into the kitchen with the dirty glass and washed it with hot, soapy water. By the time she returned, Josh was under the covers, his jeans and shirt neatly folded on the floor beside the couch. She ordered Finnegan to pick up the clothing.

Using his mouth, the retriever plucked the shirt and pants from the floor, placing them on Mary's lap.

"Good boy," she whispered, knowing from the gentle rise and fall of Josh's chest that he was already asleep, the best medicine of all.

Gently, she lifted the blanket to cover Josh's shoulder, then wheeled out of the living room to let the boy rest. She'd make some of her chicken soup to feed him when he woke up.

But right now, she wanted to call Steven Jarvis at the bank to apprise him of the situation at Winchell Manor and the discovery Abby had made regarding Beauregard's will. And she had to let Pastor Jim know why neither she nor Josh would be at the day camp today.

Suddenly she felt filled with purpose and energy. There was so much to do. She relished the knowledge that being in a wheelchair didn't hold her back from helping others.

She'd come a long way since her accident and she realized how foolish she'd been to doubt God's plan for her.

THE JUDGE'S CHAMBERS were on the second floor of the courthouse. Without taking time to comb her hair or freshen up after her boat ride, Abby hurried along the corridor. She hoped, since Judge Swink was a longtime family friend, that he would excuse her disheveled appearance.

A court clerk informed Abby that Judge Swink was presiding over a case and was not available to see her.

"Will he be taking a break anytime soon? I won't take up much of his time." At least she hoped the judge could quickly settle the matter. The old Winchell Bible weighed heavy in her arms. It held the proof that Beauregard had a sister, who was named in the will Abby had tucked back inside the Bible.

"When to take breaks is entirely within the discretion of the judge, ma'am. I will say he generally breaks for lunch around twelve-thirty."

Abby checked her watch. "But that's two hours from now," she protested.

The clerk, a young woman with silky blond hair and blue-green eyes that bulged slightly, simply gazed at her.

"I guess I'll have to wait," Abby said, repressing a sigh. "Which courtroom is Judge Swink in?"

"Number two. It's around the corner. But His Honor doesn't like spectators barging in and out, and causing a distraction."

"Thank you. I promise I'll be the epitome of decorum." She smiled, thinking her hair was probably going every which way, and her jeans and sweater were not necessarily appropriate attire to wear in court. But then, Friday Harbor was a pretty casual place.

She found the courtroom easily enough and peered through the window in the door to get the lay of the land. Judge Swink, long past the age of voluntary retirement, had aged since last she saw him and had added several new lines to his already craggy face. As a child, she'd thought of the judge as Ichabod Crane with a smile.

He wasn't smiling now. It looked more like he was lecturing the defendant.

Abby slipped quietly inside the courtroom and took a seat on the aisle behind a gray-haired woman wearing a print dress. Gratefully, she placed the heavy Bible on the chair beside her. With her fingers tapping her thigh, she beat out the persistent ticking of the clock marking the final minutes of her last chance to save Winchell Manor.

When she looked up, the judge gave her an almost imperceptible nod of acknowledgement. She smiled in return.

Within a few minutes, the judge had sentenced the defendant to thirty days in jail, less time served, recessed the court and swept from the room, his black cloak billowing behind him. A bailiff stepped over to invite Abby into Judge Swink's chambers.

The judge opened his arms wide and Abby walked into his fatherly embrace, made awkward by the Bible she carried.

"How are all our fine feathered friends these days, my dear?" the judge asked. He had a wonderfully deep voice and had been the lead bass singer in his church choir for years.

"Flying high for the most part, Your Honor."

"Your father said you had an urgent matter to discuss with me." He gestured to the leather chair in front of his desk. "Sit and tell me what the problem is."

She quickly explained the situation to him. Leaning back with his hips resting against his desk, he appeared to take in every nuance of her story, nodding occasionally to let her know that he understood. She handed him Beauregard's will.

"I believe the issue is," she concluded, "that Winchell Manor is still private property. A proper search for his heirs hasn't been conducted and the county exceeded its authority by condemning the building and attempting to subvert the land to public use. I'm asking you to issue an injunction that would provide enough time to sort out who, if anyone, is the current rightful owner."

Without comment, the judge read through the will, then looked at her. "Has this been authenticated by anyone?"

"Only so far as I found the will in this Bible, which appears to belong to the Winchell family. There's mention of Beauregard's sister, Catherine Winchell, as well as an older brother, Nelson. I know from other records that Nelson died in the Civil War."

Placing the Bible on the judge's desk, she opened it to the middle section where the family history was recorded and pointed out the entry.

He examined the page and nodded. "But you have no idea if the sister noted here has any living descendants?"

"No, sir. I'm hoping to find records at the Green Harbor Bank that would shed light on that subject. You'll notice in the will that the bank manager was named executor at the time of Beauregard's death."

"A hundred years ago," the judge pointed out. "Staff turnover would have to be awfully low if that man's still employed by the bank. Either that, or the bank's pension program is worse than the county's."

Abby smiled but didn't want to encourage the judge to make light of the situation. There wasn't enough time left to waste even a minute if she was to save the manor.

"Your Honor, not only is the manor house a historical landmark on Sparrow Island, the cellar contains a wealth of valuable furniture and period items. We need an opportunity to evaluate the remaining assets as well as conduct a search for heirs. If the demolition proceeds as scheduled, we'll lose any chance we have to save something that belongs not only to the Winchell family but to Sparrow Islanders as well."

He pushed himself up from the desk and walked around to the other side. "Apparently the county commissioners view the manor as a hazard. Not having personally visited the area, I'm reluctant to go against their determination."

Abby's heart sank.

"How long do you think it would take to get the antiques evaluated and a search for heirs concluded?" he asked.

"If I can get the furniture specialist from the Heritage Museum in Olympia to come over, I would think he could get a rough estimate of the value within a week, perhaps two. As for finding Beauregard's heirs..." She shrugged. "I suppose that could take years."

"I can't give you that much time, Abby. The county commissioners would put me in stocks on the courthouse's front steps if I did."

"I wouldn't want that to happen, sir."

"Nor would I." Reaching to the side of his desk, he spoke into an intercom. "Miss Reedley, would you please write up an injunction to halt all demolition activities on Winchell Manor for a period of ten days."

Abby breathed a sigh of relief as the judge finished his instructions to his clerk. Ten days wasn't much time, but it was a step in the right direction.

He turned back to her. "If necessary, we can revisit the question in ten days and, if appropriate, make the injunction permanent. Meanwhile, that structure has been there for more than a century. I think the commissioners can live with it for another week or so."

Abby stood and extended her hand. "Thank you, Your Honor. I really appreciate you doing this for me."

"*Humph.* At my age, I've gained a fine appreciation for not throwing either people or things away simply because they're old. Tell your father it's time we go fishing again. It's been too long."

"I'll tell him." Smiling, Abby hurried out of the judge's office. It didn't take long for the clerk to prepare the injunction paperwork and get it signed by the judge, then Abby was on her way.

Before she left the marina, however, she called Sandy McDonald on her cell phone. "Hi, Sandy. It's Abby. Is Winchell Manor still standing?"

"You bet it is! What a morning we've had. Lillian has the contractors tied in knots."

"Can you put her on?"

"I'd be happy to."

Abby heard crowd noise as Sandy went in search of Lillian, and what sounded like chanting. Abby frowned. What were they up to at the manor?

"Not a stick or stone has been harmed," Lillian announced with glee as she took the phone. "And you can bet your panty hose that we'll be on the six o'clock news all across the country."

"Terrific!" Grinning, Abby loosened the mooring lines to Stuart Lynch's boat from the dock. "That will certainly give William something to write about in *The Birdcall* next week."

"He's been scribbling in his notebook all morning, having a great time playing media mogul. Some of the TV crews even interviewed him."

"So he'll have his fifteen minutes of fame." Chuckling, Abby didn't mind a bit under the circumstances. "Is Sergeant Cobb from the sheriff's office around? I need to talk with him too."

"Yep. I'll get Sandy to round him up for you."

When Henry came on, Abby informed him she had the injunction in hand. Since he'd been briefed by Mary, he knew the situation and didn't hesitate to enforce the order.

"You may have some upset folks after I break the news to them about the injunction," Henry warned.

"I know. I'll try to calm their ruffled feathers when I get back."

Settling herself in the stern of the boat, she motored out of the harbor. She suspected the real work of saving Winchell Manor had only just begun.

WHEN ABBY ARRIVED in her car back at Arrowhead Hill, it looked like a crowd scene from a disaster movie was being filmed. Two helicopters circled overhead, both of them carrying the markings of TV news stations. Cars and trucks were parked at odd angles around the manor. Spectators milled about, some of them being interviewed by johnny-on-the-spot television and print journalists.

Lillian Trumble and her army of fifty or more protesters stood at the focal point of the scene, waving their picket signs beneath the SAVE WINCHELL MANOR banner and shouting:

"WHO WANTS TO SAVE THE MANOR?"

"WE DO! WE DO!"

"WHY DO WE WANT TO SAVE THE MANOR?"

"FOR OUR CHILDREN! FOR OUR CHILDREN!"

In the midday sun, the limestone exterior of the manor glistened as though it somehow knew there had been a reprieve.

There would be no demolition this day.

Abby noted with pleasure that her parents were among the

protesters as well as Sandy McDonald and her son Bobby, Naomi Yardley along with many of the historical society members, and even Ana Dominguez who must have closed her shop to join the crowd. Hugo was one of the few men on the picket line and looked quite dapper in a blue blazer and slacks.

Those standing off to the side—looking anything but happy about the situation—included Archie Goodfellow and others in the community who didn't favor restoration of Winchell Manor. Most of them were easily identifiable, standing with their arms folded across their respective chests and glum expressions on their faces.

Henry Cobb, looking very official in his desert-tan uniform shirt, dark-green pants and Smokey-the-Bear sergeant's hat, had positioned himself between the two factions. When Abby had driven up the hill, she'd noticed one of his deputies standing guard at the back of the manor and a second one strolling around the perimeter keeping an eye on things too.

Abby headed toward Henry.

A cheer went up from the protesters when they spotted her. In return, she waved the injunction in the air. That brought a tidal wave of reporters in her direction, led by William Jansen.

"How about an exclusive, Abby?" A bulky camera hung on a strap around William's neck. "This is big news for Sparrow Island."

"A little later, okay William?"

"What do you plan to do with the manor, Ms. Stanton?" another reporter shouted.

A camera flash popped in her face.

"Is there really a ghost in Winchell Manor?" someone asked.

Without breaking stride, she shook her head. "There is no ghost."

"Have you found evidence of a murder?"

"Did you find a body in the cellar? Whose was it?"

She reached Henry and the two of them were immediately surrounded by the mob of reporters. More camera flashes went off, making Abby flinch.

Henry took the injunction from her. "This is it?"

"Yes. We've got ten days, and longer if I can show the injunction should be permanent."

"Archie and some of the others aren't real happy."

"I didn't think they would be."

Hugo made his way through the crowd to her side. "If you'll excuse me, Abby. I think it would be wise to arrange a hasty press conference. It's the only way these creatures will give you any peace."

A reporter shoved a microphone in front of her and she pushed it away.

"A press conference?" She hadn't considered that would be necessary.

"The last time I was in Nairobi, we found it necessary to speak directly with the press. It was right after we'd discovered a new species of desert lizard. Quite an exciting find, really. The press was mad to learn more about it."

She blinked at the peculiar rationale for her to hold a press conference was because a lizard in Nairobi had caused similar excitement. "Well, all right . . ."

"If I may," Hugo said, "I'll act as your press secretary. We'll set up something on the steps of the manor where you can make a formal statement. With the banner overhead and the protestors standing around you, that will make good video."

Abby agreed, although not with a lot of enthusiasm at the thought of being televised. Her hair was windblown, her cheeks probably windburned from the boat ride, and she was barely presentable in the jeans and sweater she'd hastily pulled on that morning. But it was obvious she had to give the insatiable press something to feed on and it was an opportunity to gain public support for the restoration of the manor. Her vanity counted little compared to the good that could come from a press conference.

Like a Pied Piper, Hugo led the press away, which only provided an opportunity for Archie to express his displeasure.

"Congratulations, Abby. I hope you know what a mess you've gotten us into."

"I look at Winchell Manor as an opportunity, not as a mess, Archie."

"The whole island is being overrun by the press and you don't think that's trouble? When this story breaks, we'll have every nut and schemer from here to L.A. trying to wheedle a piece of the action. All of 'em will be long-lost kin of the Winchells. The county will be in court trying to settle the lawsuits for years. And when it's all said and done, we'll have to tear down the place, just like me and Frank voted to do in the first place."

"I've got faith that won't happen, Archie." In her heart, she knew she was doing the right thing.

Archie muttered his disapproval.

Deciding there was only one way to convince Archie she hadn't totally lost her mind, Abby turned to Henry. "After I speak with the press, I'd like to take you and the members of the town council and Naomi Yardley on a tour of the manor. Particularly the cellar." She'd ask William Jansen to come along too. He'd love having the exclusive report for *The Birdcall.* "I think everyone will understand the situation better after they see what a treasure we've found. But I'll need help keeping the press out."

"I'll tell my men. And if this place and its contents are as valuable as you say they are, I'm going to have to hire some guards. I don't have enough deputies to provide security here twenty-four/seven, and you can bet the county commissioners aren't going to like the idea of spending the money."

That was something else Abby hadn't considered. "Let me give that some thought." She could dip into her own savings to pay for a few days of security, but she hated to do that if there was any other choice.

When she stepped up onto the porch for the press conference, the protesters applauded her. She thanked them and gave Lillian, who had unlocked herself from the porch's post, a hug.

"I don't know what I would have done without you," Abby said.

"Shoot. I haven't had this much fun in ages." Lillian grinned broadly. Her face was flushed with excitement and her age lines had all but melted away. "I'm thinking of getting back into the battle. You know, there's some countries out there where women still can't vote. Maybe they could use an old warhorse like me to get things stirred up."

Laughing, Abby said, "I'm sure they could."

With a quick finger comb of her hair and a deep breath, Abby turned to face the press.

BY THE TIME ABBY FINISHED dealing with the press and had shown the treasures of Winchell Manor to the members of the town council and others, it was mid-afternoon. William Jansen had perhaps been the most excited of the entire group. He had his big story, including several rolls of film.

Except for two sheriff's deputies, Abby and Naomi Yardley appeared to be the only ones left to tour the exterior of the building.

A breeze was blowing up from the harbor, making the wild grass in the former alfalfa field wave in emerald ripples and teasing the tops of nearby fir trees. The air was fresh.

"The foundation looks solid to me," Naomi commented. "That landslide in the tunnel is a little troubling, though. Certainly we'd need an engineer to go over the place with a fine-tooth comb to make sure it's all structurally sound."

"You said *we*. Does that mean the Sparrow Island Historical Society would like to have a part in the restoration, if we can find the funding?"

"Abby, I'm practically salivating at the possibility, which isn't a pretty sight I can assure you."

Abby chuckled. "I'm so glad you're excited about the idea because antiques and building restoration are way out of my sphere of experience. Forget that I wouldn't have time to take on a project this large. I've already been neglecting my job at the conservatory."

"I'm sure Hugo agrees the effort was worthwhile. This has the potential to be a major historic center for study of all the islands, even the entire Pacific Northwest."

"Well, I'd certainly be happy to turn over the restoration and operation of the manor to your group." They walked slowly toward the back of the house. "I would like to see this smaller building turned into something like a youth hostel. It probably once housed the servant's quarters, but if it could be converted to housing, I'd like to see ornithology and history students using it as a base camp here on the island."

"That sounds reasonable to me. Assuming," she emphasized, "there's funding available for any of our grand plans."

"Too true." Spotting the telltale splash of yellow fur, Abby knelt next to the porch of the smaller building. "There's a small family of resident cats we'll have to do something about."

Albert, the braver of the two kittens, came bounding out from under the steps. Victoria II peered out more cautiously.

"It's possible these kittens are the descendants of a cat Beauregard gave Theadora in 1875," Abby said. "She wrote about getting a cat and naming her Victoria in her journal."

"Really?" Squatting next to Abby, Naomi let Albert nuzzle her hand.

"I haven't spotted the mother cat yet. She must be very wary. But I've been meaning to at least find the kittens a good home. Maybe when things settle down in a few days."

Victoria II found enough courage to approach Naomi, who gave her a long pet and rubbed her tummy when the kitten rolled onto her back.

"Why don't you leave the cats here?" Naomi asked.

"Here? But there's no one to care for them. Without a regular source of food, they'll become predators and hunt voles and other prey that several of our bird species need for survival."

"After generations of surviving off the land, maybe these two little ones deserve to become the official mascots of Winchell Manor. In time, volunteers will give them lots of loving care."

Sitting back on her haunches, Abby considered the idea. "We'd have to catch the mother cat and have her neutered, as well as the kittens when they're old enough. I wouldn't want more feral kittens born."

"And I could take these two little dears home with me and keep them until the manor is ready for occupancy. I lost my own cat to old age about a year ago. It'll be fun to have kittens in my life for a little while."

"I think Albert and Victoria II would love that."

Picking up the two kittens, Naomi stood and rubbed her cheek against their soft fur. "Perfect names. And I can hardly wait to get my hands on Theadora's journal. That's truly an amazing find."

Abby agreed, and the two women continued around the manor back to their vehicles that were parked in the front on the gravel drive.

As she glanced up at the third-floor tower room, something caught Abby's eye. A flash of light. The image of a face in the window disappeared almost as fast as it had appeared.

Her breath caught and she blinked, trying to focus on what she had seen. Or imagined.

"What's wrong?" Naomi asked.

"Nothing. It's just that. . . I think I saw someone in the tower room."

"There's no one left inside. Except for the deputies, everyone went home."

"Maybe not everyone." *Maybe not the ghost of Winchell Manor*, she thought foolishly, still trying to shake the image she'd seen.

Suddenly, the tower window opened and the face reappeared, smiling. "Hi, Abby. Can you see me?"

She nearly fainted. "Bobby McDonald, what are you doing up there?" she shouted up to him.

"Lookin' for the ghost," he yelled back. "I borrowed Mom's

camera, and Mr. Jansen said he'd pay me big bucks if I could get a picture for him."

Torn between laughter and a few choice words, Abby planted her fists on her hips and called up to the boy. "Is your mother up there with you?"

"No, ma'am. It's just me. Mom went to pick wildflowers behind the house."

"Well then, get yourself down here, young man. Winchell Manor is off-limits and you know it."

"Ah, gee . . . I promised Mr. Jansen."

"*Now*, Bobby, or I'll find your mother or send a deputy up there to bring you down."

Sandy appeared from the forested area. "I wondered where that child went. I'm really sorry. I should have been watching him more carefully." She looked up at the tower window. "Bobby, you get down here this minute or you can't use your microscope for a week."

"Ah, Mom . . ."

"I mean it!"

His head disappeared, though Abby imagined with considerable reluctance.

Shaking her head, Sandy walked to the front of the house to meet her wayward son.

Chuckling, Naomi said, "There are some youngsters who are just too smart for their own good."

Or for their parents' peace of mind, Abby suspected, feeling a fair amount of sympathy for Sandy. Thinking about children reminded her that she should get home to find out how Josh was faring, although she knew he was in good hands with her sister.

CHAPTER ❦ SEVENTEEN

Mary wheeled to the door to the garage to greet Abby the moment she heard her sister arrive home. She was so proud of Abby and what she had accomplished.

"We saw you on TV! You were wonderful with the press. And you stopped the demolition!"

"Stopped it for now. But I'm afraid that was the easy part. Finding the funding to do something useful with the manor will be the hard part." She glanced around. "Where's Josh?"

"In the living room. He had a nice nap. His temperature's down, and now he's eating some chicken soup."

Abby lowered her voice. "Did you ask him why he ran away from home?"

"Not yet. I wanted him to rest first and feel more relaxed here. And I thought you'd want to hear his story too. Between us, maybe we can sort things out and decide what to do."

Agreeing that was a good plan, Abby followed Mary into the living room. Josh was sitting on the couch, a blanket wrapped around him, and a bowl of soup and a glass of orange juice on a tray in his lap. His color was much better than it had been that morning when Mary had brought him home. He had company too. Blossom was perched on the back of the couch keeping an interested eye on the chicken soup, and Finnegan had picked a spot on the floor where he could keep track of both Mary and their guest.

"Hey, Josh. You're looking much better than the last time I saw you," Abby said.

"Hey," he responded with a shy smile. "Mary's soup tastes great. You should try some."

"I plan to." Abby sat in the upholstered chair opposite the couch while Mary positioned herself next to the couch. "Are you feeling well enough to tell us why you ran away from home?"

"I don't want to go back to Idaho."

"Josh, honey, tell us what made you leave home," Mary said.

Thoughtfully, he took another spoonful of soup, then looked up. "My folks, they're like always fighting and yelling and stuff. They're gonna get a divorce, see? And Grandma died a few of months ago, so everything's changing. They don't need me around. I'm just something else my folks have to fight over."

"Oh, Josh," Abby said sympathetically. "I'm so sorry."

"Did they hurt or abuse you?" Mary asked. If that was the case, she'd see to it Josh would have somewhere safe to live.

He looked surprised she'd suggest such a thing. "Gosh, no, Mary. My folks have always been great, at least up 'til now. Both of them. Then they just changed, you know, and fight with each other all the time."

Mary remembered a high school friend whose parents divorced and the hardest part for the girl had been how to be loyal to one parent without hurting the other. "Are they arguing over who you're going to live with?"

"Yeah. Dad says us men ought to stick together and that just makes Mom cry all the more. So they ask me where I want to live. I mean, how am I supposed to decide?" Blinking his eyes, he looked down at his nearly empty soup bowl as if that was where he'd find the answers he needed. "I love them both, you know? I don't want to hurt either of them. And I miss Grandma a lot. So I . . ." His shrug was one of helplessness. "So I left."

Mary couldn't help but think Josh might have misunderstood the situation. Most children feel torn and lost when their parents start talking about divorce, and then with his grandmother's death he felt doubly at a loss. Adolescents, particularly, could get stuck on an idea—like their running away would solve the problem—and didn't want to let it go. They make everything about *them*, including that divorce is somehow their fault.

The last thing she wanted to do was undermine parental authority. But maybe she could show Josh that being on his own would create more, not fewer, problems for him.

"How old are you?" Mary asked in a quiet, reassuring manner. "Seventeen?"

His gaze darted between the two of them. "Yeah."

"I thought so, and that's pretty grown-up," she acknowledged, although a seventeen-year-old still had much to learn. "Another year and there wouldn't be any question. You'd have every right to decide whether to stay on your own or go back home."

He thrust out his jaw. "I don't see why I can't decide that now."

She desperately hoped she was taking the right approach in granting that he did have some choices, although they'd be poor ones. "Actually, you can."

Josh looked up in surprise. "I can?"

Abby looked a little shocked too.

"You could petition a court to become emancipated," Mary said. "That would mean you'd have the rights of an adult. And the responsibilities. You could decide where you wanted to live, what you spend your money on, if you go to school or not."

"I could handle that."

"You're certainly mature enough," Mary said, mentally crossing her fingers that wouldn't be his ultimate choice. "It would mean you'd have to get a full-time job to support yourself, of course. A court wouldn't allow you to be homeless."

"I was thinking about doing that when vacation Bible school was over. Maybe Pastor Jim would have something else for me or would know somebody who'd hire me."

"Possibly. Of course, the rental prices are pretty steep here on Sparrow Island, so it would have to be a job that paid a decent wage." Mary tried to appear to be giving that possibility some serious thought. "Let's see . . . Have you graduated from high school yet?"

"Naw. I just finished my junior year." He coughed, though not as hard as he'd been coughing that morning, and pulled a tissue from a box beside him.

"*Hmm*, it's hard to get a good job without a diploma," Mary pointed out. "And you did have ambitions to go to college. You said you wanted to study urban planning?"

"Well, yeah. But I don't have to. I mean, lots of guys don't graduate from high school or go to college. It's no big deal."

Mary suspected it would be for an intelligent young man like him. "You know, without a good education you might never be able to fully use the talents and abilities that God has given you. That would be a shame."

Frowning, he rubbed his forehead. "Maybe I could go to college later, you know? After I've been on my own for a while."

"That's possible," Abby agreed hesitantly. "Ida Tolliver at the Springhouse Café is hoping to do that. But it won't be easy for her."

Mary took over again. "Well, you have a lot to think about. Meanwhile, it's clear your parents are very worried about you and will want to know you're safe. I'm sure you don't want to cause them any more distress than you have. That wouldn't be fair to them."

"I guess not."

"Then, if you don't mind, we'll ask the local authorities to notify your parents that you're safe and in good hands. After that . . . Well, we'll take this one step at a time."

He hesitated before lifting his shoulders again. "I guess."

"Unless you want to call your parents yourself," Abby suggested.

He shook his head. "I wouldn't know what to say."

Reaching for the tray, Mary gave the boy an encouraging smile. "Everything will be all right. You'll see. Now, lie back down and rest some more. If you need anything else, just call. I'll be in the kitchen or in my room."

"It sure is nice, your taking care of me and all."

"*Shh*, now. You're not the first sick young man I've taken care of, and you may not even be the last."

Mary wheeled herself away and Abby followed her.

"My, you're good with that young man," Abby said softly. "But emancipation? That's pretty extreme."

"He's a sweet boy and smart too. I hope his parents can

work out their differences. Divorce can be so hard on children, even the one's who are almost grown." She placed the tray on the counter and ran water to rinse out the bowl. "I wanted him to feel that going home wouldn't be forced on him, but I'm praying it won't come to that."

"I certainly hope not. But we don't really know all the circumstances, do we?"

"No, we don't. His running away may have changed things at home too." Mary remembered when Zack had briefly run away. In her case, after he returned home, she'd made sure she listened more closely to what he wanted. "Would you like me to warm up some soup for you?"

"That'd be great. I haven't had a minute to even think about food, much less eat anything today."

"That's not good for you, you know."

"Yes, Mother," Abby teased.

Abby was just about to sit down to dinner when the phone rang. Abby quickly picked it up. When she answered, a woman's voice said, "Please hold for County Commissioner Hargrove."

Abby grimaced. This call wasn't likely to be a pleasant one.

Once the commissioner acknowledged her greeting, he launched right into a nonstop tirade. "I want to make it clear, Ms. Stanton, that the county is not going to spend one dime to either protect or restore that blighted structure you're so proud of. You maintain it is private property. Excellent. In that case, the owner is liable for all costs, including the expense of the crew that was to demolish the building today. I have ordered my staff to file a suit against any owner who comes forward, to recover any and all costs the county has incurred thus far, plus all back property taxes, including penalties and interest."

"Mr. Hargrove—"

"The county's position on Winchell Manor has been widely publicized. Had you stepped forward earlier—"

"I didn't know until recently that—"

"—certain accommodations might have been made. But under the circumstances—"

"Mr. Hargrove! You and the county are missing an opportunity to preserve a wonderful piece of San Juan's history that should be celebrated not destroyed."

"That's your opinion, Ms. Stanton." A click announced that he had concluded the conversation.

Abby stared at the phone in her hand. "That man is a hard-headed, narrow-minded, lacking-in-vision political hack! Why, if I had my way . . ." Expelling a breath, she hung up, leaned her forehead against the wall and tried to regain her composure.

"I gather our favorite commissioner didn't announce you'd won the lottery," Mary said calmly.

She glanced at her sister. "No. And losing my temper isn't going to help matters either. I apologize."

"No need. There are a lot of voters in the county who would agree with your rather colorful description of Mr. Hargrove." Wheeling around, she ladled some soup into a bowl and brought it to the table. "Eat. You'll feel better."

Abby sank into her chair. "I don't think food's going to solve my problem. I may well have bitten off more than I can chew."

"Oh? Where's your faith, Abby? Didn't you tell me that you were sure God had led you to the manor and Theodora's journal for a purpose?"

"I know, but—"

"Then you'll find a way to overcome whatever obstacles Mr. Hargrove or anyone else puts in your path."

Abby hoped that was true and sent up a quick prayer to ask for the insight to do God's work as He saw fit.

The first spoonful of Mary's delicious soup seemed to hit the bottom of Abby's empty stomach. But she'd only managed two more spoonfuls when the phone rang again.

She rolled her eyes. "If that's Hargrove . . ."

Picking up the phone, she said, "Yes?"

"Is this Abby? Ms. Stanton?"

"Yes. Who is this?" She sounded more testy than she meant to be, but Hargrove had really set her off.

"I'm Steven Jarvis, branch manager of Green Harbor Bank. Your sister called me this morning to apprise me of Beauregard Winchell's last will and testament. Since that time, I've been doing some research. I believe I have some good news for you and wondered if you could meet with me tomorrow morning here at the bank?"

Abby brightened considerably. "Yes, of course. I wonder if I could ask Naomi Yardley to join us. She's the head of the local historical society and has a serious interest in helping to restore the manor."

"That would be excellent. I know Mrs. Yardley and I'm sure she'd be able to contribute to the conversation."

"Thank you. I'll look forward to meeting with you tomorrow."

When Abby ended the call, her mood soared. Good news could mean almost anything. At the very least, perhaps she wouldn't have to worry about Hargrove's threats. Quickly, she punched in Naomi's phone number to tell her they had an appointment with the banker.

LATER THAT EVENING Mary called Henry to let him know about Josh, and the sergeant dropped by the house around eight.

"Evening, Abby," he said, removing his hat. "Your protest and the injunction sure did stir up a hornet's nest with the county commissioners."

"So I understand. Commissioner Hargrove called me." Abby was still sorry she'd let the man upset her so much. "I apologize if my actions got you into trouble."

"Don't worry about it. All part of the job. But maybe you should arrange a tour of the Winchell place for all the commissioners. I know the tour sure changed my mind about tearing the manor down. Might work for the county's head honchos too."

"Good idea. I'll try to make that happen in the next few days." She'd missed so much work at The Nature Museum, she really needed to talk with Hugo about her absences.

Mary had been freshening up in her bedroom and she rolled out into the entry, smiling fondly at the sergeant. "Thank you for coming, Henry. I hope you were able to reach Josh's parents."

"I did. Is the boy around?"

"In the living room watching TV," Mary said. "He has a terrible cold but he's going to be all right, I'm sure."

The three of them went into the living room. Josh looked up, his expression wary at the sight of a uniformed officer. Blossom had moved her position to the cushion next to the boy, relishing the extra attention she was getting.

"Josh, I'm Henry Cobb from the sheriff's office." Henry extended his hand to the teenager.

As they shook hands, Josh started to stand up, but Henry gestured for him to stay where he was on the couch.

"Am I in trouble?" Josh asked.

"Not with me, you're not. Officially, you were trespassing at the manor, but I think we can let that pass." Sitting down in the upholstered chair opposite by the couch, Henry leaned back. "I talked to your folks. They're mighty glad you're all right. They've been real worried about you, son."

Josh hung his head. "I didn't know what else to do."

"I think they've figured that out now. In my experience, the parents of runaway kids go through stages. First, they're madder than hops that their kid has run off. Then they get scared, real scared, that something bad might of happened to him. Finally, they begin to wonder what they did wrong to upset their kid so much that he had to leave like that." Henry fingered the wide brim of his hat. "That's where your folks are now, wondering what they did wrong and how to fix it."

"They can't. They're gettin' a divorce."

"Maybe. Maybe not. Your mom said she and your dad were talking to their pastor, getting some counseling so they can work things out."

Slowly, Josh lifted his gaze. "They are?"

"Yep. Sounds like your running away opened their eyes to what's really important to them. Namely you."

Josh seemed to mull that over, and Henry waited patiently for his response. "Guess it wasn't all bad then that I ran away."

"Wouldn't go so far as to say that," Henry said. "There's usually better and safer ways to handle problems than running away. A lot of youngsters get themselves into deep trouble when they try to go it on their own. I think you were lucky to hook up with Rev. Hale and the church. But maybe that's because you're a smart kid."

"So smart that I caught this stupid cold." Josh's cough emphasized his point.

"Tell you what." Leaning forward, Henry patted the boy's

knee. "Why don't you give your folks a call. They'd be relieved to hear your voice, and I'm sure Mary won't mind your using her phone."

"Not at all," Mary said. "Please call them, Josh."

Looking unsure of himself, Josh said, "What do I say?"

"Why don't you start with, 'Hi, Mom, it's me'?" Henry suggested with an encouraging smile. "From what your mom said when I talked with her, I imagine they'll take it from there."

Running his fingers through Blossom's long fur, Josh hesitated.

"You can use the phone in the kitchen," Mary said. "We'll stay in here so you'll have some privacy."

"You don't think they're too mad at me?"

"They'll be so happy to hear your voice, they'll forget they were ever angry with you," Mary assured him. "That's how I felt when my Zack ran away to join a band thinking he'd become a big star in Hollywood. Of course, he was only ten at the time and didn't get any farther than the ferry landing. But I was sure relieved when a friend found him and called me."

Mary's story lightened the atmosphere and they all chuckled at the thought of a ten-year-old going off to join a band. In fact, Zack may not have run away again, but he hadn't given up his musical ambitions. He was now a successful musician, playing keyboard and touring the country with his jazz group. The only downside was that Mary didn't get to see her son as often as she'd like.

Nodding, Josh got up. "I won't talk long."

"Talk as long as you need to," Mary said.

Abby met Mary's gaze as the adolescent walked into the kitchen, and she smiled. Mary seemed to have exactly the right touch with the boy. Henry had done well too. And if Josh's family could get back together, they all could feel proud of their efforts.

From the kitchen they heard Josh say, "Hi, Mom. It's me.... I'm okay. Really.... It's just a cold ... Yeah, I know ... I missed you, too, Mom. And Dad ..."

The conversation was so touching, yet so personal, Abby forced herself not to listen. Instead she prayed. *Lord, help Josh and his parents find their way back together again, all three of them. Let them learn the lesson You've taught me, that family means more than simply blood ties. It is where love can be best nurtured. Amen.*

When Josh returned to the living room, he was coughing, but grinning too. "My folks are coming out here, to Sparrow Island. They're hoping maybe it'll be okay for me to stay here a couple of days, Mary. Until they get here. Then we're all gonna get a hotel room or something. Spend some time together."

"I think that's perfect," Mary said. "And Abby and I will be delighted to have a young man like you around the house for however long you'd like to stay."

His face flushed a bright red. "Thanks."

Abby said, "If there's a vacancy, you and your parents might like to stay at The Bird Nest bed-and-breakfast in town. Martin and Terza Choi are wonderful hosts. Of course, The Dorset is nice, too, if a bit pricey."

"Great. I'll ask Mom. She said she'd call tomorrow after they get plane reservations and stuff. There aren't that many flights out of Lewiston, and then there's the drive from Seattle and the ferry schedule to worry about. She'll let me know when they can get here."

Josh looked so pleased with himself, and relieved, Abby was

sure his family had taken the first step toward becoming whole again.

Now she had to hope her meeting with Steven Jarvis at the bank tomorrow would be equally productive. She and Naomi would be meeting with him at nine, when the bank opened.

What would come next? Abby didn't know, but she would simply have to place her faith in the Lord.

CHAPTER ❦ EIGHTEEN

I N ORDER TO FIT IN HER morning devotionals, Abby made it a point to wake early so she could begin her days in prayer and meditation. Today could be an important day for the future of Winchell Manor. She wanted to approach the challenges she might face with a calm spirit.

She considered reading more of *Imitation of Christ* in order to better understand Beauregard's life following the death of his wife and the decisions he'd made. But that was heavy going, requiring a good deal of concentration to understand what the fifteenth-century author meant.

Instead, she picked up her daily devotional book from the bed table and adjusted her glasses. The day's reading was based on a Bible reference that was both simple and profound: *Commit to the LORD whatever you do, and your plans will succeed* (Proverbs 16:3).

After Abby read the short homily that followed the verse, she bent her head and silently prayed. *Dear Lord, today I will commit myself to Your will and faithfully put the future of*

Winchell Manor in Your hands. I thank You for and ask Your blessing on my family. I ask a special blessing for Josh and his family, and Your help in restoring love and harmony to them. Amen.

Feeling at peace with herself, no matter the day's outcome, Abby showered and dressed and went downstairs. The smell of bacon cooking in a frying pan made her mouth water.

Josh was sitting at the kitchen table, which was nicely set for three with bright placemats and napkins. The plate in front of him was heaped with scrambled eggs, bacon, hash browns and toast.

Abby placed her hand affectionately on Josh's shoulder. "Looks like Mary's trying to fatten you up."

"I bet he hasn't had a breakfast like this since he got on the island," Mary said, pouring three glasses of orange juice at the counter. "Besides, he needs his strength to get over that cold he's got."

"I'm much better this morning," Josh said around a mouthful of hash browns. "This is really good, Mary."

Mary smiled fondly at the teenager. "I cooked up some bacon for you too, Abby. Would you like some eggs this morning?" She delivered the orange juice to the table on a tray, then wheeled back to the counter.

"I'd better stick with cereal, but the bacon will be a special treat. Thanks."

"I'm going to make you some lunch, Josh," Mary said, "and put it in the refrigerator. You can eat it whenever you get hungry. There's a pitcher of lemonade and some soft drinks if you want them. I'm going to have to go to the day camp. I don't want the children to have another day without a craft project."

"I'm okay to help Bea today," Josh insisted.

"Oh no, you're not, young man," Mary announced in a

firm, motherly tone. "In the first place, I don't want you exposing the children to your cold. But more than that, I want you to get lots of rest so you'll be healthy when your parents come to visit. The church can get along without you for one more day. I'll help Bea as best I can."

"I have an idea." Taking down a box of cereal from the cupboard, Abby filled a bowl. "Why don't you ask Bobby McDonald to volunteer to fill in for Josh? He'd be a big help, I'm sure, and he clearly has too much time on his hands this summer." *And too vivid an imagination*, she thought.

"I hadn't thought of that. I'll give Sandy a call," Mary said. "I'm not sure Bobby's old enough to help with the cooking, but he could take care of the cleanup."

"You might suggest," Abby continued, pouring milk on her cereal, "that afterwards Bobby could write up his church camp experience and get it printed in *The Birdcall.* William is always looking for local stories. Bobby might even start a regular column about summer activities for kids on the island."

"Perfect. That boy is certainly smart enough if William will go along with the idea."

"Maybe I should put a bug in his ear. He does owe me a favor after I gave him that exclusive tour of the manor yesterday." Abby would willingly give up her dinner with William if it meant Bobby could have a productive summer and maybe even get paid a few dollars for his articles.

Before Mary left for church camp, she made sure Josh had everything he needed including her cell phone number. "Maybe I should ask my mother to drop in on you to see if you're all right," Mary said, hesitating at the last minute.

"I'll be fine. Honest. I've got the TV, and if I get too bored, I'll sit out in the sun and catch some rays."

"All right, dear. If you're sure. I'll be home as early as I can. I promise."

Abby was still getting ready for her meeting at the bank when the phone rang.

"Ms. Stanton, my name is Kendrick Kerstan. I'm with the Heritage Museum," the caller said. "I believe you spoke with our head curator recently about a rather nice discovery you'd made on Sparrow Island."

"Yes, that's true." The fact that Mr. Kerstan, the museum's furniture specialist, was calling her instead of the other way around was a pleasant surprise.

"We saw the news story on television this morning and we can't say how delighted we are that you're considering a collaboration with the Heritage Museum."

"Really? Well, we're still working out the details."

"I understand that, of course. I was hoping I might visit the manor and make a preliminary estimate of the value of the collection you've uncovered."

"I think that would be excellent."

"Good. Would this afternoon be convenient?"

She frowned. "I thought you were filming an antiques show for public television."

"I am. But if the newscast was correct, I believe it's imperative the Winchell family collection be thoroughly inventoried and protected. I'd like to get started as soon as possible."

Suddenly the situation was moving much faster than Abby had anticipated. At this point, she wanted to do whatever she could to preserve the manor and its contents, but she didn't want to make a misstep.

"I'd be happy to meet with you this afternoon," she said. "But I want to make it clear that the current ownership of

Winchell Manor is still unclear and I'm not in a position to make a firm offer regarding collaboration or management of the property. But your advice would be most welcome."

There was a moment of hesitation before he said, "I understand, Ms. Stanton. I plan to be on the island by two o'clock, if that would be convenient."

"I'll meet you at the ferry dock." She gave him her cell phone number in case he missed the ferry and thanked him for calling.

As she hung up, she marveled at what a difference media coverage made and mentally thanked Lillian Trumble for her public relations skills.

The next phone call, only minutes later, was from the president of the Washington Island Preservation Trust, who had also been watching the news. Abby made the same arrangement with him as she had with Mr. Kerstan—to meet at the ferry that afternoon—but she cut the conversation short. She didn't want to be late for her meeting at the bank. Winchell Manor was taking on a life of its own at warp speed.

ALTHOUGH THE GREEN HARBOR BANK had kept up with the times and changes in the industry, it had retained much of the old feeling of a family bank. The wood floor was dark with age and polish, the tellers' windows still had the ornate metal bars that had been installed just before the turn of the century, and the counters were a deep mahogany. Overhead was an open-beam cathedral ceiling with antique lighting on long chains that had been converted from gas to electricity in the 1920s.

The general impression was that this bank had been around a long time and was here to stay. Your money was safe with Green Harbor Bank.

Steven Jarvis exuded the same sense of stability despite his relative youth. He greeted Abby and Naomi, then ushered them to his desk, which was set off to one side of the bank.

"Please have a seat," he said, indicating the two chairs in front of his large mahogany desk, which looked to be a part of the original bank decor. He seated himself in his swivel chair. "I'm afraid what I've discovered is somewhat embarrassing for Green Harbor Bank in terms of our management of the Winchell estate."

Abby's heart leaped into her throat. "Is the estate worthless?"

"No, no. Nothing so dire, thank goodness." He pulled a thick file from his drawer and placed it on his desk. "I've located Beauregard Winchell's instructions and a copy of his original will, which provided that Filmore Hoskins, then manager of this branch, should act as executor." He slid a handwritten piece of paper across the desk for them to examine. It looked much like the will Abby had found in the Winchell family Bible.

"From these records, it appears that Mr. Hoskins performed his initial duties efficiently. He made a thorough search for Beauregard's sister, Catherine Winchell Thurman, and discovered that she and her husband both died of illness on a wagon train coming west in 1868. Although the disease wasn't identified, it could well have been typhoid. Many of those immigrating by wagon train were lost in that way."

"Did she have any children?" Abby asked.

"Mr. Hoskins was unable to locate any offspring. The initial wagon train census, if you will, indicated that Mrs. Thurman was pregnant when they left St. Joseph, Missouri, but there's no record of a birth along the way."

"That's so sad," Naomi said sympathetically. "So many people died coming west. Such a hard life."

Abby concurred. "But that means the Winchell estate should have been put to some good use for Sparrow Island if Beauregard's will had been executed properly."

"That is where the bank—inadvertently, you understand—failed in its duties." Steven passed his hand across the top of his shaved head as though he were brushing back a lock of invisible hair. "I discovered through other records that our Mr. Hoskins passed on unexpectedly right about the time the bank received confirmation that there were no living heirs to the Winchell estate. That was in early 1908. Because of communication difficulties and the economy at that time, no successor for Mr. Hoskins was appointed for more than a year. Frankly, the executor duties simply fell through a crack and the Winchell accounts have lain dormant all this time."

Troubled, Abby cocked her head to the side. "What does that mean exactly?"

"Several things. First, the monies we've been holding in trust have been gathering interest all these years. The current balance is, to say the least, extensive."

When Steven named the total amount in the account, Abby felt her jaw drop.

Naomi giggled and covered her mouth with her hand. "I'm amazed. That has to be more money than the entire wealth in Sparrow Island."

Steven disagreed. "Not quite that much, I'm afraid. But it is substantial. It's also encumbered to some extent."

"How's that?" Abby asked.

"I've checked with the county assessor, and it seems Winchell Manor and the accompanying property is seriously in arrears on the property taxes. Had all of the records been properly kept, I believe the county would have been within its rights to claim the property as abandoned, which would have been the fault of Green Harbor Bank for its poor stewardship, I'm afraid."

"Can the county still do that?" Abby asked, fearful that Commissioner Hargrove would leap on the possibility.

"Our attorneys are researching that question, but I'm optimistic we can negotiate an arrangement to pay the back taxes in order to clear the title. As the executor for the estate, the bank was not notified of the tax liability."

Still trying to grasp the situation, Abby said, "I thought if bank accounts fall inactive for some number of years, the state takes them over."

"That's quite true—*if* the bank reports them inactive. In this case, our failure to do so benefits the estate." He shook his head as though attempting to dislodge the thought of his bank failing a depositor. "For such a thing to happen is quite unusual, I assure you. Although in this case, I'd say it was a blessing in disguise."

"I think you're right." Leaning back her in chair, Abby tried to relax. "So what happens next?"

"I plan to assume the responsibilities of executor. After taxes, the remainder of the estate would provide a substantial endowment if we want to develop plans to turn the manor into a museum, which I understand both from Mary and this morning's news reports is the case. The development would have to be under the auspices of some responsible nonprofit organization." He looked directly at Naomi. "The Sparrow Island Historical Society might be such an appropriate organization."

Naomi all but came up out of her chair to lead a cheer, she was so excited by the prospect.

Equally thrilled with Steven's proposal, Abby took a

moment to send up a quick prayer of thanks, then hurried to fill them in on her phone calls from both the Heritage Museum and the Washington Island Preservation Trust. As they discussed the situation, they agreed that the best arrangement might well be a collaboration among all three of the nonprofit groups with Steven Jarvis, as executor, overseeing the project from a financial perspective and the formation of a joint board of directors.

"The first thing I think we need to do with the estate," Abby suggested, "is to hire round-the-clock security and probably put up a fence to keep out trespassers. The sheriff's office is providing some security now but I doubt that will last long once the county discovers we have our own funds."

"Excellent idea," Steven said. "I'll take care of that this morning."

"There is one other problem that you may be able to help me with," Abby said.

"Anything."

"Commissioner Hargrove called this morning. He was quite upset about what went on at Winchell Manor and how we blocked the demolition. He threatened to sue to regain the money the county was out for the construction crew."

"Oh, what nonsense!" Naomi said.

Abby agreed. "I'm hoping your bank attorneys could include that item in their negotiations along with back taxes."

Nodding, Steven jotted a note on a yellow pad of paper. "I'll see to it, Ms. Stanton."

"I have the feeling you and I are going to be spending a lot of time together in assorted meetings about Winchell Manor," Abby said, smiling. "I think it would be all right if we used first names."

"Absolutely, Abby. And Naomi." He acknowledged them both with a smile. "It will be my pleasure to work with you both."

After they left the bank, Abby and Naomi went to the Springhouse Café for an early lunch and to talk over plans for the manor. From there, Abby stopped by the conservatory, a part of her life she'd been sorely neglecting lately.

Hugo greeted her in the workroom where he was putting together an interactive display of a vole habitat.

"Hello, Abby. That was quite a brilliant performance Lillian put on yesterday, wasn't it?"

"She's an amazing woman, all right. And I appreciated your being there. It looks like we'll be able to save the manor and turn it into a museum as I'd hoped." She ran down what she had learned at the bank about the Winchell estate and how things appeared to be coming together.

"Then it's been an especially good day for you, Abby. We had a call from the Washington Community Foundation this morning. They've agreed to fund your field trip program for sixth graders in the San Juan County schools. We'll have the money starting in September."

"Wow!" She couldn't help but be pleased and excited about providing an introduction to ornithology and ecology for young students. "This has been a *great* day. But I do feel guilty that I've spent so much time away from The Nature Museum this past week or so."

"Nothing to feel guilty about at all. I fully approve of your efforts to save Winchell Manor, and view the time spent well worthwhile. Perhaps down the road a year or two, our Nature Conservatory and Winchell Manor will be able to find many ways to collaborate."

"I certainly hope so," she agreed, once again appreciating what a fine gentleman Hugo was and how much foresight he had.

She visited awhile with Hugo, picked up her mail and then had to hurry to meet the afternoon ferry. She then drove Mr. Kerstan of the Heritage Museum and his counterpart from the Preservation Trust up to Winchell Manor for a tour. Later, with a promise that they could both return next week, she drove them to the ferry.

By the time Abby returned home, Mary and Josh were already eating dinner.

"Sorry I'm late," she said, washing her hands at the sink.

"Not to worry," Mary said. "We're just having hamburgers and fruit salad. I put yours in the oven to stay warm."

"Thanks." She took a minute to put condiments on a bun and help herself to some salad, then sat down at the table. "How are you feeling, Josh?"

"Great. My folks will get here tomorrow morning. They're gonna rent a car at the Seattle airport, drive up to Anacortes and take the ferry. We're gonna stay at that bed-and-breakfast you told me about."

"Good." Abby was pleased to see the boy happy about his family's arrival. At heart, she suspected Josh had been homesick for his parents all along. That was a positive sign.

She bit into her burger, which must have been a full quarter pounder. This was another of Mary's efforts to fatten Josh up—which was likely to put a few pounds on Abby, too, if Josh were to stay with them much longer.

Mary asked Abby about her meeting with Steven, and she reported the good news about the wealth of the Winchell estate and how three different groups might well end up working toward the same goal of renovation and restoration of the manor.

"That is so exciting," Mary said. "I do wish I could help in some way."

"You might be able to. When I met with Lillian at her house, she read me parts of her grandmother's diary. She also told me how her grandmother had described the manor in incredible detail, including things like the draperies and floor coverings that are now gone. I'm hoping we can recreate the manor as it was during Theadora's life as accurately as possible. With your artistic talent, you could be a big help."

Mary looked pleased at the prospect. "Do you really think so?"

"I'd bet you could read the descriptions, research them and come up with very close copies of the fabrics. It would be quite a project, though. I suspect it will be years before all of the renovations are complete."

A confident smile slowly crept over Mary's face. "I can do that. I'm sure I can."

Nodding, Abby forked a slice of fresh peach into her mouth. "Absolutely."

"I bet you'd be good." Josh started on his second hamburger.

"You know, the sad thing about all this," Abby said, "is that Beauregard's sister, who was his primary heir, and her husband died of an illness coming west on a wagon train. Apparently, she had no children so there aren't any descendants to inherit the manor."

"Which is good for us, isn't it?" Mary questioned.

"Of course. But it's sad."

Josh gulped down half a glass of milk. "One of my great-great-grandfathers came west in a wagon train. Dad used to tell me how this great-great-whatever was orphaned when his mom and dad got sick. The guy—my great-great-whatever—was just a baby, I guess. One of the other families on the train adopted him after his parents died. That's how come we're Walkers. After the wagon train fiasco, they settled in Idaho and started a cattle ranch. For years, they supplied the army posts in the West with beef. My grandpa finally moved into town and opened a feed and grain store. My dad still runs the business."

Laying down her hamburger, Abby gazed across the table at the teenager. "What was the name of the baby before he was adopted?"

"I dunno. Something like Thurgood, Thurman. Something like that. I never paid much attention, you know?" He drank the rest of his milk, then wiped his mouth with a napkin. "That was great, Mary. Sure beats a peanut butter sandwich for dinner."

Abby's mouth went dry. Thurman was the married name of Beauregard's sister—and his heir. "Josh, did you ever hear your father mention the maiden name of that baby's mother?"

"Gee, I dunno."

Abby took a deep breath. "Could it have been Winchell?"

The boy returned her stare for a moment. "I'd have to ask my dad, you know? It sounds kinda familiar, but I can't remember. Honest."

"Was there any particular reason you came to Sparrow Island? Had you heard of it before?"

"Not really. I was just trying to get as faraway from my folks as I could. I headed west on a bus, hitchhiked some. I was careful about that. I mean, I'd heard stories and stuff. This is sort of where I ran out of money. Besides, the next stop would've been Japan, and I didn't want to go that far."

"Was it purely a coincidence you ended up here and staying in Winchell Manor?"

"Yeah, I guess." He grinned. "You think maybe that's how come I felt so at home at the manor, 'cause it was built by my great-great-great-uncle or something?"

Abby didn't really want to consider that possibility as she looked at Josh. Still, she had a terrible feeling the ghost of Winchell Manor had come back to haunt her in ways she never could have imagined.

Or one of God's amazing coincidences had landed squarely on Sparrow Island.

What had seemed like an incredibly good day for Abby and Winchell Manor had just taken an unpredictable turn that could change everything.

CHAPTER ❧ NINETEEN

When we've been there ten thousand years,
Bright shining as the sun,
We've no less days to sing God's praise
Than when we'd first begun.

JOSH'S PARENTS ARRIVED
on the island the next morning and Abby knew what she had
to do. She had to tell Sue and Brett Walker that it was possible
they were the rightful heirs to Winchell Manor and the huge
Winchell fortune.

If that was true, they might decide to move to Sparrow
Island and take over the property, even restore it themselves.
Or they might tear it down. Or, heaven help her, sell everything to developers who would do who-knew-what with the
land. Condos. Townhouses. An amusement park.

She shuddered at the thought.

Nonetheless, the truth had to be told. That was the only
way Abby would be able to live with her conscience.

She let the Walker family have their reunion on their own,
then picked them up at The Bird Nest to take them up to see
Winchell Manor.

Brett Walker was tall and sinewy, slender like his son, but with darker hair and a face lined by stress. In comparison, Sue was short and a little plump, with naturally blond hair that curled around her face. She exuded the warmth of a loving mother. She could barely keep her eyes off of her son or a smile from her face. If Abby had had questions about Josh's parents, they evaporated when she saw how they interacted with their son—and with each other, for that matter.

When they reached the manor, Josh led the way up the stairs to the tower room.

"This is where I slept, Mom. You should see the stars at night from here. And the ships going by in the straits are all lit up like Christmas trees. Awesome."

Sue gave her son a quick hug. "I'm so upset you were alone. Please don't ever scare us like that again."

"Sorry. But it wasn't so bad, really. I mean, I made friends at church and stuff. 'Course, I got kinda tired of eating peanut butter sandwiches, you know?" He grinned shyly at his mother.

Tousling the boy's hair, Brett said, "You can have all the steak and fries you want when we get home, son."

Like most teenagers, Josh shrugged off their affectionate touches as though he didn't care, but Abby could see he was pleased his family was back together again. Apparently the rift between Brett and Sue had mended some and communication had been restored because of their mutual concern for their runaway son.

"Let me take you down to the cellar and show you what Josh was sleeping on top of," Abby said. "It's the pièce de résistance of the Winchell Manor." And, she thought, what might well sway the Walkers' decision about pursuing their inheritance.

Sue's first glimpse of the antique furniture stored in the cellar room had her gasping with delight, and every piece Abby uncovered brought her further elation.

"Why, this is way more exciting than Aunt Annabelle's Attic. That's an antique store on the highway near where we live," she explained, touching everything she could reach with loving care. "Brett sometimes accuses me of owning a half interest in the shop since I buy so many things there. But none nearly as nice as these. What I wouldn't give to furnish my house with just a couple of these end tables, or that writing desk. Oh my..."

"This collection is exquisite," Abby agreed. "What we're hoping to do is to restore the manor, redecorate the rooms just as they were in the mid-1800s and turn it into a museum. We thought that was what Beauregard Winchell would want done after all these years." And what God was leading her to, as well, unless Abby was way off base, which now seemed entirely possible.

"That's a pretty ambitious plan," Brett commented.

"Yes, it is. Let's go back upstairs." She turned her flashlight back toward the tunnel and the opening in the brick wall to the wine cellar. "There's something I need to discuss with you both. All three of you, actually."

She took them up to the library and stood in front of the portrait of Theadora Winchell. Despite the sunny June day, the interior of the house was cool and Abby felt a breeze ripple across her neck, raising the hair on her nape. Either the ghost of Winchell Manor was on the loose again, or her own fears and uncertainties were feeding her imagination. No doubt it was the latter.

"Josh told us the story of your ancestor who was orphaned on a wagon train when his parents died of a disease," Abby began.

"Yes, that's true." Brett looked a bit puzzled she'd brought up the topic. "He was my great-grandfather."

"And he was adopted by the Walker family?"

Brett nodded and shot a curious look at Josh, who was rubbing a century of dirt from a window pane so he could peer outside.

"Do you know his surname before he was adopted?" Abby asked.

He glanced at Sue, who said, "It was Thurman. Why do you ask?"

"If you'll bear with me, I'll get to that in a minute. Do you happen to know the maiden name of your great-grandfather's mother?"

Brett turned to his wife again. "Sue's done all the family history research. I haven't paid much attention."

"That part of the family tree has been a little difficult to trace since the Walkers apparently didn't know the Thurmans very well," Sue explained. "When the wagon train formed up in St. Joseph, people joined the group from all over the eastern part of the country. There were a couple of possibilities for the Thurman family in question. As nearly as I could figure out, Brett's great-grandfather's family could have either been from Georgia or South Carolina. In either case, chances were good they were Confederates leaving the South. It was after the Civil War. We're not exactly sure of the year."

Abby acknowledged the information with a nod. "So you don't know the maternal surname?"

"Sorry. Is it important?" Sue looked at her expectantly.

Abby slid her hands into her jeans pockets and steadied herself with a deep breath. "It's possible that Brett and Josh are the direct descendants of Beauregard Winchell's sister, Catherine Thurman. If that's so, you would be the rightful heir to the Winchell estate, which includes a substantial amount of money, as well as the manor and the land around it."

Brett and Sue stared at each other for a moment, then Brett burst out laughing.

"See, Susie-Q," he said, obviously using his affectionate nickname for his wife, "that's what I always told you. You married me for my money and not my good looks!"

"Oh, you . . ." She gave him a loving tap on his arm. "But what would it mean if he is the heir?"

"You'd have to be able to prove the relationship to the satisfaction of the estate's executor, who happens to be the bank manager here in Green Harbor, or to the courts. Then you'd inherit everything." Gesturing around her and feeling sick to her stomach with dread, Abby indicated the house and all it contained—material things she had coveted for the good she thought they'd bring to Sparrow Island, the symbols of Beauregard's acceptance of Christ and the credit such an accomplishment would bring to her. Perhaps, like Beauregard, she should have been storing up treasure in heaven rather than here on earth. Certainly she should have made sure her ego wasn't the driving force behind her effort to restore Winchell Manor.

Josh rejoined the group. "I told Abby that maybe I ended up here 'cause it was my great-great-great-uncle who built the place."

"That wouldn't be easy to prove," Sue pointed out, considering her son with affection. "Post-Civil War records aren't always easy to trace. Informal adoptions, like your dad's great-grandfather, often weren't recorded at all. The children simply started to be known by the adoptive parents' name. There wasn't any legal paper trail to follow."

"What would happen to the plans to turn this into a museum?" Brett wanted to know.

"If you inherited the manor, its disposition would be entirely up to you."

Brett speared his fingers through his hair and put a fatherly hand on the boy's shoulder. When he turned his attention back to Abby, he said, "I think the three of us need to talk about this. What you've told us has been quite a surprise. If we decided to pursue the possibility that I'm the heir, it could change our lives considerably. And not necessarily for the better."

"I agree," Sue said. "We're going to have to give this a lot of thought before we make any decision. Inheriting property this extensive . . ." Her gestured included the entire estate. ". . . could easily change more than just our bank accounts. It could change who we are."

"Cool to think we could own the place though," Josh said, grinning. "Could I have the tower room? Like for my own bedroom?"

"You're jumping the gun, son. We'll talk about it."

For herself, Abby intended to do a lot of praying. Although—given that she liked Josh and his parents—she wasn't entirely sure what she should pray for.

"You'll have our answer tomorrow before we leave for home," Brett announced. "We're on the afternoon ferry."

More than once after meeting with the Walkers, Abby realized how easy it could be to misunderstand God's will. It was possible she'd been led to the discovery of Theodora's journal and all that followed because God wanted the manor restored to the Winchell family, and not used as a testament to Beauregard's conversion and faith in Christ, as Abby had believed.

At this point, either scenario seemed equally plausible and just as worthy in its own way.

Time and again she had to remind herself that she'd put the future of Winchell Manor in God's hands. Letting go of her worry and her need for control was one of the hardest things she'd ever had to do.

ON SUNDAY, Rev. Hale based his sermon on Isaiah 40:30–31: "*Even youths grow tired and weary, and young men stumble and fall; but those who hope in the LORD will renew their strength. . . .*"

Mary felt inspired by his words. Certainly, the accident had caused her to stumble and fall, and she wouldn't be able to get up again in a physical sense. But helping at the Vacation Bible School had raised her up in ways she hadn't expected. Through working with the children—and especially by getting to know Josh—she had discovered her worth as a person wasn't diminished because she was in a wheelchair. She still had talents to share with others.

When the congregation sang the final song, "Amazing Grace," tears of joy filled her eyes. If she had been lost for a time, she felt she had at last found herself again.

Pastor Jim closed the service with a benediction and everyone began to file out.

"Hi, Mary," Bobby said as she was rolling down the aisle.

"Hello, young man," Mary said.

"Know what?"

"What should I know?"

"I wrote the article for Mr. Jansen, like you said."

"Good for you. Did he like it?"

"Yep. He's gonna put it in the paper next week. And he *paid* me five dollars!"

"That's wonderful, Bobby. I'm very happy for you, and I'll look forward to reading your story." The crowd of departing parishioners at the door edged aside so she could get through.

"I put the five dollars in the collection plate this morning."

Surprised, Mary brought herself to a stop on the walkway outside. "You gave the money you earned to the church?"

Grinning, he said, "Yep. See, I was praying and praying I'd find a way to make money this summer. There's a really neat telescope I saw in a catalog that I wanna buy."

"But you gave the money away."

"I figured God answered my prayers so I owed him first. Then I can start saving for the telescope. Mr. Jansen says I can write a story every week this summer. He's gonna call it 'Kids Speak.'"

Mary framed Bobby's face between her hands and kissed him on the forehead. "You are a very nice young man, Master McDonald. And very clever. I love you very much."

Still grinning, he shrugged his shoulders. "What's not to love?"

"Oh, you . . ." Laughing, Mary shooed him off to find his parents.

Having overheard the conversation, Abby said, "He is a little rascal, isn't he? A little too smart for his own britches maybe but still lovable."

"He'll grow up to be a fine young man. I'm sure of it."

Outside the church, Abby and Mary spotted their mother and father talking with Pastor Jim, and joined them.

"Wasn't the sermon wonderful?" Ellen said to Mary and Abby. "I understand you've both had an exciting week."

"More exciting than I'd like," Abby responded. "And it's not over yet. We're going to see Josh's family off on the ferry this afternoon."

Mary added, "That's when they'll tell Abby if they intend to pursue the possibility that Brett Walker is the heir to the Winchell fortune."

"Are you worried?" George asked.

"I'm trying not to be, Dad. But it isn't easy."

"Then I'll need to dust off my sermon about being patient and believing that God knows what He's doing," Pastor Jim said. "I've certainly learned that lesson more than once, including again this morning."

They all turned to the preacher.

"A gentleman came up to me just a few minutes ago. He's been vacationing on Sparrow Island for several years now. Whenever he's here, he visits Little Flock Church. He told me that a sermon I gave last year not only had an impact on him, but his whole congregation in Spokane as well."

"How's that?" Abby's father asked.

"The sermon was about how a church isn't about a particular minister or some fancy stained-glass windows. It's about finding God in your heart."

"I remember that sermon," Abby said. "Mary and I were just talking about that the other day."

Rev. Hale looked pleased. "It seems this gentleman's home congregation had experienced a turnover in ministers and the new preacher had a different way of doing things that upset him and many of his friends. When he went back home, he gathered the members of the church who were disgruntled, sat them all down and they prayed together asking for God's help with the changes that were going on."

Little Toby came running to his daddy, who hefted him up into his arms.

"That seemed to be a turning point," he continued. "Not only did the congregation's attitude change, so did their pastor's. Together, they worked things out and the church is one happy family now."

"That's wonderful," Ellen said.

"It's also an example of how God's Word spreads. You see, I admit I was tempted by the job offer in Southern California, thinking I could reach thousands of people via television. A real ego trip." He grinned a little sheepishly and looped his free arm around his wife, who had joined the group.

"They offered you the job?" Mary asked, her heart suddenly in her throat.

"They did indeed, and with a salary and benefits that were quite generous." He smiled gently at Mary. "What I hadn't understood is that I can touch a lot of lives from right here at Little Flock Church. I don't have to move to a big city to do God's work."

"Thank the good Lord," Ellen Stanton said. "After having you here for five years, we couldn't imagine how it would be without you."

Relief swept through Mary. "I, for one, am delighted we won't have to adjust to a new pastor's ways anytime soon."

George Stanton extended his hand to Pastor Jim. "I'm sure I speak for the entire congregation when I say we're extremely glad you'll be staying on with Little Flock Church."

"No more than we are," the pastor said.

As the group broke up to head for their cars, Ellen said,

"Girls, since you can't make it to Sunday dinner, why don't you two come to supper tonight? I'll do my special tamale pie. I know that recipe is one of your favorites."

"Perfect, Mom," Mary said. "We'll be there." After they learned the Walkers' verdict about being the possible heirs to Winchell House, whatever their answer, Mary knew her sister would need a break and time to relax.

On the lawn in front of the church, a group of children was playing, and a couple of the youngsters from day camp had cornered Josh, who had attended church with his parents.

"You're gonna come back, aren't you, Josh?" P.J. asked.

Young Terry from the class seemed equally hopeful of Josh's return.

"At least for a visit, okay?" Josh said. "So you guys gotta be good, huh?"

"We will be," P.J. answered for them both.

Josh gave them high-fives. "I gotta go with my folks now. We're gonna drive out to the ol' lighthouse out on the point. They want to learn everything they can about the island. So I'll see ya." The teenager jogged over to where his parents had been waiting, watching their son with pride in their eyes. After speaking to his parents, Josh turned and waved one last time to the boys.

Mary had been especially pleased that the Walkers had attended church this morning. If nothing else, seeing where Josh had been working would reassure them he'd been in good hands while he was away from them.

Still, that didn't answer the ultimate question of whether they would some day take up permanent residence at Winchell Manor as the rightful heirs.

THREE JUVENILE WESTERN SANDPIPERS foraged along the shore not far from the ferry dock, where they were joined by a curious crow. Reluctant to get his feet wet, the crow hopped out of the way when a waved lapped up onto the beach.

Not wanting to fret about whatever decision the Walkers had made, Abby concentrated on the instinctive behavior of her feathered friends. Birds, in all their variations, had often provided her with the same sense of peace and well-being that she found in prayer.

"Here they come," Mary said.

Turning away from the shore birds, Abby saw the Walkers park their rental car in the line waiting to board the ferry. All three of them got out of the sedan and walked toward Mary and Abby.

"Do you think they look like they've just come into a multimillion dollar inheritance?" Mary asked.

"I don't know. I haven't met many multimillionaires." But her stomach was knotted in anticipation of their decision.

Brett extended his hand to Abby. "Thank you for coming to see us off."

Mary rolled over to Josh and raised her arms. "No way would I let Josh get away without a good-bye hug."

Blushing, the teenager bent over to accept her hug. "Thanks for everything, Mary. You're the greatest."

"You're pretty good yourself, young man." There was a sheen of tears in her eyes as Mary patted his cheek. "Behave yourself now, you hear? And write to us once in a while. We want to know how you're getting along."

"Yes, ma'am."

"Before we leave," Brett began, "I'd like to tell you a story about our family. My father opened Walker Feed and Grain when he was a young man. He started with almost nothing and built it into a fine business. Then he passed it on to me."

He slipped his arm around his wife's waist and drew her closer.

"I wanted to prove to my dad that I was as good a man as he was. So I worked as hard as I could. I opened a second store in a neighboring town and then a third store. I wanted him to be proud of me.

"But I'd stretched my resources to the limit, which meant I had to work even harder. I spent so much time on the road and in my stores, I was almost never home, and when I was, I was stressed out and exhausted. That almost cost me my family. When Josh ran away, it made me take stock of what's really important."

"It's a lesson we all have to learn," Abby said.

"Among other things," Brett continued, "I figured out more money isn't going to make me happy and maybe it would cost me what I already had. And the fact is, financially we're pretty comfortable." He glanced down at his wife and smiled. "Sue and I don't know if we're related to your Beauregard Winchell, though it's been fun to think that we might be filthy rich if we were."

"I was gonna buy myself a Corvette, if we turned out to inherit the manor and stuff," Josh said. "But Dad said he wouldn't let me either way 'til I'm thirty-five." Grinning, he shrugged. "So the inheritance doesn't mean much to me one way or the other."

Abby's laugh was one of relief.

"We're going back to Idaho," Brett continued. "Many generations have lived there, and it's home. I'm going to close down the third store, or maybe franchise it, and maybe even do the same with the second one, and concentrate on my family. If you need me to sign something that waives my rights to the inheritance—assuming I have any—I'd be happy to do that. But I'm not going to waive my rights to the people I love."

His wife beamed a smile at her husband and Josh looked proud about the family decision too.

"Thank you, Mr. Walker," Abby said. "Given what you've told us, I think you're doing the right thing. Your son and your wife are very special people. For that matter, you are too. After all, we know what a fine son you've raised."

"I agree," Mary said. "And you can be sure Winchell Manor will be well cared for. Abby will see to that."

"I'm sure she and all the good people on Sparrow Island will do just that. We certainly owe both of you a lot for taking care of our boy."

"It was our pleasure," Mary said.

"We hope all of you will come back to visit us often," Abby added. "You'll always be welcome here."

"Now that my Brett is going to slow down at work," Sue said, "maybe we'll actually get to take a vacation once in a while."

"I promise." He gestured toward the ferry, which was admitting vehicles and passengers. "We'd better go. We don't want to miss our flight home."

With more hugs and thank-yous, Abby and Mary waited as the Walkers got back into their car and Brett drove it onto the ferry. A few minutes later, Josh appeared on the top deck, waving frantically. They waved back.

Abby sent up a heartfelt prayer of thanks, both for the decision the Walker's family had made and for the guidance God had provided her. Winchell Manor would become what she had hoped, a monument to the history of the San Juan Islands and the power of God's love.

When the ferry sounded its deep bass horn, Abby pushed her sister back to the van. They both got inside, Finnegan between them, and sat watching as the ferry pulled away from the dock.

Abby's thoughts slipped back to the church service they had attended earlier in the day. "When we all sang 'Amazing Grace' this morning, I thought about Josh, how he was lost and then found. What a wonderful story of a family becoming whole again through love.

"It seems to me Beauregard was lost, too, after his wife died. He struggled so hard, but finally found himself through God."

Mary nodded. "And through your hard work, the lost treasures of Winchell Manor have been found and will be restored in a way that everyone can enjoy them."

"I think God did most of the work on that project," Abby admitted. "My biggest problem was keeping focused on the fact that He knew what He was doing and how He was using me for His ends, whatever they were."

Mary took Abby's hand. "When you graduated from college and took that job in New York, we were all afraid you were lost to us. We're all so glad, Mom and Dad and especially me, that we've found you again. Just look at all of God's miracles."

Abby felt the press of tears behind her eyelids. "I have come home, haven't I? And found much of what I've been searching for all of my life. I love you, Mary."

Squeezing her hand, Mary nodded, and there were tears in her eyes, too, and all the love Abby could want. "Mom promised to make her famous tamale pie tonight. Why don't we go see if we can help her?"

As they drove out of the parking lot, Abby marveled at the incredible blue sky and the soaring birds that flew over the harbor and stretched their wings above the forests of the Sparrow Island Nature Conservatory.

She thought of Winchell Manor on Arrowhead Hill, glistening in the sunlight, a beacon to those searching for the place where they belong.

Like Josh and Beauregard's treasures, Abby had found her way home. Surely one of God's miracles.

Amazing grace! How sweet the sound,
That saved a wretch like me!
I once was lost, but now am found;
Was blind, but now I see.